P9-CKH-040

Dear Charlotte,

Just a note to let you know that you and Zoey aren't the <u>only</u> two to find your first love—I've found mine!

Only, he doesn't know it, of course. And I'm not telling. He's a lawyer now—still has a "bad boy" motorcycle, though—and he's got a darling little girl. Guess who introduced us? His ex!

Zoey, as usual, is giving me plenty of advice. I hope you're having a wonderful time in Bermuda and I'm so looking forward to the three of us getting together when you return. See you soon!

Love,

Lydia

Dear Reader,

Just what is "keeping house"? In the barest sense, it means keeping a family safe, secure and healthy by providing the essentials of warmth, shelter and food. But beyond the physical necessities of life, "keeping house" also means providing for grace, beauty, hospitality, friendship.... The list goes on. Not just sustaining life, but what makes life worth living.

A *home* is much more than a house.

Lydia Lane wants to do all these things, only she doesn't have a family to practice on. She decides to turn her knowledge into a business, teaching the "homely arts" to others. One of her first clients is Sam T. Pereira, the "bad boy" she'd once secretly loved with all the passion in her fifteen-year-old heart.

Now a street lawyer and a divorced single dad who works out of his house so he can spend more time with his daughter, Sam can't believe how his buddy's little sister has grown up. He decides he doesn't just want her turning his house into a home; he wants her in his life.

I hope you enjoy the story of Lydia and Sam as they discover that true love can happen to people who care deeply about the things that give life its meaning—home and family.

With Lydia's story, we end the three girlfriends' search for their first loves. Zoey chases her man down (or so she thinks); Charlotte accidentally falls for hers all over again and, to turn the tables, Lydia's first love finds her.

Warmest regards,

Judith Bowen

P.S. I love to hear from readers. Write me at P.O. Box 2333, Point Roberts, WA 98281-2333 or check out my Web site at www.judithbowen.com.

Lydia Lane
Judith Bowen

HARLEQUIN®

TORONTO • NEW YORK • LONDON
AMSTERDAM • PARIS • SYDNEY • HAMBURG
STOCKHOLM • ATHENS • TOKYO • MILAN • MADRID
PRAGUE • WARSAW • BUDAPEST • AUCKLAND

ISBN 0-373-71032-1

LYDIA LANE

Visit us at www.eHarlequin.com

Printed in U.S.A.

To Linda Earl,
loyal, generous, enthusiastic—always an inspiration

CHAPTER ONE

"AMBER!" Sam slapped the pizza box onto the coffee table in the family room, pushing aside the week's accumulation of newspapers and comic books. He whistled loudly, then yelled up the stairs. "Mommy's show is on and the pizza's here."

He flicked the channels on the big-screen television until he got to TownTV, Channel 14, and the familiar opening medley of his ex-wife's late-afternoon talk show, "What's New with Candy Lou?" Her name was Candace Penelope Downing, no Lou at all, but the producers thought the rhyme sounded better.

"Yippee!" His daughter raced into the room with her friend from three doors down, Tania Jackson, right behind her. Amber carried the microphone from the play karaoke set that had been a Christmas present. Tania never said much. The two girls, both eight, were practically joined at the hip, and now they skidded to a stop as one, each grabbed a slice of pizza—the two largest, of course—and scrambled onto the oversize recliner where they settled down happily. Nothing to wipe their fingers with. Should he bother?

Yeah, might as well, even though the whole room was due for a major cleaning.

"Who's Mommy got on today?" Amber asked, her mouth already stuffed with Hawaiian pizza. Sam was so sick of Hawaiian he could scream. Oh, for a lacing of hot peppers and anchovies. Feta cheese and Greek olives—he could dream, couldn't he? Cappicola or, damn, even oysters!

"Don't know, honey." Sam dropped a couple of paper towels on the arm of the girls' chair and then settled into the other recliner with his slice of pizza. Come to think of it, he was sick of pizza, period. "We'll see."

Watching Candace Downing's show with his daughter was a ritual Sam tried not to miss. Amber lived with him. The single women who drifted in and out of his life and the regular visits from Amber's grandmother and his sisters didn't provide enough feminine influence, in his opinion. This—watching Candace's show once a week—was supposedly one way of maintaining maternal contact. Candace's idea, naturally.

What kind of world was that—where you had to catch your mother on afternoon TV if you wanted to see her?

Sam shook his head and told himself to pay attention.

"—a new and unusual business. Do you really teach people like me how to polish silver?" Candace's high-pitched giggle had always bothered him. Sam frowned; he'd seen that woman before, Candace's guest.

"—if you happen to own silver. Many people, of course, don't. But the service I provide helps busy Toronto families learn some of the skills involved in running a household efficiently and well. There can be a lot of satisfaction in knowing that the people you love are being taken care of—"

"I'll take your word for it!"

"So many of the homemaking arts our grandmothers knew have been lost over the years. These skills used to be passed down as a matter of course from mother to daughter. I learned a lot of them from my great-aunt. Since the sixties, our mothers have been too busy forging careers outside the home to worry about housekeeping skills, so, over the last few decades a lot of know-how has disappeared. Often, today, there's no one to ask. That's where my company, Domestica, comes in. We can teach you the skills that will make your home a sanctuary in a hectic world."

"How intriguing. Literally turning a house into a home, you mean?"

Sam glanced around the family room. It looked like a tornado had been through. It *always* looked like a tornado had been through when his mother was away, which she was, or he'd lost another cleaning lady, which he had, just before Christmas. He could go for some of that sanctuary business....

"That's right." The woman on the screen gave his ex a cool look—one that was very appealing, Sam thought—and slowly crossed her legs. Long, slim, very nice legs, he noted, pizza slice halfway from his plate to his mouth. He frowned. *He definitely knew this woman from somewhere.* A client? No way!

"Homemaking skills are important but sadly undervalued in the modern world. Once, a good housekeeper kept her drains scalded and her kitchen clean to preserve her family's health. Today, with vaccinations and chlorinated water, we don't have to worry so much about those kinds of germs, but good housekeeping skills can affect your health even today."

"They can?" Candace was all attention.

"Yes. For instance, did you know that a properly made bed will contribute to a good night's sleep? And wouldn't a good night's rest make a stressed-out day a little easier? Science proves—"

"You mean you don't just toss a duvet over the sheets, grab a coffee and race out the door? That's what *I* call making the bed!"

Sam was sure Candace thought she was speaking for the entire civilized world. He was intrigued. *A well-made bed...*

"Yes. A properly made, properly aired bed is comfortable, clean and allergen-free, all of which adds up to a more restful sleep. Our grandmothers knew about the benefits of fresh air in the bedroom. The pillow should have a zippered microfibre cover to prevent dust mites, a source of allergies, from passing through. Over that, a pillow cover and a nicely ironed pillowslip, preferably pure cotton or linen—''

''Ironed?'' Candace squealed. ''You've got to be kidding!''

Her guest smiled but did not reply and Candace leaned forward in a phony confidential way that Sam had seen many times before. ''Okay, besides ironing tips, what else does your company offer us? Can you teach kids anything? And dads? I mean, if you can, lots of moms out there would be thrilled to hear about it.''

''Certainly.'' There was that calm, assertive look again, a look Sam found incredibly appealing. The woman oozed sensuality and icy cool competence at the same time. ''I've taught Boy Scout troops how to iron their own shirts, pack their own tasty, well-balanced school lunches and polish their own shoes. I've conducted executive retreat weekend workshops on cooking—''

''Cooking, too?''

Candace's guest nodded. ''Yes, cooking. In fact, Domestica offers a personal chef service as an addition to our homemaking workshops. You'd be surprised how many people want me to organize their

kitchens, shop for their groceries and prepare a
week's worth of nutritious meals they—''

"*Lydia Lane!*"

"What, Daddy?"

"Lydia Lane," Sam repeated, feeling a little rush
of blood to his knees, a sensation he hadn't felt for
quite a while. It was the *well-made bed* that had done
it. He'd pictured this tawny goddess sprawled out on
that well-made bed.... "Daddy knows that lady, Amber. Remember my friend, Steve Lane? We went
fishing with him and Uncle Avie last summer and
Uncle Avie accidentally caught that mud turtle?"

"Oh, yeah. Yuck." She turned to her friend. "We
let him go back in the water."

"Yeah, well, that's Steve's little sister Mommy's
talking to." *That* was it.

"Oh. Isn't Mommy pretty today?"

"Sure is, baby," Sam muttered. Was she? Of
course she was. Not that Candace Downing did anything for Sam anymore. Their four-year marriage had
been friendly but not passionate. Their divorce was
cordial and they were on good terms, always keeping
Amber's interests foremost. In fact, he'd been relieved when Candace had decided that if he was cutting down his corporate law practice—where he had
a chance to make something of himself, in her opinion—so he could expand what she described as his
"street people" practice, she was calling it quits.
She'd always regretted leaving her barely hatched

TV career so she could marry him and have his baby a year later, and she decided to give it her best effort again before her looks and energy were gone. Candace liked society and parties and grown-ups, she informed him. She found full-time care of a three-year-old just too…too trying. Sam always thought it ironic that the pinnacle of her renewed career so far was this snoozer of a talk show.

Their daughter, Candace had reasoned, would do just fine with him. Lots of kids had day care and nannies and were brought up perfectly well by single dads. Sam could afford help. Candace would take Amber on weekends whenever she was in town, and on holidays and shopping trips to New York and Montreal when she got a little older. That would be fun—a real mother-daughter experience. Sam working out of a home office; Candace pursuing her media career. It couldn't be more perfect, she declared.

Perfect. Sam glanced around. The room was a disaster. The carpet and upholstery needed cleaning. Amber's jeans had holes in the knee. Why didn't she put on a new pair or tell him when she needed to buy some? The fridge was empty—again. The Christmas tree had turned brown; Sam had forgotten to put water in the receptacle. There was still some balled-up Christmas paper behind the tree, jammed into a corner along with a whole lot of dust. The last housekeeper had left before the holidays and Sam hadn't had the heart to look for another one yet. How many did this make this year? Three? Four? *Five?*

Several glass ornaments had fallen onto the carpet, bowling balls for Punch, the cat, who belonged to Tania but spent as much time at their house as he did at home. Only one string of lights worked. And now—Sam groaned—someone would have to take down the damn tree and get rid of it and store all the little decorating doodads—

Someone meant him.

He ran his hands through his hair and picked up the empty pizza box to carry through to the kitchen, which was another kind of disaster. Why hadn't he listened to his mother's advice and just gone to one of his sisters' houses for Christmas? Let his brother-in-law worry about Christmas trees. But, no, putting up a tree every year for his kid was something he figured he should do.

His daughter deserved some family traditions and it was up to him to provide them. No mom around, and a dad who wasn't doing the world's greatest job of running a household on his own. But this was his *family,* even if it was just him and Amber. If that meant dead Christmas trees, and Thanksgiving and Christmas dinners at the Royal York Hotel, so be it. For Easter they usually went to his parents' place, along with his sisters and their families. He couldn't have managed without his mother's help and while he appreciated her tremendously, she could be…well, quite ornery about doing things her way. Candace would have said *pushy*.

Now his parents had gone to Portugal for six weeks, visiting relatives, and look at this place! Straight downhill. It was exactly what Lydia Lane had said, he didn't have the faintest idea where to start. Or how to do anything. Taking care of a house was a hell of a bigger job than he'd thought and he had renewed respect for his mother and other women like her, who always seemed to know exactly what needed to be done and when.

Sam had been doing his best for the past four years but this single dad business wasn't working out the way he'd planned.

Perfect? If only!

THE TOWNTV BUILDING, a redbrick, three-story converted warehouse, was on a quiet street on the edge of the Danforth-Pape neighborhood, not far from Lydia's loft.

In the second-floor Studio A, "What's New with Candy Lou?" was just finishing up. The program was taped in the morning for broadcast at five that afternoon. Lydia's appearance had been followed by a puppeteer who specialized in pet birthday parties—he did mostly animated bones and mice—and a playwright whose first play, "A Time to Laugh, a Time to Cry" was opening New Year's Day in a tiny local theater.

Aptly titled, no doubt, Lydia thought skeptically as she dug through her change purse for a subway token. That wasn't fair, she reprimanded herself; she'd try to see the play for the sake of the starry-eyed author. Her aging minivan had been making weird noises and she'd left it at the garage to be checked out. Fingers crossed—her budget was extremely tight right now. There was no room for repairs on top of the mortgage payments, not unless business picked up and that was highly unlikely at this time of year. People would be getting their Christmas credit-card bills soon and paying someone to reorganize their households was not a top priority.

She had no idea how the show had gone but she hoped it brought in some new business. Every little bit of publicity helped. She'd watch the interview at home later, when the show aired. She and who else? Who watched afternoon television between Christmas and New Year's Eve? Anyone with any kind of life was busy with holiday activities, going away somewhere warm with a lover, skiing for the week with the family in Vermont. Something a little more exciting than going to the after-Christmas sales by herself. If only Zoey and Charlotte weren't so busy right now…

This week she had two small jobs and then Charlotte's wedding was coming up on New Year's Eve, next Monday. *That*, at least, was something to look forward to.

"Oh, there you are!" Candace Downing slipped into the cloakroom, closing the door behind her. "I was hoping you hadn't gone yet—did you catch the rest of the show?" Her eyes were sparkling and her hands fluttered.

Lydia nodded. She'd been curious to see the puppet guy. How weird was that—doing a puppet act for pets? Plus, she was always looking for interesting party acts so she could recommend them to clients who asked, an old habit from her days with Call-a-Girl, the little do-everything business she and Charlotte and Zoey had run when they were in college. She'd met Zoey Phillips and Charlotte Moore ten years ago when they all worked at Jasper Park Lodge in the Alberta Rockies the summer after high-school graduation. That fall, they'd started Call-a-Girl. Cutting grass, shoveling snow, catering birthdays, housesitting, walking dogs—they did anything to pay the bills.

Now Charlotte was getting married at City Hall on New Year's Eve, Zoey was marrying some cowboy from out West just before Valentine's Day—and Lydia was cooking no-fat meals for a ladies-who'd-rather-lunch breakfast club and organizing closets for an industrial tycoon who'd bullied her on her fee to the point where she'd nearly turned down the job even though she needed the work. You could see why these people got rich; they never let go of anything.

"You wanted to see me?" Lydia smoothed on her gloves. Bright, bright red, to match her cashmere beret from Holt's, a pre-Christmas sale present to herself.

"Nice gloves," Candace said.

"Thank you." Lydia smiled.

"Listen, have you got time for a coffee?" Candace glanced at her watch. She was a small woman, much more petite than she appeared on television. Thick dark hair, blue eyes, very pretty.

"Sure. Why?" Lydia was mystified. She'd done a good interview with Candace Downing, she thought. The invitation to be a guest on her show was welcome, particularly during the slow holiday season. She'd expected a bit of a put-down for the work she did with Domestica—she often got one—so had been prepared with her answers. Lydia believed passionately that her work had a positive effect on people's lives. Had she made a convert? Maybe. Candace probably wanted to hire her. Some people were so furtive about it. As if aspiring to a well-run household should be some kind of...of *secret!*

"Let's go down to the caf," Candace said, opening the door again. "I've been thinking about what you said on the show. I may have a client for you."

They both ordered lattes in the cafeteria that served the building and the neighborhood and took a seat by the window. Although it was late morning, they were the only people there. It was Boxing Day,

December 26, and Lydia assumed most office staff in the area had the entire week off between Christmas and New Years.

"You ever do longer jobs—you know, a couple of weeks, maybe months if necessary?" Candace stirred her coffee vigorously. Lydia had the impression that Candace did everything full-tilt.

"No, but I'd like to find something like that," Lydia said. "A longer job would allow me to prove that the things I do can make a real difference to a real family. You can't adequately judge results doing a weekend closet job." She eyed her companion over the rim of her coffee cup. "Depends what it is, of course."

"I'm thinking of my ex."

"Your ex?"

Candace's blue gaze met hers steadily. "Yes. His life is one big mess. I wouldn't mind so much, but he's raising our daughter and I worry about her. His mother helps out a lot and she's very Old World—Portuguese—not that I have anything against the Portuguese, of course. But she's very—" Candace gave her a girl-to-girl look "—you know, quite *persuasive,* and I'm worried that Amber isn't getting the type of influence she should have...."

"How old is Amber?"

"Eight," Candace replied. "Her nana is totally traditional. No offence, of course, considering what you do, but you know the type I mean? Cooks and cleans all the time? Believes a woman's place is in the home looking after her man, garbage like that? She's giving Amber the wrong idea about modern women.'' Candace took a sip of her coffee, put it down and stirred in more Sweet'n'Low. She shook her head. ''*Very* wrong.''

''What would you want me to do?'' Lydia shrugged. ''And surely your ex-husband would be the one to talk to?''

''Of course! Your Domestica thing sounds perfect, though. I'll mention it to him. He takes my advice on most things to do with Amber.'' Her expression was rather smug and Lydia wondered what kind of wuss she'd been married to. ''He's one of those guys who's never done anything for himself domestically. Mama did everything. Ironed his shirts, picked up his socks, cooked his breakfast, tied his ties. Don't get me wrong. *I* was never a great housekeeper—''

Candace laughed, looking thoroughly pleased to acknowledge her shortcomings in that department, which irritated Lydia. But she'd seen the attitude a million times before, especially with career moms like Candace.

''—but it didn't matter. I hired people to do the nitty-gritties—and I have tremendous respect for someone like you who's made a business out of it. Sam went straight downhill after we split up. And now, since he's had a home office—whew! Seriously, you don't want to know. Everything's totally disorganized.''

"Where exactly do you see me fitting in?''

"Everywhere!'' Candace leaned forward. "You could start with the cleaning thing, get that house of his sanitized. That's number one. Then you could organize him. He's totally helpless. He sends out all their clothes to a laundry, even Amber's pajamas. They can't keep a maid—they've had about half a dozen this year alone. Seriously! No one will stay. I don't blame the housekeepers. These days they interview the clients, you know, not the other way around. They can get all the work they want at easier places.''

Lydia bit her lip. Sounded bad. "It would be a...challenge.''

"You could do it, I know you could. You're smart, you're organized, it's your business, for heaven's sake! Charge him as much as you want, he's got money. Teach him how to shop and cook. You do that, don't you? Yourself?''

"Yes. And I've got part-timers who work with me.''

"What clients do you have now—for food preparation, I mean?''

"A ladies' breakfast club. That Raptors guy, Griff—''

"Not Griff Daniels! The basketball player? Is he as sexy as they say?''

"I guess so. If you like your guys seven feet tall." Lydia made a face. "I don't."

"Hey, to each her own." Candace giggled. "I'm going to try and get him on my show. Never mind that, you've got credentials, that's the main thing. Sam can't cook. They live on cornflakes, pizzas, Chinese takeout, Swiss Chalet. Or his mother brings food over. Isn't that terrible? And I haven't even got to the worst part yet!"

Candace studied her for a reaction. Lydia decided not to ask what the worst part was. "Listen, if things are so bad," she began gently, "why don't you have your daughter live with you?"

"Oh, no! That's out of the question." Candace breezily waved a well-manicured hand. "Sam and I made a deal when we split up so I could pursue my TV career. Anyway, he's the better parent. I travel a lot and I have long hours, so I'm never home. Plus, well, you know—" she lowered her voice confidentially "—I *like* it this way. He's a terrific father. Reliable, responsible. A natural. And Amber adores him. It's just the chaos factor in his house, that's all."

Why, Lydia wondered, had Candace had split with such a prize? Obviously she wasn't telling all. "Okay, I know there's more—what's the worst part?"

"The home office thing." Candace set down her cup. "He used to do corporate law when we were married, but then he decided he didn't like the hours, especially after Amber was born. So he cut back on the corporate stuff so he could do more of what I call street law.''

"Street law?"

"Hookers, ne'er-do-wells, B & E artists, old broken-down has-beens of one kind or another." Candace shuddered delicately. "You name it. Waiters who've been robbed of their holiday pay by bosses, people who say they've been framed by the police, you get the picture." Candace rapped her lacquered nails on the tabletop. "He won't give it up. Feels sorry for those people. Luckily, he still has regular clients who actually pay their bills.''

"Does he deal with *murderers?*" Her ex sounded like quite a guy.

"Oh, no!" Lydia frowned. "At least I don't think so. Heavy-duty criminals, like serial killers or bikers or anything, would get some big downtown lawyer, don't you think? No, I'm sure it's not *dangerous,* just that it's no place to bring up a girl with these *people* running in and out of his house.''

"Surely not his house!"

"Well, home office. But he ends up making friends with half of them and they end up in the house. He's very social. Anyway, that's next on the list. First we get him organized, then we get rid of that home office. We can work on that later.''

"We?"

"Well, me." Candace giggled again. She had a

very girlish laugh. "But I can see that we're going to understand one another very well, Lydia. And that's half the battle, isn't it? Will you consider taking him on—*please?*"

Lydia smiled. She liked Candace, one of those pretty women who were an inch deep and a mile wide and didn't care who knew. "I will. Of course, I'll need to talk to your ex—what's his name again?"

"Sam." Candace scooped up the bill. "Sampson T. Pereira and you know what he always tells people the *T* stands for?"

"What?"

"Trouble!"

CHAPTER TWO

SAM STEPPED AWAY from the shower and walked nude over to the wooden bench he and Avie shared by their lockers. He grabbed a towel and began to mop his streaming head. "Candace called yesterday, Av."

"Yeah?" Avie Berkowitz, his pal from grade school and regular partner—perennially losing partner—at Tuesday and Thursday squash sessions, was already dressed. He examined his chin in the mirror inside the locker door. "To talk to the kid?"

"No, to me."

"Ah. Let me guess—she's on your case again."

"That's it." Sam rubbed his face briskly. "She wants me to make some changes. New year coming up and all that. Get the house under control. She's got a point. You know what it's like around there." Sam managed to squeeze out a chuckle. "Matter of fact, she's already got someone lined up for the job. A guest she had on her show."

"That's our girl Candace. Why do something yourself when you can get someone else to do it? And, preferably, get our boy Sam to pay for it."

"You're too hard on her, Av."

"She's a bitch."

"She's Amber's mother. She's not a bitch—she's just superficial. That's allowed."

"If you say so." Avie ran a comb through his sandy hair. Sam stopped toweling to admire the way his friend expertly camouflaged the shiny spot on the crown of his head with a few quick strokes. Avie was only thirty-three, Sam's age, but he was already a little soft around the middle and a little thin on top. "So, she wants you to get someone in to redo your life? We're talking about a woman, I presume."

"Yeah." Sam finished drying off and reached for his jeans. "I'm definitely thinking about it. Trouble is, it's kind of weird. You remember Steve Lane?"

"Of course I do. Graduated bottom of our class, lineman for the B.C. Lions for two years, went into real estate, last I heard. What's he do now?"

"Stockbroker—"

"Bay Street?" Avie looked incredulous.

"No, Winnipeg. Listen, this woman is Steve Lane's little sister, believe it or not. She runs this trendy one-person business, shopping, doing closets, cooking, basically straightening out people's lives."

"Doing closets? I could use someone like that," Avie muttered. He turned to Sam. "Good-looking?"

"A babe. *Major* babe. I saw her on Candace's show." Sam stepped into his briefs and jeans and pulled them up.

"Even better. Do I detect some hesitation, pal? Is there a problem?"

"Yeah, history." Sam grinned. "She used to have a big crush on me. Some coincidence, eh?"

"No kidding?" Avie studied him with real interest. "That a factor?"

"Well, no." Sam sucked in his stomach to do up his button and zipper. Avie wasn't the only one getting a little soft. Time to go back to Guido's Gym and start punching bags again. This uptown squash stuff was great, but pumping serious iron was what he really needed. "I never went out with her. Never even *talked* to her that I can remember. Steve told me she had the hots for me. When I heard that, I avoided her like a bad case of the—well, you know."

"Why?" Avie slipped on his jacket.

"She was fifteen, for crying out loud!" Sam reached for his shirt. "Sixteen, maybe. I just feel weird about it."

"Hey, she won't even remember. Believe me, at fifteen, they've got crushes on anything with an Adam's apple. No kidding, my sisters used to go through guys like penny candy at that age." Avie should know; he had four sisters.

Sam had two sisters himself. Why didn't he recall stuff like that? "Yeah?"

"Yeah." Avie slapped him on the shoulder as he buttoned his shirt. "Trust me, she won't remember you. And even if she does—so what? Listen, I gotta go. Meeting somebody at five.'' He winked and Sam laughed. ''By the way, you got anything on for New Year's?''

''Nope. Maybe go skating or watch the fireworks down at Ontario Place.''

Avie gave him a skeptical glance. ''Really?''

''Yeah, we did it last year. It's fun. This someone new you're seeing?''

''Not exactly.'' Avie winked again. ''Brainy type from Accounting I've had my eye on for a while. We're on for New Year's Eve, too. You still seeing that pro tennis player? Delores something-or-other?''

''No.''

''Jessica? The art-school babe?''

''Not really.'' Sam shrugged. ''I'm going to a gallery launch with her in January, that's all.''

''Okay. See you later.''

''Good luck.''

Sam picked up the socks he'd worn to the gym, walked over to the sink area and dropped them in the garbage can. He pulled a new pair from the twelve-pack of white athletic socks he kept in the locker. Shoving aside his motorcycle helmet, he sat down on the bench to pull them on.

Come to think of it, he hadn't washed socks for years. Or briefs. He was embarrassed to send them out to the laundry, along with everything else. He recalled a law clerk laughing hysterically as he told Sam he'd read in the paper that Sylvester Stallone, the actor, always put on brand-new briefs straight out of the package, never wore a pair twice. They had to provide him with new ones wherever he went, on location. Brand-new briefs every day! Could you beat that?

Sam had tried to work up a laugh for the clerk's sake—but, hey, what was so funny about that?

He zipped his leather jacket and picked up his helmet by the visor. Keys? He patted his jeans pocket. He'd brought the Harley although it was cold today. Maybe he should've taken a bus. But he couldn't disappoint the street kid who kept an eye on his bike for him when he came to the Y. Sam always dropped him a twenty, which made for expensive parking, but the kid needed the cash. Now he had to get Amber from the community center day camp. On the Harley. In zero-degree weather. Bad planning.

Sam sighed. Candace was right; he could use some organization in his life. A sense of order and what had Lydia Lane called it? Oh, yeah—sanctuary.

THE DAY AFTER the television show, on the way back from finishing the industrialist's closets, Lydia peered into her mailbox at the entrance of the converted warehouse building that housed her loft. Aha! Letters.

She opened the brass wicket and pulled out three cards, two flyers and a nice fat envelope from Wolverine Productions. Finally!

She ripped open the envelope and scanned the contents. Bull's-eye—they wanted to rent her loft for six weeks. The contract was enclosed, if she was still interested.

Was she! Her new loft was a big financial worry. And now the van's horrible engine noises were giving her heart failure, plus it had stalled twice in the last week. It was still at the garage and she'd put off calling to find out what was wrong. She didn't want to know. Bad news, for sure.

She'd bought the loft on impulse last summer, unable to resist the location or the price, but her finances weren't really solid enough to take on a big mortgage. Then there were taxes and utilities and various property owners' expenses she hadn't really considered. She'd made all her mortgage payments so far—a thrill after so many years of pouring money into the black hole of rent—but she'd overstepped her meager decorating budget this fall and been forced to economize drastically at Christmas.

Right now, with the usual midwinter, post-Christmas slowdown, she couldn't afford to spend much on the loft or—heaven forbid—major repairs to her vehicle. But neither could she bear to live with no closets, raw cement floors and uncurtained windows. She absolutely *had* to fix the van, if it was broken. She couldn't conduct her business without it and she couldn't afford a new one.

Two weeks before Christmas, a friend in the movie business had mentioned that Lydia's loft was a perfect location for one of her clients, and last week someone from Wolverine Productions had come around.

Now they were offering big bucks to take over her loft for a month, possibly six weeks. With the money, Lydia could fix up the apartment the way she wanted. It was terribly tempting. Her friend had told her that any improvements the movie people made you could keep if you wanted. Like paint, carpets, drapes. Even furniture. Whatever wasn't rented, they'd sell you for almost nothing.

Lydia hurried to the elevator. The big drawback all along had been where she'd stay while the movie was being filmed. She'd tested the waters with her mother, but the invitation had been very reluctantly extended. Marcia Lane had a new boyfriend and Lydia knew she wasn't keen on reminding him that no matter how fun and frisky she was, she was still on the far side of fifty and had a daughter of twenty-eight to prove it.

There was the possibility of using Charlotte's place while she and her new husband were away on their honeymoon for three weeks, but that wasn't long enough. She'd have to find a second place if the movie people wanted her loft for the full six weeks. Zoey? Maybe. Now, with the possibility of a longer job coming through for her...

Lydia punched the elevator button again.

Sam Pereira. After all these years.

Somehow she'd known he'd end up married to am

airhead. It was justice, really. Lydia stared at the big
steel doors as they slowly opened. Her loft was on
the third floor. She hadn't let on to Candace Downing, of course, but Lydia knew very well who
Sam T. Pereira was.

And the *T* standing for trouble? He wasn't far off.

She'd met Sam Pereira when she was fifteen.
Chubby, naive, painfully shy and…well, fifteen. Her
brother Steve had already graduated and was working at a menswear store, a job he hated. He'd been
scouted for football in high school—as had Sam,
Lydia found out later—but Steve's marks weren't
good enough and the scholarship offer had been re-
scinded. Instead, he'd lived at home, worked out at
Guido's Gym and dreamed of being scouted by the
CFL in a trans-city league game. Mostly, Lydia
knew, he wished he had the money for a big, noisy
motorcycle like the one Sam Pereira had.

Sam Pereira was hot. Hot, hot, *hot*. There was just
no other word for it. He was tough and handsome.
Tall, dark-haired, brown-eyed, with a sexy smile and
a body hard as a rock, not that Lydia had ever *felt*
any of it. But she could guess. He wore jeans and
sunglasses and black T-shirts with the sleeves torn
off. He swaggered, and women loved him. Even her
mother giggled and got rosy-cheeked when Sam
came to the house with Steve. He was always full of
compliments for her hairdo, her taste in clothes and
decor.

Like Steve, Sam was an athlete. But instead of

playing football after high school, Sam worked in a garage and concentrated on boxing, of all things. Lydia and her friends didn't know anything about boxing except that it was an icky, stinky, sweaty sport where guys wearing baggy shorts bashed away at each other until one fell down or one was declared a winner. According to Steve, the judges were all on the take. So why did they do it?

Lydia and her group sometimes used to skip school on Fridays and take the streetcar to Guido's Gym on Fisher Street to watch the matches when Steve or Sam was fighting. They were all in love with Sam Pereira. Exhibition matches were free, and Lydia thought that was because the gym was just glad to get a few spectators. She and her friends would each buy a hot dog and a soft drink and stand on the sidelines and scream and yell like the rest of the crowd, most of them men. If Steve happened to spot them, he'd always make a big fuss, send them home and warn her he'd tell their parents if Lydia came to Guido's again. It was no place for a girl, he insisted.

Early that spring, goaded by her best friend, Carly Dombrowski, Lydia wrote a note asking Sam if he'd escort her to a Valentine's school dance, a fund-raiser for the graduation festivities planned in June. Lydia thought it was a good thing. She knew that lots of past graduates of Selkirk High were attending the fund-raiser. Why not Sam Pereira?

She'd written the note—on pink, scented notepaper, she recalled, to her endless embarrassment—because she couldn't bear to speak to him in person, even though he was a regular at their house. She was too shy, and what if he turned her down? A note was easier. If he didn't want to go with her, he could write her back. No one needed to know.

The big mistake was giving it to Steve to deliver. Steve, of course, read it. He was furious with Lydia and reamed her out for being sex-crazed. A ludicrous accusation, since she was fifteen and planned to remain a virgin until marriage. He said she was just a baby in ninth grade, way too young for his friend—who had to be all of about nineteen or twenty—and too bold and too dumb and too just-about-everything-else. She'd yelled back that this was just a stupid dance they were talking about; she wasn't asking Sam Pereira to *marry* her. She'd screamed and wept and complained to their mother—who'd put her fingers in her ears, Lydia remembered—and then ran to her bedroom, slamming the door so hard it nearly popped off the hinges. She'd cried herself to sleep.

Rather suddenly, Sam had disappeared from her life. Steve told her he'd gotten a job in Montreal, at an athletic club, which, she knew, was guy-talk for another seedy gym. Lydia always wondered if Steve had told Sam about her note. Surely not. What would be the point? At the time, Lydia hadn't understood the reason for Steve's behavior.

Later, when rumors about Sam's escapades in Montreal and elsewhere penetrated their neighborhood, she began to understand. Steve obviously knew his friend a lot better than Lydia did. She'd certainly never heard that Sam had cleaned up his act and gone to law school and become a responsible citizen. What *she'd* heard was that he was always in and out of trouble—with the law, with women, with ex-girl-friends, with the shadowy figures who frequented the clubs and boxing world. He lived on the edge, no matter where he was.

By the time she graduated herself, Lydia had much more sympathy for her brother's reaction. No way did Steve Lane want his little sister mixed up with the likes of his best friend.

At least not when she was fifteen years old.

Lydia opened the robin's-egg-blue door to her loft and deposited the few groceries she'd picked up on the kitchen counter. The light on her machine was blinking—Zoey, wanting to know if she could meet her for lunch on Saturday, to go over some last-minute details for Charlotte's wedding. Yes, that would be fantastic; she'd return Zoey's call after she'd had something to eat. No messages for Domestica.

It was so odd, thinking about Sam Pereira after all these years. Steve never mentioned him. Until yesterday morning when she'd had coffee with Candace Downing, after the show was taped, she'd even forgotten about that little crush she'd had on him thirteen years ago.

After graduation, she'd gone to the summer job at

Jasper Park Lodge where she'd met Zoey and Charlotte, who were still her best friends. Sam had obviously joined the real world, had a daughter and an ex to prove it, and she was no longer a virgin. She'd held out until twenty-two, a lot longer than most of her friends, and then given herself, heart, body and soul to a park ranger she'd met while working at a kids' summer camp in Algonquin Park. That had lasted two months, before Lydia realized he was more interested in bears than he was in her.

Since then, she'd had several boyfriends. She was currently without a man in her life, hadn't really been serious about anyone since Joel Monday, a guitarist and part-time clerk in a music store, who'd told her after they'd been seeing each other for over a year that he'd done some soul-searching and decided he was finally ready to make the big commitment. It was embarrassing to recall. Lydia had been poised, heart racing, wondering if she'd say "yes"—and then he'd said he was committing to his career and going to Chicago to join a boy band. Boy band! He was twenty-seven!

Since then—nearly three years—she'd started Domestica and had been too busy to invest much energy in her love life. Who *had* been her last date casual or otherwise? Let's see—Tag Blanshard, the circus guy. Trained trick horses or something. He'd gone off to Germany on a circus contract and she hadn't heard from him again. He'd been fun. Weird, but fun. What was it about her that attracted such oddballs?

Lydia glanced into her living area. Charlie, her lovebird, chirped his loud "how ya doin'" greeting. The "What's New with Candy Lou?" tape stuck out of the VCR slot. Maybe she'd watch it again tonight, after a nice supper and a long bath. She'd plan tomorrow while she watched; there was only tomorrow's breakfast club to get through before Charlotte's wedding. Charlotte getting married! She almost had to pinch herself to believe it.

First things first. Lydia let Charlie out of his cage to fly around the loft, then she poured herself a glass of Australian chardonnay and put the bottle back in the refrigerator. The phone rang.

She briefly considered letting the machine take it, but after the third ring she picked up. "Hello."

"Is this Domestica?"

"Yes, it is. Can I help you?" Good—she crossed her fingers for luck—some new business.

"Lydia Lane?" She felt it coming, like a buzz in her elbow joints.... A sexy male chuckle. "Hey, you'll never guess who this is."

She thought about guessing, but he didn't give her time.

"Steve's friend—Sam Pereira. Remember me?"

CHAPTER THREE

FOR A SPLIT SECOND, Lydia thought about playing dumb, but decided that was giving Sam Pereira more importance in her life than he had: he was a potential client, according to his ex. That was all. "Sure I do. How are you, Sam?" she asked pleasantly.

"Fine, fine. Yourself?"

"Very well."

"Married? Kids?"

"No." She racked her brain for something to say. Funny how you could obsess about a situation like this—well, she had when she was fifteen—and come up with a million clever remarks but when the time came, your mind went blank. "How about you?"

"Divorced. One daughter."

"That's nice—not about the divorce, I mean. I meant your daughter, that must be nice." She took a deep breath. "So, do you still see Steve much?"

"Now and then. We spent some time together last summer near Peterborough. I was with him and Avie—you remember Avie Berkowitz?"

"No." She remembered a Jill Berkowitz, who was probably related.

"He graduated with me and Steve. We went fishing, the three of us and my little girl. Rented a cabin for a week. Caught some northern pike."

"Great." Lydia was starting to feel silly. Where was this conversation going? "Well, it's good to hear from you, Sam, after all this time—"

"Fourteen years."

Had it been that long? Thirteen, Lydia had thought. "As a matter of fact, Candace Downing mentioned your name to me yesterday."

"That's what I'm calling about," he said quickly, the charm evaporating as he picked up on what she hoped were her cool, attention-to-business tones. "Candace is, uh, she's my ex, you know."

"Yes, she told me. She mentioned you might call me regarding Domestica—"

"That's it. Candace thinks I could use your company's services. Organizing my house or whatever it is you do. I'm not a hundred percent convinced but I told her I'd talk to you."

"I understand. Domestica isn't for everyone," Lydia said stiffly. Honestly, she was so tired of people being skeptical about the joys and rewards of making a house a home, even people who desperately needed it.

"That's what I told Candace. Can we get together to talk about it?"

"This is a busy season but I think I could work you in." It would have been a lie, except that with

Charlotte's wedding, this actually *was* a busy time. "We could discuss your needs tomorrow or Saturday. Or toward the middle of next week? I have a wedding to go to on Monday."

There was a horrifying split-second pause. "My...needs?"

"What you want me to do. You know the services Domestica offers clients?" she said hastily. From the frying pan into the fire!

And, of course, Sam didn't miss a beat. He chuckled. "Hey, for a minute there..."

"Does tomorrow afternoon work for you?" she interjected frostily. Really! Mr. Charming hadn't changed his ways much. "Say, two o'clock?"

"Two o'clock is fine. My place or yours?"

"It'd better be your place, Sam, since it's your place I'll be organizing, right?"

"Right. See you at two." He gave her directions to his house and Lydia put the phone down, realizing that her hand was shaking. She wished she didn't know him. She wished she was meeting him for the first time and could safely call him *Mr.* Pereira, as she addressed all her clients. It was part of the professional attitude she tried to maintain, which was hard when so many people seemed to automatically look down on the "menial work" they thought she did, even though they were paying big bucks for her expertise.

Just hearing his voice after all this time...

Would she be able to pull it off? The cool, competent Ms. Lydia Lane? Of course she would. This was just another job and a particularly interesting one, considering what Candace had said. It was ridiculous to even *think* anything else! She was no besotted fifteen-year-old who went tongue-tied and weak-kneed at the sight of a macho guy on a noisy motorcycle.

Not anymore.

And, besides, what was she worried about? He had no idea she'd ever had a crush on him. As far as he was concerned, she was just Steve Lane's little sister. She was lucky he'd remembered her at all.

SHE HAD the breakfast club assignment in the morning, which meant allowing time to zip back to the loft and change out of her uniform of the past two years—black leggings, a loose hip-length striped black-and-tan linen tunic that said ''Domestica'' on the back and a chef's apron. Sometimes, on a cooking job, she'd don a big chef's cap, too. Kids loved that. When she was doing closets or helping a client organize other parts of his or her life, she added a slip-on apron that had a million pockets in it. Lydia had sewn the aprons herself, plus tunics for her part-timers, all of whom had families of their own and had booked off through the holiday season, until the middle of January.

The breakfast club ladies were full of post-

Christmas gossip and entertained themselves while
Lydia whipped up breakfast in the middle of Mrs.
Laverty's big kitchen. There were seven regulars, all
longtime friends in their fifties, who rotated their
meetings at each others' houses every Friday morning. They'd played cards for a while, shopped and
even hired a personal trainer for six weeks once.
Now they were trying a no-fat breakfast club. This
was the last one of the year, and Mrs. Laverty told
her they'd decide next month if they were going to
continue with the club or try some other activity.

The ladies were always dieting. Lydia prepared
poached eggs with smoked salmon and grilled tomatoes with feta cheese and basil. She juiced man-
goes, strawberries and kiwis for beverages and
popped a batch of apple muffins in the oven for those
ladies who preferred low-fat to no-fat. There were
always two or three who caved and had muffins or
coffee cake or whatever Lydia baked.

Then she rushed home to change. She'd been
thinking about Sam all morning. She was curious
about him. Where he lived, how he lived, what his
daughter looked like. What kind of father he was—
a wonderful one, according to his ex. Whether law
school and responsibility had changed him at all.

She checked her messages when she came in the
door, as was her habit.

"Lydia? Sam here. Listen, my daughter would really like to meet you. What about joining us for din-

ner this evening so Amber could be there? Nothing fancy. Six o'clock? If not, see you at two.''

Well. Lydia was moved. She *did* want to meet Sam's daughter. See what kind of child had been produced by the union of a sexy Portuguese-Canadian tough guy and a delicate, Barbie doll TV-host mom. And, of course, she'd be spending time with Amber if Sam offered her the job.

Eight years old? The girl was probably either a terror or hopelessly adorable.

So afternoon businesslike was out and casual social evening was in. Lydia opened the door of her overstuffed antique armoire—she'd order built-ins when the movie money came in—and started pulling out and discarding outfits. She had an impression to make—on *two* people—and she wanted it to be exactly right.

SAM LIVED in a three-story brick Victorian on Parry Street, a block from High Park. It was one of those roomy older houses meant for a big family. The streets in the area were lined with mature elms and maples and Lydia passed a group of children playing hockey under the streetlights as she inched along in her minivan, which she'd retrieved from the garage that afternoon.

By this time of day, in midwinter, it was nearly dark. Luckily, she was able to park right in front of the Pereira house. Her mechanic had told her the van needed major repairs—a valve job, among other things. She didn't want to think about it.

She reached over to the passenger side to grab the mixed bouquet of flowers she'd brought as a neutral-but-appropriate offering to her host and prospective client. Wine, she'd decided, was too personal and presumptuous for what was essentially a business meeting. She also retrieved her leather project case, a converted briefcase in which she kept notes and plans concerning the individual projects she had on the go, both the ones she was doing herself and those she'd farmed out to part-timers. With the Christmas holidays underway, she was on her own, and her agenda pages were dismally empty.

She had mixed feelings about accepting Sam's revised invitation. She wanted the job, but she also wanted to remain on strictly business terms with Sam, something that might be harder to do while sitting down to a meal with him and his daughter. On the other hand, she was anxious to meet Amber in an informal setting. Father and daughter were both part of this project. Candace didn't want Lydia just to straighten out Sam's life and organize his shopping and menus, she wanted her to function as something of a role model for Amber. Not that a month or two of her influence would make much difference with a child who'd be at school most of the time Lydia was around.

And of course, she'd be working for Sam—not

Candace—if the job was offered. Sam was the person she needed to convince.

She got out of the minivan, which had ping-pinged all the way over—the valve problem, apparently—and balanced on the icy sidewalk. It had snowed the day before but the sidewalk leading to the Pereira residence had been neatly cleared, the snow piled on either side. At the bottom of the steps that led to the front porch, Lydia noticed a professionally lettered sign, with an arrow pointing to the side of the building: *Sam T. Pereira, Barrister & Solicitor.* His home office obviously had an outside entrance. There was a buzzer, but Lydia raised the old-fashioned brass door knocker—incredibly tarnished, she noted—and rapped smartly.

The door was opened almost immediately. Lydia felt the blood rush to her cheeks. *Sam Pereira! And ten times handsomer than she remembered.*

"How you doing, Lydia?" He grinned and extended his hand. "You look great." Was he going to *kiss* her?

She quickly thrust the flowers at him. "Here. Merry Christmas and Happy New Year. You don't look so bad yourself." The understatement of the year.

"Flowers?" He seemed dumbfounded, then pleased. "Hey, how about that? You can give Amber her first flower-arranging lesson." He held the door wider and Lydia stepped in.

The vestibule was warm, and Lydia could smell smoke from a wood fire crackling somewhere. There were no pictures on the wall and only a vinyl boot mat at the door, no carpet of any kind. He kept smiling at her, which made her blood jangle from her knees to her earlobes. Lydia fumbled with the buttons on her coat. He reached out one hand, still smiling, "Here, let me take that."

Lydia pulled off her boots and allowed Sam to take her jacket. While he hung it in the hall closet—crowded beyond belief with coats, hats, umbrellas, tennis rackets, boots and school bookbags, to name just part of its burden—she slipped into the low-heeled black suede shoes she'd brought with her.

"Very nice," he murmured as he turned to her again, eyeing her embroidered twin set and trim gray slacks. She'd thought the outfit faintly festive and yet businesslike at the same time.

She ignored the comment. "Well?"

"Come in," Sam said, leading the way. Lydia picked up her project case and followed him. He was wearing jeans and a navy polo shirt, short-sleeved, which showed off his biceps. Despite the law degree, he still resembled a neighborhood tough, from the shaggy dark hair to the well-muscled physique. He even had a vestige of the swagger she remembered.

"This is my daughter, Amber," he said proudly as they entered the kitchen. "Amber, this is Lydia Lane."

"Hi!" A sweet-looking girl with dark hair and brown eyes was stirring something in a bowl. "Dad and I are making supper."

Dropping the flowers on the counter, Sam turned to Lydia and whispered. "Do you want to be *Ms.* Lane?"

"Lydia, please," she returned quietly.

"You can call her Lydia, honey. Uh, Lydia—" His warm dark eyes swept over her again. "Can I get you something to drink? Wine? Beer? Fruit juice? Water?"

Lydia hesitated a split second. "A glass of wine would be very nice." She moved closer to the girl. "What are you making, Amber?"

"Some salad." The girl stirred whatever she had in the bowl. *Stirred* salad? "It's our special salad, me 'n' my dad's. We make it all the time. Even for picnics in the summer and at the lake when we go fishing."

"I see." Lydia stepped a little closer and saw that the girl was stirring shredded green cabbage, flecked with a few grated carrots and a bit of red cabbage. She noticed the empty cellophane bag marked "coleslaw" on the counter beside the bowl. "That looks yummy."

"It is," the girl said with a shy smile, giving the cabbage an extra stir. "Very yummy."

"Tonight's our big night to cook, right, honey?"

her father said, opening the refrigerator and pulling
out a bottle of wine. "Riesling do, Lydia?"

"Just fine." Her curiosity was aroused. "What
else is on the menu, Amber? I'm presuming you're
the cook here and your dad's just the helper."

The girl giggled. "Yes. Dad!" she said impor-
tantly, addressing him. "I need the bottle out of the
fridge, the stuff for the salad."

"Ta-da!" He plunked a bottle of creamy coleslaw
dressing on the counter and Lydia watched the girl
glug at least half the bottle into the grated cabbage
and start stirring vigorously again. "We're having
chicken and salad and little buns out of the fridge."

Little buns out of the fridge? Sam poured wine into
two glasses.

"Have you got a vase?" Lydia could see that no
one was going to do anything about the flowers. She
had the feeling it wasn't because they weren't appreciated, just that no one realized they'd die if they
weren't put into water immediately.

Sam reached into a cupboard over the refrigerator
and brought down a dusty cut-glass vase. "Never
been used," he said with a smile, giving it a quick
wipe with a paper towel. "I think it was a wedding
present. I have no idea why Candace didn't take it
with her. It's not my kind of thing."

Lydia knew he was joking but his casual mention
of his ex unnerved her. "Knife?"

"In the drawer." Sam regarded her curiously.

Lydia pulled a carving knife out of the drawer he indicated and sawed off the bottom inch of the stems. The knife was dull. She ran warm water into the vase and thrust the flowers in, arranging them very hastily. It didn't matter; they looked lovely. Shaggy and wild. She moved one cluster of chrysanthemums to a different part of the arrangement, then set the vase on the counter near Amber. ''There!''

Sam silently handed her a glass of white wine.

''Thank you,'' she said.

''No, thank *you*.'' He picked up a glass himself and gazed admiringly at the flowers for a few seconds. Then, with a smile, he gestured toward the family room, which opened off the kitchen. The fireplace, with a fire blazing in it, was the source of the smoke she'd sniffed earlier. *Sooty chimneys.* She glanced around the room quickly. A very dead Christmas tree sagged in one corner. Other than that, it was a pleasant, comfortable room, but sadly in need of care. Dust on most of the horizontal surfaces, fingermarks on the woodwork, and the mirror over the mantel didn't look as if it had been cleaned in a while.

Sam raised his glass and smiled. ''To old friends.''

''To old friends,'' she repeated, although it wasn't at all true, and took a sip of the reisling, which was crisp and cold. They'd never been friends. She didn't think she'd even *spoken* to him until now.

"Quite a coincidence, isn't it?" he asked. "You being Steve Lane's kid sister?"

"Mmm." Lydia perched on the edge of the loveseat that fronted the bay window. "Isn't it? Steve and I aren't that close anymore. He lives in Winnipeg, has a family."

"I know. You're what, three or four years younger than him?"

"Five."

"Then Candace having you on her show like that." He shook his head and smiled. *He still had a killer smile....* "How are your parents, by the way?"

"Mom's fine. She has a new boyfriend."

"Yeah?" He looked rather shocked. "What about your dad?"

"Oh!" She realized he thought her mother was having an affair. "He lives in New York State. Albany. They've been divorced for ten years. Right after I graduated from high school, actually. I thought Steve might have mentioned it."

"No." Sam shook his head and studied her over the rim of his wineglass. Lydia wished he wouldn't stare. She didn't really want this visit to become personal in any way. Maybe she could hurry things up in the kitchen. "Do you want to talk business? Or is there anything I can do to help with the meal?"

Sam laughed. It was a very familiar sound, one that sent little skips of sensation down her spine. "Hell, no. It's our usual Friday night supper, when we don't eat out, that is. Cabbage salad, those pre-made biscuits in the refrigerator roll. Amber loves them—''

The buns out of the fridge.

''—and some chicken from a *churrasqueira* on Bloor Street. That's my part.'' He checked his watch. ''I'm expecting the delivery kid any minute.''

''I thought you said this was your big night to cook,'' she reminded him, taking another sip of wine. She sat back, feeling slightly more comfortable. What had she been so worried about? Sure, he was sexy and handsome as ever, but now that the initial shock had worn off, she knew she was fine. She'd met handsome, sexy guys before. Even the circus guy was handsome and sexy, although he sported a few too many tattoos for her taste.

''Hey, we *are* cooking—biscuits and salad.'' He set his glass on a table beside him, the surface of which was littered with magazines and newspapers. ''What can I say? At least it's not pizza.'' He made a face and she smiled. ''Candace was pretty impressed with you the other day. She thinks you could probably do a lot for me.''

''And you don't?''

He picked up his glass. ''Damned if I know. I've had five housekeepers this year. Or six, I can't remember. I'm game to try anything.''

''I'm not a housekeeper,'' she warned.

''No.'' He watched her carefully for a moment,

then took a sip of his wine. "I understand that. But I'm not sure exactly what you do."

"I teach people how to look after themselves in their own homes. That might sound strange, but a lot of people just don't know how to do it anymore. They lurch from one crisis to the next, whether it's no bread or milk in the house at breakfast time or no clean laundry when they need it. They've never learned the organizational skills to create the kind of quiet, efficient surroundings they want to live in and to maintain those surroundings with the least possible effort. They haven't learned how to balance their busy lives with the requirements of a smoothly running household. And that's what I teach them."

"Wow." He actually looked impressed, which Lydia found encouraging. It was her standard pitch. "The kind of things moms do," he murmured.

"Some moms." She gave him a skeptical look. "Maybe your mom. And mine, when Steve and I were little. In the past, yes, these were the skills passed down from mother to daughter. Life has changed."

"Sure has."

She crossed her legs. "People are different, too. It's not one size fits all. Everyone wants a different kind of home. I try to design systems to suit my individual clients."

"Sounds interesting. We're not too formal here, as you've noticed."

"Yes. Some people like formal surroundings, with everything in its place, and others prefer to live more casually. The trick is to organize your home so that *you* like it and you have some control over it. That way, in the end, you actually save time, which you can then spend enjoying your home or being with the people you love and everyone's happier all around. It works, believe me."

Sam laughed and Lydia's fingers tightened on her drink. "Almost too good to be true. I've tried cleaning services. Live-ins. Housekeepers..." He glanced around the cluttered family room. "Hell, I've had so many housekeepers I've got the employment service on speed dial. No one ever stays. Seriously, I have no idea why. Then, when things get really bad, my mother steps in. She's our lifesaver. Right now they're in Portugal—"

"And it's hardly her responsibility, is it?"

"No," he said slowly. "Of course not. She's raised three kids. She doesn't need to be worrying about my household as well as her own."

"Exactly. You're a grown man. You should be able to look after yourself."

He stared at her. Lydia wondered if she'd overstepped her bounds. "You're right. I should be able to handle this. So tell me what you'd suggest for a hopeless case like me."

Whew! For a few seconds there, she wondered if he'd taken offense. She reminded herself just how desperately she needed this job. "Nobody's hopeless."

"Promise?" He grinned. "Is that a money-back guarantee?"

"First we'd have some detailed talks about what exactly you want to achieve here." She waved one hand to include the room. "Throughout the house. Then I'll start teaching you whatever is necessary to accomplish that. Everything from the basics of how to wipe down and sanitize a kitchen counter to how to do laundry—" Lydia smiled but noticed that Sam didn't "—to more complicated stuff like, oh, I don't know—ironing tablecloths properly, making brioche, freezing perfect ice cubes. Depends on how much you want to do—"

"Hold on!" Sam held out a hand. "Forget brioche. Basic stuff, yes. Fancy stuff, no."

"Like laundry?"

He shrugged nonchalantly. "Maybe..."

Lydia wanted to laugh, considering what Candace had told her about Sam's overworked laundry service, but she managed to maintain a straight face. "Basics are critical, of course, but you'd be surprised how much of a difference what you call the 'fancy stuff' can make to people's lives. The happiness it can create. The serenity."

"Yeah, I heard you talk about that on Candace's show." He looked at her as though he expected her to leap right in with a demonstration. She found the admiration in his eyes exhilarating and cautioned herself that she wasn't here to be admired, pleasant as the sensation was. This wasn't a social occasion.

She could hear sounds from the kitchen. Banging sounds. What was going on in there? "Do you want to talk about specifics now? Shall I give you a quick example?"

"Sure. Chicken's not here yet." Sam glanced at his watch, then leaned back and put his feet up on the leather ottoman in front of him.

"Okay." He folded his arms over his chest and regarded her attentively. "Shoot."

CHAPTER FOUR

LYDIA WAS VERY AWARE of his interest in her as a woman but realized at the same time that Sam Pereira liked women. Always had. *Any* woman interested him. "Prices? Services? Timetables?" she said briskly.

"Services."

"All right. From the bit I've seen and from what Candace has told me, I'd start by overseeing a complete overhaul of your house, top to bottom."

"Which would involve—what?" He frowned.

"Getting everything cleaned, first of all. Carpets, furniture, kitchen cabinets, floors, walls—"

"Wow. You do that?"

"No, I don't clean. But I can go through your house and make a list of what's needed and hire a crew to do the actual work. I deal with several firms in town that specialize in cleaning. They do a thorough job."

He nodded. "Okay. Sounds good."

"It would probably be best if you and Amber left for a couple of days, while the cleaners are here," she added, doubtfully. This was a recommendation that a lot of her clients didn't like. They thought it wouldn't matter if they were on the premises but it always did. People got upset seeing commercial cleaners handle their furniture, move their goods around, clean behind their family pictures. It was human nature. Then there were damp carpets to dry, which took a day, sometimes strong odors in the house....

"As it happens, Amber's away on a ski trip next weekend with a family from the neighborhood. Would that be too soon—if we go ahead with this?"

"I'll check. I can let you know." Lydia heard a clatter and a yelp from the kitchen.

"You okay?" Sam called over his shoulder.

"Okay, Dad! Just dropped the rolling pin. Don't worry, it didn't break."

"I'm more worried about your toes, honey," he called back.

Lydia raised one eyebrow. *Rolling pin?*

"She's doing the biscuits, I guess. Okay, cleaning. I'd be in town but I'd stay out of your way, I promise. What about you? What would you be doing?"

"Me? Besides supervising subcontractors, I'd come in on the organization side. We'd go through everything together. For example, I'd guess that you want your closets done—that hall closet looks pretty bad. Also kitchen cabinets, linen closets, drawers, things like that."

"Linen closets. Hmm."

Lydia's cheeks were hot. The fire was blazing and
it was very warm in the room, especially with two
sweaters on. The wine didn't help.

"Sanctuary. Harmony. Isn't that what you promised on television?" He smiled. "I admit, it sounds
very appealing. You'd be doing this…this organizing
yourself, right? Not someone who works for you?"

"Is that a factor?" She wondered why her heart
was racing.

"Yes, it is," he said with a shrug. "I know you.
Well, I *sort of* know you from the past. Right?"
When Lydia nodded he continued. "Amber knows
Steve. I think I told you we went fishing last year.
Now Candace has had you on her show. Let's just
say I'd like to—you know, keep this personal. In
fact, I insist. That's why I preferred to have you meet
Amber casually tonight. Almost as though this is an
ordinary social occasion."

She wasn't convinced by his reasons but, regard-
less, his position fit in with her plans.

Oh. She suddenly got it.

"That way if Amber didn't take to you or I decided not to do this, we could just drop the whole
thing and she'd—well, you're just a family friend
who stopped by for dinner once." He smiled wryly.
"Then I could start interviewing housekeepers all
over again, like we've done before."

"Dinner!" Amber came into the dining room with
the bowl of cabbage salad in her hands, her eyes

shining with pleasure. "Everything's ready, Dad." Her jeans were rolled up, obviously too long for her, and her feet were bare. Lydia realized how proud and pleased the girl was to participate in the dinner preparations for her father's guest. Somehow, Lydia couldn't see Candace allowing an eight-year-old to muck about with a salad or touch a hot oven to bake biscuits. If it was a safety issue, maybe Sam shouldn't either.... Lydia didn't know.

The doorbell rang. Sam stood and took Lydia's empty wineglass from her nerveless fingers.

"You understand, don't you?" he said softly, moving very close to her. She met his gaze, difficult as it was with him so near.

"Yes," she said. "I understand."

The doorbell rang again.

"You go join Amber at the table, okay?" he said, touching her shoulder lightly. He looked apologetic but she supposed he'd actually done her a favor by letting her know how things stood. "This is her big event. I'll bring in the chicken."

DESSERT WAS Rocky Road ice cream. A premium brand, Lydia noted, but then she hadn't thought for a moment that Sam was a penny-pincher or that his domestic problems were a result of being reluctant to spend money.

Lydia learned quite a lot during the meal, without prying at all. Amber, she was relieved to see, took

to her immediately, maybe because Lydia had com-
plimented her warmly on her salad.

The girl had had a series of nannies since her
mother left, then there'd been an exclusive day care
for a while followed by up-and-down relationships
with a series of housekeepers. Sam Pereira had tried
everything in his attempts to do the best for his
daughter and run his household smoothly at the same
time.

Everything except Domestica. Her services didn't
come cheap, but she didn't think Sam would object
to the expense. He seemed desperate.

As for the salad, it *was* quite good. Kind of mushy,
but tasty—the way leftover coleslaw tasted. Lydia
had caught Sam's eye once or twice as Amber rattled
on, telling her about school and what Santa brought
her for Christmas, and had been hard-pressed to keep
a straight face. He'd been worried that she wouldn't
get along with his child! Surely the only objections
he could have now would be to the price, possibly,
and the service she could provide. She crossed her
fingers under the table; she *needed* this job.

Toward the end of the meal Sam casually asked
Lydia what she had planned for New Year's Eve and
Lydia reminded him that she was going to one of her
best friends' weddings. At the news, Amber stared
at her so raptly that Lydia almost felt embarrassed.

"Oh, I *wish* I could see a bride. I've never been
to a wedding." She glanced at her father.

"Never?"

Amber shook her head and Sam looked uncomfortable. "Never. My best friend has, Tania, her cousin got married and she got to go...." The girl's voice trailed off and Lydia felt a pang of sympathy.

"Excuse me." Sam cleared his throat and left the table. He carried the empty ice cream dishes into the kitchen, where he piled them on top of a stack of soiled dishes already in the sink. Lydia followed him with some glasses and cutlery. She wondered how one small girl could dirty so many dishes making salad-out-of-a-bag and refrigerator dinner rolls.

"Coffee?"

"Do I dare?"

"Of course you do," he said with a grin. "I make excellent coffee. It's one of my prime domestic skills. Trust me." He reached into a cupboard for mugs. "So, your best friend's wedding, huh?"

"One of my best friends. Charlotte. The other best friend, Zoey Phillips, is getting married in February."

Lydia was sorry the conversation had veered to weddings. She went back to the dining room for the dish containing the remaining coleslaw and the chicken bucket, which had been plunked down in its cardboard container in the center of the table. Even though she was technically a guest, there was no ceremony here....

"And you've never been married?" he continued, when she returned.

"No." He knew that, didn't he? Why had he asked?

"Not even close?"

Why did he look so interested? It was annoying. Lydia shrugged. No way was she telling this man about the almost-proposal from the unemployed musician!

Sam poured coffee beans into a grinder. "Poor kid. No weddings! What kind of single parent am I? I'm afraid I just don't get all this girl stuff. Maybe I ought to start haunting churches on Saturdays instead of taking her skating. At least she'd get to see a few brides and limos."

"It's her age, don't you think? Girls like weddings, especially little girls. They see it as a fashion event, like dressing up Barbie dolls, not a marriage between two people who want to make a life together."

Sam laughed softly. "Yeah, I think you're right. Hey, sometimes even grown-up girls see it as a fashion event, not a marriage," he said. Lydia wondered at the faint note of bitterness in his voice. It had been four years—was he still in love with Candace Downing? Or was he thinking of the tangled affairs of some of his clients?

Lydia returned to the dining room, where Amber was still sitting quietly at the table, apparently daydreaming. Lydia felt sorry for her. She'd be delighted to take her to Charlotte's wedding. Of course, she didn't dare mention the possibility until she'd talked to Charlotte or, at least, Zoey. Charlotte's marriage to her first love, Liam Connery, the man she'd rediscovered on her trip to Prince Edward Island this fall, was anything but formal. It was City Hall in the afternoon and a party at the King William afterward. A New Year's-cum-wedding party. One more small guest wouldn't matter....

"I wish you could meet my friend Tania," Amber said, her brown eyes meeting Lydia's seriously. "She's been to a real wedding and she knows how to make chili and everything!"

"Oh?" Making chili was quite an accomplishment for a child Amber's age. "Good for her."

"Her mom showed her how." Amber looked rather pensive for a few seconds. Lydia had a fleeting glimpse of the fashionable Candace in the kitchen with her daughter. "My nana helps me cook sometimes, but she won't let me turn the oven on by myself," the girl said. She brightened. "Dad does, though. Dad lets me do everything."

"Is Tania the friend you're going skiing with next weekend?"

"Boarding!" Amber scoffed, looking cheerful again. "Nobody skis, that's for sissies—"

"Like me," her father said, coming into the room with two steaming mugs topped with whipped milk foam. When Lydia had seen the coffee grinder, she knew he was serious about making a decent cup of coffee. Nice to see he wasn't entirely helpless. "I ski. I'll bet Lydia does, right?"

She nodded. "Not as much as I'd like to. But two or three times a winter."

"Bo-o-oring," Amber said with an impish grin.

"You used to box, too, as I recall," Lydia said, taking her mug from him. "You still do?"

"*Box?* You mean my dad used to be a boxer like that creepy old Larry Mozzarella—"

"Amber!"

"He is, Dad! Mom said. He's a creepy old, broken-down boxer—"

"Upstairs, young lady," Sam ordered. When it seemed Amber might ignore him, he added, *"Now."*

His daughter went to the door, red-faced. "How long?"

Sam glanced at his watch. "Fifteen minutes. Then you can come down and we'll see how polite you can be." He shook his head when the child left. "Sorry about that."

Lydia followed Sam back to the family room, carrying her mug of coffee and cleared her throat softly. "Larry *Mozzarella?*"

"Yeah." He grinned. "Actually it's Massullo, but the girls, she and Tania, always call him that. Larry doesn't mind. He's a client." He was silent for a full minute, frowning. "I just wish my ex-wife would keep her opinions to herself. Amber's never made fun of Larry before. I don't like that—''

"She knows him?"

"I've known Larry for a long time and, yeah, Amber's met him.''

"It's my fault, I guess. I didn't know your boxing career was a secret.''

"No secret." He bent to poke the fire. "And some career! To answer your question, yeah, I still put on the gloves from time to time. These days, it's mainly to take a beating from the young guys—like Steve and I used to be.''

She stared at him, shocked.

He gave her a crooked grin. "Keeps a guy humble.'' He set his cup on the mantel and threw another log on the fire. Sparks and bursts of flame, blue and orange, shot up the chimney and a small puff of smoke wafted into the room. Having the chimneys cleaned was high on any agenda for this place. *If* she got the job.

Sam sighed and picked up his mug. "Now, back to business. Can we talk money?''

"Sure." She was surprised he'd changed the subject so abruptly. Maybe he'd remembered that neither his personal nor professional life was any of her concern—which they weren't. He didn't blink at the hourly fee she mentioned, plus an initial assessment fee. "Or, if you like, I could give you a quote for the full job once I've had more of a chance to see what's involved.''

''That might be a good idea.'' Sam lapsed into silence again, staring at the flames. The incident with his daughter had obviously disturbed him. Lydia regarded him, unobserved for a moment. He was still such an incredibly handsome man, clean-shaven now instead of wearing the three-days' growth he'd affected as a teenager. Rugged, fit, with charisma and appeal that made a woman's pulse jump. At least, hers did. She was curious—was Sam still as much of a ladies' man as he'd once been? Probably. He'd obviously changed a lot from the days when he and Steve used to fix up old cars and drag-race at midnight. Lydia remembered her parents finding out and having a fit. Now he was a single parent, a responsible lawyer, a property owner.

Some things changed; some didn't.

Lydia put down her mug and Sam glanced up at her. ''I have a lunch date tomorrow but I could come over in the morning, if you don't mind me being here early, about nine,'' she said. ''Or we can make it midafternoon.''

''Let's go for the morning,'' he said. ''I'd like to do something with Amber in the afternoon, maybe take her to the Leafs' game.''

''Fine with me.'' Lydia stood. ''Time for me to be on my way. Thank you for the meal. It was very nice.''

"And you're very diplomatic, Ms. Lane," he teased. He accompanied her to the hall closet, where he retrieved her coat. Here was a Domestica lesson....

"You see?" she said, smoothing the wrinkles from her coat. "When your closets are overstuffed, like yours is, you can't find things—am I right?"

"Yeah, you got that right."

"And," she continued logically, "when you do find something, it's all wrinkled from being packed in—right again?"

He laughed and smoothed the shoulders of her coat after she'd put it on, a teasing, caressing gesture that gave Lydia cramps in her toes. "There! All smooth again. Drive carefully."

"I will."

He opened the door and held it for her.

"And, no question, you've passed the most important hurdle for the job. My daughter."

CHAPTER FIVE

THE ICE FOG SETTLED IN overnight. It was almost half-past nine by the time Lydia made it back to Parry Street the next morning. Traffic was hideous, plus she drove more slowly than usual due to visibility problems.

"Lydia!" Sam opened the door and threw his hands over his face in an exaggerated gesture, as if he'd forgotten she was coming over this morning, but she knew he hadn't. It was early and he clearly wasn't a morning person. She was. She'd been up since seven.

"Actually, I'm late. Sorry, the traffic was terrible," she said as she handed Sam her gloves and jacket and watched him cram them into his hall closet. She took off her boots and slipped on a pair of moccasins. Today, she'd gone for a casual businesslike image and was wearing chino trousers and a blue sweater. Under her arm, she carried her project case.

Sam, in jeans and a T-shirt, looked rumpled and sleepy—and sexy enough to want to kiss. If she'd been fifteen, she'd definitely have swooned.

"You had breakfast?" Sam ran a hand through his hair. He'd obviously showered, but that was about it. "You won't mind if I have some toast or something before we get started? I think I'm going to need fortification. How about you?"

"I've eaten." She followed him to the kitchen. Bare feet. Very *sexy* bare feet. "Ages ago," she added.

He gave her a humorous look and rummaged in the fridge, bringing out a loaf of bread. Lesson Number Two...

"Is Amber still asleep?"

"Amber? Oh, she's at Tania Jackson's. There's some show they watch together on Saturday mornings—Binky or Batty? Biffy? I don't know. Some girls' type of show. It's the Jacksons' turn to have them."

Sam popped two slices of bread into the toaster that sat on the kitchen counter. "Barbara Jackson makes sure they get a decent breakfast. It's a little competitive thing she's got going with me. Coffee?"

"Thanks." She perched on a stool behind the counter, which ran partway into the kitchen, a sort of working island that separated the kitchen proper from the breakfast nook. At some time, this house, at least the kitchen area, had been updated. "Competitive thing? What do you mean?"

"They get muffins and milk and juice here. Or something you can microwave. Like burritos." He grinned. "Over there, it's waffles, scrambled eggs, things with soy in them, the big all-out nutritious breakfast."

Sam ground some beans and there was a whoosh as he did something else with another machine, this one stainless steel. Suddenly there was a fragrant cup of coffee steaming in front of her. "Cream? Sugar?"

"You do take your coffee seriously!" She laughed as she poured in some cream and stirred.

"Yeah, if my law practice tanks I could always hire on at a Starbucks somewhere." He made another cup, for himself, and turned to her, holding his high. "You know, there are very few absolute pleasures in life...." He inhaled deeply, his eyes half-closed. "*Ahhh.* Good coffee is one of them."

"What else?" she asked, sipping at her own coffee as his toast popped up.

He buttered one slice before looking directly at her. "Sex. Chocolate. Fly-fishing. Not necessarily in that order."

Lydia set her cup down unsteadily. Well, she'd asked. "Have you ever noticed that your bread's always stale, even when you've just bought it?"

He stared at her. "*What* are you talking about?"

"The art of keeping house. What I'm here for. Last night I mentioned a few drawbacks to living with overstuffed hall closets. Today I'm giving you a tip about keeping bread fresh."

He laughed out loud, put his two pieces of toast

on a plate, opened the fridge and retrieved a jar of jam. Then he pushed the door shut with one bare foot and came over to sit on the stool beside her, still grinning. "You take this stuff seriously, don't you?" he said, echoing her earlier remark.

"So should you, since you're going to be paying me."

He inspected his toast. "Good point." He took a big bite and looked attentively at her as he began to chew.

"It's knowing these little things that makes life pleasanter and easier. Good household management. I'm sure you find it vaguely irritating to always have stale bread."

"Definitely. How did you know? I'm always cussing out the bakery for selling me day-old."

"It's not their fault. They sell you fresh. As soon as you put it in the fridge, you ruin it. Bread should never be refrigerated. Either keep it at pantry or shelf temperature, or freeze it."

"No kidding! I thought keeping stuff in the fridge meant things lasted longer. Doesn't that make sense?"

"It *seems* to make sense, yes. But not for bread. There's data somewhere, I know I could find it in one of my books, that proves bread deteriorates fastest at temperatures just above freezing. Refrigerator temperatures in other words. One day in the fridge is the same as five or six days in a breadbox at room temperature.''

He nodded, and once again seemed impressed by her knowledge.

''You're better off to buy it sliced and then freeze the part you're not going to use right away. You can take out each slice as you need it and use the microwave or toaster to defrost it. You'll always have fresh bread on hand.''

''Really?''

''Really. Of course, there's a limit to how long you can keep it in a freezer.''

''But that's another lesson, right?''

Lydia liked the genuine appreciation she saw in his eyes. Sam was going to be a keen student and a pleasure to teach—particularly since he didn't know much. He was starting at near-zero. Some of the toughest pupils were people who thought they already knew the correct way to do things, and balked at Lydia's efforts to change their habits. She always wondered, in those cases—why had they hired her if they were doing so well on their own?

''Right,'' she told him. ''We'll get into all that later.''

''Okay.'' He picked up his plate and knife and dropped them in the sink. ''Let's take a look at the rest of this place.''

Lesson Number Three? Lydia decided to postpone a lecture on keeping the kitchen clean and making better use of the dishwasher to contain and hide soiled dishes.

She followed Sam through the house, taking notes as she went. She had a checklist for each room, with estimates for the time required to put it in order, including cleaning and organizing, and also, if necessary, the time involved in planning, purchasing and installing organizational aids.

Like laundry baskets or hampers. Or shelving units. Sam didn't have any system at all. Amber put her dirty clothes on the floor of her closet and so did he, from what she could tell. Towels were piled in one corner of the bathroom. Sam seemed a little embarrassed as he showed her through his house, but she'd actually seen much worse. The carpets and curtains could stand a cleaning, yes, but his house wasn't particularly dirty, probably because his mother made sure the essentials were done, plus he'd had cleaning help and housekeepers most of the time—until they quit.

But there was no rhyme or reason or apparent method to anything she saw throughout the house. To her delight, Sam seemed utterly fascinated by her comments and advice.

"Do you wash your own towels?" She assumed he did, as the white ones were dingy and the dark ones were linty. And, after all, *anybody* could operate an automatic washing machine.

"Yeah," he said sheepishly. "How can you tell?"

"I can see you're not separating colors," she said, picking up one towel that was supposed to be white, she presumed, but was covered with pink blotches. "What's this?"

He shrugged, obviously mystified. Lydia could tell he'd probably washed it with the burgundy towels she'd seen on the bathroom floor.

"Red dye. Evidence that you don't wash your colors separately."

"There never seems to be enough of one color to do a load," he said, frowning. "So I just throw in some other colors. Saving water, right? Which is a good thing."

"Wrong. Well, you may be saving water which *is* a good thing, but you're ruining the appearance of your towels. Who wants to use towels that look like they're already dirty? There's a simple solution to your problem. Save water *and* save your towels. Do you know what it is?"

"No. You tell me, Ms. Lane," he said, arms crossed. "You're the professional." They were standing in the main bathroom on the second floor. It was a good-sized bathroom, with beautiful, old-fashioned cast-iron fixtures, a black-and-white mosaic tiled floor and a big window to the south, overlooking the back yard. The house, what she'd seen of it, was well laid out and the rooms were high-ceilinged and large. Very much a family home, with three bedrooms not even used. She hadn't seen Sam's bedroom yet.

"You buy towels of one color. All white, or all blue or all burgundy, or whatever you prefer. I like white. They're easy to bleach and they make good cleaning rags when they're worn out."

Sam stared at her. "Why didn't I think of that? Damn! It's so simple. All one color!"

Lydia couldn't refrain from laughing. Sam's astonishment did wonders for her self-confidence. She believed passionately that improved housekeeping skills really did make people's lives easier. She'd seen the magic over and over with closet and drawer organization, with personal shopping and menu-planning, with special textile-care workshops she'd done for clients. It was going to be terrific fun proving her theories with a whole house, top to bottom, and the family who lived in that house—Sam and his daughter.

"WELL, OF *COURSE* she can come to the wedding!" Zoey leaned forward and tapped her fork on the edge of Lydia's plate. They were dining at Limpopo, a new favorite restaurant of Zoey's. Lydia couldn't keep up with Zoey's favorite restaurants. This one, despite the name, was Thai.

"I suppose Charlotte won't mind," Lydia said, toying with the last of her stuffed chicken wings.

"You know she won't. Imagine! The poor little

kid's never been to a wedding or seen a bride,'' Zoey continued, shaking her head. She looked terrific. Of course, she always did, but since she'd come back from spending nearly two months out West, she had a special glow. That, undoubtedly, had something to do with the handsome cowboy she'd brought back with her, Cameron Donnelly. Lydia had met him and been totally impressed.

"She won't be seeing much of a bride, mind you," Zoey went on. "Charlotte's not wearing a traditional wedding dress. Doesn't that surprise you?" Her blue eyes probed Lydia's for reaction.

"I guess so," Lydia said with a shrug. "I never thought of Charlotte as having a quickie City Hall ceremony."

"No way! Of all of us, I figured she'd be the one with the big la-di-da Forest Hill wedding, the men in morning suits, ladies in hats, the horse-and-carriage stuff." Zoey struck a pose and Lydia giggled. She was thrilled to have her two best friends back in town after both of them had been gone for months—at opposite ends of the country, yet.

"What about you, Zoe?" Zoey was planning a wedding the Saturday before Valentine's, which fell on a Thursday.

"I'm on major fast-track. I want the full wedding, no corners cut, my family, Cam's family, all my friends. You and Charlotte as bridesmaids. Your little Amber can come to my wedding if she wants to see a *real* bride. I'm only doing this once, believe me. In fact, I have a fitting this afternoon—can you come? The seamstress is working overtime, bless her. The only thing left to decide is the menu. You could help me there. Oh, Lydia, Cameron is the most wonderful, wonderful man—I'm so happy!''

Lydia smiled. Her two best friends, both getting married. Lydia hadn't quite absorbed it all. Especially Zoey's news, which had come just before Christmas. She'd gone out to British Columbia to track down and romance her first love and ended up falling for his brother.

It was a dream come true for all of them. And to think it had happened because of the silly challenge thrown out at the Jasper Park Lodge summer staff reunion last spring. Someone had suggested they each look up their first crushes, just for the fun of it. Look where it had landed them—or at least, where it had landed Zoey and Charlotte.

"You've got something to wear next week?" Zoey glanced her way as dessert arrived, some delicate-looking coconut concoction.

"Yes. I bought the perfect dress the other day. Very forties. I find I'm in a forties mood these days, d'you know what I mean?"

"Not really." Zoey liked modern—modern fabrics, modern styles, modern everything.

"Glam. It's a wrap-around, sheath sort of thing. Boxing Day sale at Magique," Lydia said, putting her spoon into her dessert. She'd bought it the afternoon after she'd taped the "What's New with Cindy Lou?" show. "You?"

"No, I need to get something this afternoon. It's been a hectic week. You're sure you can't come with me?"

Lydia wanted to, but she still had a few things to finish so she could start making plans for Sam's house, now that it looked like the job was definite. She'd feel better with the contract signed and in her hands. "Sorry, Zoe. Business first."

"I guess you're right." Her friend sighed. "So, tell me about this new job you've got coming up. What's the guy like?"

"It's the weirdest thing, Zoey. It turns out he's someone my brother used to know—still does. They went fishing last summer." Lydia scooped up a spoonful of the cool creamy dessert. It was delicious. She wouldn't mind getting the recipe for this.

"Handsome? Single? Rich?"

"Divorced. His ex is the host of that afternoon show I was on last week. She's the one who put me on to him."

"*She* did?" Zoey frowned. "What kind of sense does that make?"

"I don't know." Lydia shrugged and spooned up more of the coconut dessert. "Anyway, she set up the whole thing. I had dinner at his place last night to meet his little girl and I went over there this morning to give him an estimate. I'm sure he's going to hire me.''

"And? What's he like?'' Zoey's frown had turned back to glee. "Did he remember you?''

"Yes. And to tell you the truth, I remember him. I had a bit of a crush on him back then.'' She threw her friend a look of appeal. "I was fifteen and of course, he didn't know I existed—''

"*First* crush?'' Zoey asked, her voice incredulous. Lydia knew why—it was all because of that silly challenge.

"Oh, I don't know about that,'' she replied calmly. "You know, when you're fifteen or sixteen you have a lot of hopeless crushes on a lot of impossible guys.''

"Come on, Lydia—*first* crush?''

"Couldn't have been, I was fifteen.'' She wrinkled her nose, trying to remember. There *had* to have been other heartthrobs. But none stood out in her mind.

"That's it!'' Zoey gestured to the waitress to bring the bill. "I'm telling Charlotte she can depend on two extras. This poor little Amber girl who's never seen a bride and her dad, who's your first love. Charlotte and I need to get a peek at him before she goes traipsing back to Prince Edward Island with her guy and I head over to British Columbia as a rancher's bride.'' She smiled a little self-consciously.

"Oh, I couldn't bring them both!'' It seemed so...excessive. Amber *and* her dad?

"Oh, yes, you could. Face it, Lydia, you hardly know the girl, so she needs her father with her, right? If Lissy was invited somewhere, I know she'd want her dad." Lissy was Cameron's daughter from a previous marriage. Zoey was acquiring a child as well as a husband. "What if she, you know—got homesick or something? Or threw up? You wouldn't want to deal with that."

Zoey picked up the bill and waggled her eyebrows at Lydia, who laughed. It was Zoey's signal to her friends, at least to Lydia and Charlotte, that they would do exactly what Zoey wanted and there would be no further argument.

"A WEDDING!" Sam couldn't contain his surprise. He changed the phone from one ear to the other and stepped over the clothes he'd been stuffing into the duffel bag that went to the cleaners once a week.

"I've talked to my friend—it's okay, honest!" She laughed nervously. "It's a very informal affair."

He could hear that she was getting a little embarrassed at his dismay. "Well, okay. Amber will be thrilled. I'd tell her now, except she's already in bed."

"My friend thought Amber might be uncomfortable without you, since she's only met me once...."

"I'm invited, too?"

"If you're not otherwise engaged, of course. I realize it's New Year's Eve."

"I'm not." Sam did some quick thinking. He wasn't keen on weddings. Definitely not. He'd been to one he particularly regretted—his own. If it weren't for Amber, he'd wouldn't mind never having met Candace. Although they were superficially friends now, it was only since they were divorced that Sam understood how little they'd had in common all along. Why had he married her? He couldn't remember. He must have been in love—or in lust— with her at the time. That was nine long years ago.... If he got married again, he hoped he'd have more sense.

At least he had a wonderful daughter to show for the experience. Candace was Amber's mom and, like it or not, she'd always be part of his life.

"I'm sure Amber will be just fine without me," he began—and then he imagined Lydia dressed up in some elegant sexy dress, maybe even dancing with him. "Hell, why not? I'd just planned to go skating with her and Tania or go to the fireworks at Ontario Place in the evening. Okay, What should she wear? A dress? Pants? Not jeans, I guess."

Lydia suggested that if Candace wasn't available to take Amber shopping, he should see if Tania and her mother would take her to a mall to buy a suitable outfit. And suitable meant a skirt or possibly dressy slacks. Whatever Amber was comfortable with. Lydia didn't seem to know any more than he did what an eight-year-old girl might consider appropriate for a wedding, but she figured Tania's mother would. All of which struck him as completely logical. He wondered why he hadn't sent Amber shopping with Barbara Jackson before.

"Fine. I'm looking forward to it. And Lydia—"

"Yes?"

"I did two loads of towels after you left."

"You did?" She didn't sound that impressed. Face it, washing towels was pretty mundane. Even *he* washed towels although he sent out almost everything else. Everything he didn't buy new, like socks.

"One white load and one dark. Separate. Blue and green are dark, right?"

"Right." She giggled. It was a delicious sound, even over the phone. "Good for you, Sam. You're a fast learner."

"You bet I am. Let's get this contract straightened away and get started. Next week? Tuesday?" He hadn't asked about working hours, when she'd be here, how long she thought it might take. "Do you have an estimate for me yet?"

"I'm working on it. Tuesday's a holiday."

"Oh, yeah. I forgot." Not that he had any plans for New Year's Day. "How about Wednesday, then?"

"I have plans for Wednesday. How about if I call you? And I'll reserve the housecleaners for Thursday so if it's a go, they can start right away."

Ms. Organized, that was for sure. A very good sign...

Sam hung up the phone and bent down to finish stuffing laundry into the canvas bag. Where the hell was the white shirt he wanted to wear to court next Friday? Every Monday morning the duffel bag went out to Cheerful Modern Laundry, a very auspiciously named business, he'd always thought. Wednesday it came back miraculously transformed, shirts starched and ironed, sweaters and pajamas folded, pants on hangers. They'd even pressed the jeans until Sam told them not to.

Son of a gun—a wedding! With cool-as-a-cucumber Ms. Lydia Lane looking like a goddess, he was sure, in whatever she decided to wear. Maybe he was letting his imagination run a little wild, but it was hard not to—Stevie Lane's younger sister had turned into a real babe. And, like Avie had predicted, there'd been no hint that she remembered him as anything more than a long-ago friend of her brother's.

It was a slight blow to his ego that he'd been that forgettable, but he was glad all the same. No baggage. All options open. She intrigued him. He was a sucker for her casual upswept hair that made a man's fingers itch to take it down, the sleepy hazel eyes, the hint of voluptuousness she probably thought well-hidden beneath sweaters and snappy charcoal trousers, like the outfit she'd worn to dinner. Or the casual slacks and covered-to-the-chin pullover she'd worn today. Her business look.

Sam had a good feeling about Lydia Lane. And he always trusted his instincts.

Lydia rearranging his household. Lydia rearranging his life.

Why not enjoy it? *Domestica*. He couldn't wait.

CHAPTER SIX

SAM THOUGHT ABOUT taking the Harley to the wedding since December 31 was turning out to be so mild that the snow was actually melting on the sidewalks. In the end, he decided, no, that might not make the best impression.

Amber didn't want to go in the Land Rover in her new dress. Sam was stunned to see the confection she'd returned with from the mall. He could understand why she preferred to avoid the Land Rover, which was more of a beat-up twenty-year-old utility vehicle they used for weekend excursions and to go fishing in the summer. They'd take a cab instead. The actual wedding was at three o'clock. Sam hadn't thought Amber would care about it, but he was wrong; she cared very much.

"Daddy!" She'd nearly burst into tears when he suggested they go to the hotel later and just catch the party. "That's not the wedding part. The wedding part is where they have rings and kiss and *get married!*"

True enough.

At first he'd been a little disturbed at how she

appeared to be lording it over her friend Tania, but soon realized that Amber's attitude was part of the experience. And Tania seemed only too happy to play the eager sidekick, asking questions—to which Amber generally didn't know the answers, but to which she didn't hesitate to respond—and offering to help do up buttons or lend Amber shoes. Once, when Sam stopped in the hall to listen, he heard Tania ask about the bride—was she a cousin?—and his daughter respond airily that, no, the bride was someone their friend Lydia knew and she was probably a princess.

Their friend Lydia!

Of course, it had escaped his mind that this would be one of the worst days of the year for cabs and they had to wait half an hour longer than he'd planned, which meant they were twenty minutes late pulling up to City Hall. They found a seat at the back of the room, just as the magistrate began his opening remarks.

The place was jammed with spectators, most of them belonging to the current bride and groom, he hoped. He knew there were lonely people whose hobby it was to attend weddings, any weddings. Funerals, too. Some of them were his clients.

Sam scanned the crowd quickly. Lydia would be at the front somewhere. As one of the bride's best friends, she'd undoubtedly have some vital role to play in the proceedings. If he didn't have a chance to talk to her here, he'd find her at the hotel later.

"I can't see anything, Dad!" Amber whispered desperately. There weren't many occasions anymore when his daughter would tolerate him lifting her onto his knee. This, however was one of them. He put his arms around her, relishing the warmth of her small, energetic body, remembering the long-ago days when she was happy to curl up on his lap, to read a story or talk or just sit there dreaming with her thumb in her mouth while he read the paper over her head. People like his mother constantly remarked on how quickly time passed, inevitably acting surprised. But the cliché had power. It didn't seem that long ago since he and Candace had brought Amber home from the hospital, one blue April day with the wind blowing and the first shoots of tulips and grape hyacinths poking through the weedy beds at the house they'd rented on Ossington Avenue. A big step up from the apartment, they'd thought. Sam's corporate practice was taking off and with the birth of their baby, all their dreams had come true.

Now they were divorced, he and Amber lived in the big house on Parry Street and Candace was deliriously happy without them, a bright but extremely minor star in the media firmament. He was happy, too. He had his daughter and his law practice, the kind he wanted, not the kind he felt he'd been forced into and—once Lydia helped him whip his household into shape—life would be easy again.

Sam watched the tall, dark man at the front of the room take the slim, dark-haired woman in his arms and kiss her soundly. Then again. The crowd's approval was evident, in smiles and murmurs to neighbors. Closing his eyes, he listened to the bat-wing sound of hands feeling about for gloves and hats in preparation for leaving.

"Ooh," his daughter whispered as the magistrate beamed at the newlywed couple. "Look, Dad! They must be married now. They're kissing!"

Ah, yes. If only it was that simple.

THE KING WILLIAM Hotel was a Toronto landmark—old, exclusive and swank. Sam had been there many times with clients, mainly dining in its richly paneled, very expensive restaurant, the Pelican.

He'd never been there as a kid, the only son of working-class Portuguese immigrants. His father was a stonemason. The kids who might've been brought to the King William for Sunday brunches or special dinners were the sons and daughters of lawyers and bankers, not stonemasons.

Sam had brought his parents to the hotel for lunch once or twice, just because he was a respected attorney now and—mostly—because they couldn't kick him out anymore. But he'd given it up when he realized his mother wasn't really comfortable having penguin-suited waiters anticipate her every need.

Frankly, the snobbish waiters still annoyed him. But they weren't dining in the Pelican, they were going to the Sussex Room, where the wedding party was being held.

Amber was in her glory, all pink cheeks and bright eyes. Sam felt a stab of guilt that he'd never realized how starved his daughter was for a little glamour in her life. Her various activities—school, girls' hockey, dance lessons, sporadic weekends with her mother and a couple of fishing trips in the summer with him—obviously weren't enough. What it came down to, he was starting to think, was the lack of a civilizing feminine presence in their household. His mother didn't count; she was very traditional and old-fashioned. Not that there was anything wrong with traditional, but Amber needed more than her grandmother in her life. Candace had settled into more of a big-sister role than a motherly one.

All of which led him back to the question of marriage. He wanted to be married—he *liked* the idea of being married—but in the last year or so he hadn't met a woman he was remotely interested in spending the rest of his life with. Delores, the tennis pro? Miranda, the stockbroker? Nope. Maybe he was too picky, but the kind of partner he wanted—and he was doubly wary after his experience with Candace—was a rare creature in his world. He wanted a modern woman, yes, independent, free-spirited and bold, but at the same time, he yearned for the secure, happy sense of home that he'd grown up with. Not just a place to come back to at the end of the day, where you warmed up microwave dinners and went to bed. That was a house. A residence. He wanted a *home*.

It didn't mean his wife had to meet the stay-at-home standards of his mother—did those women even exist anymore?—but it certainly meant she'd have to value family life the way he did.

The first person he saw when the white-gloved attendant opened the brass-and-wood doors of the Sussex Room was Lydia Lane. He'd only managed to catch her eye briefly as people were leaving City Hall. As he'd expected, she was one of her friend's witnesses to the marriage and had been standing up front, by the action.

"Lydia!" Amber immediately ran to her and Sam noted with interest how she welcomed the girl with a smile, gently placing her hands on Amber's shoulders as his daughter looked up, chattering nonstop. Lydia gave the child her full attention.

"Sam!" She came toward him, hands extended, and he enjoyed being the focus of that same smile. This was the public Lydia Lane, polite and polished. She had on a pale-pink dress made of some soft material, not tight but form-fitting. *Very sexy.* Lydia Lane had a great figure and she didn't try to disguise it or make herself resemble a stick insect. Not that she could; she had curves. He liked that.

"I was just telling Amber there are some children here she might enjoy meeting," Lydia said. "Do you want to come with us, so I can introduce you, too?"

"Sure." Sam smiled and offered her his arm. After a moment's hesitation, she accepted. He could see the warring reactions in her eyes—business and pleasure. She'd obviously decided that since this was a social occasion, his presence counted marginally as pleasure. Good. They had an acquaintance, after all, that went back many years, although she seemed determined for some reason to discount that....

"I didn't think you'd make it to the ceremony," she murmured as they eased their way through the crowd. There were quite a few people in the room, more than Sam would have expected, considering the low profile of a civil ceremony.

"We were late, unfortunately," he said, holding her arm a little tighter as they skirted a knot of young teenagers. "But it wasn't due to my usual disorganization." He raised one eyebrow, wondering if she'd concluded that it was.

"No?"

"No. Actually, I'm always on time. Dressed or undressed, I'm there...." He let the image sink in, then added, "I had a hard time getting a cab."

"So," she continued, with the slow smile he found utterly fascinating. "I might call that being a *tiny* bit disorganized—'' her eyes twinkled ''—since you didn't consider how busy taxis would be on New Year's Eve.''

Sam laughed. She was absolutely right.

''Zoey!'' Lydia stopped to greet a pretty red-haired woman with a rugged-looking guy in tow. Cowboy or truck driver was his guess. ''Zoey, this is Amber's dad, Sam Pereira. Sam—this is one of my best friends in the whole world, Zoey Phillips, soon to be Zoey Donnelly.'' Lydia glanced up at him. ''I talked to Zoey about bringing Amber to the wedding, and it was her idea that I invite you, as well.''

''Ah.'' Sam shook Zoey's hand, surprised to see a certain calculating light in her eye. Sizing him up? Surely not.

''This is my fiancé, Cameron Donnelly,'' Zoey said, putting her arm around the man's waist and smiling up into his face. There was no mistaking the look of love and devotion he returned. ''We're getting married in February and Amber's definitely invited to my wedding. You, too.'' She turned toward Lydia, and Sam wished he could see Lydia's expression. *Another wedding invitation.* ''It'll be the whole nine yards, not this hole-in-the-wall affair that Charlotte's having.''

Sam laughed and whispered, ''Better not let the management hear that.'' The King William Hotel was no hole-in-the-corner establishment. He shook the fiancé's hand, whose grip was that of a hard-working man. "You from around here?"

"No," Cameron Donnelly said. "British Columbia. I run a cattle ranch in the Chilcotin area."

"Daddy!" Sam turned to see that Amber, who had gone ahead of him and Lydia, was gesticulating wildly at them. "Hurry!"

"Looks like your daughter's met up with Cameron's little girl, Lissy," Zoey said, smiling. "She's here somewhere, playing with the kids."

Lydia took his arm again. "We'd better go. I wanted to introduce Amber to the Macdonald children who came from Prince Edward Island for the wedding. Sam hasn't met the bride and groom yet either."

"Charlotte's your other best friend, right?" he said as they walked toward Amber, who was with two other children.

"Right. The three of us met ten years ago working at Jasper Park Lodge for the summer. We've been best friends ever since. Oh, I see you've already met someone, Amber!"

His daughter appeared to be instant bosom buddies with a girl of about her own age, black-haired and blue-eyed, wearing a confection of a dress almost as over-the-top as hers. Another little girl, younger, with china-blue eyes and short blond hair, wearing a green velvet dress, stood with them.

"Mary Macdonald. She's my new friend, Daddy,

and we're going to go see if her little sister's okay
'cause Mary's supposed to be baby-sitting and she
lost her in all the people's legs. She's only four. This
is Lissy—'' she pointed to the blond girl ''—and her
dad's here somewhere, too. We're going to get some
cake and lemonade and then we're going to dance
with Mary's brothers. She said they'd let us—''

''Wow. Okay, honey. Off you go. Don't forget to
save a dance for me.''

''Oh, Daddy!'' Amber blushed and, with one
knowing eye on her new friend, spun around, mod-
eling the full skirt of her dress to best advantage.
Mary followed suit, while Lissy watched them both,
eyes like saucers. Then the three girls hurried off.

''What a sweet child Amber is!''

Sam felt his chest swell with pride. ''I think so.''

''You've done a good job with her,'' Lydia said
softly, still watching the girls from a distance.

Sam was amazed at the pleasure the compliment
gave him. No one had ever told him he was doing a
good job as a parent. Not even his mother, who regularly mentioned his shortcomings in that—and
other—departments.

''I think you have. She's sweet, she has a natural
dignity and charm, is clearly self-confident and she's
polite. What more could you ask for?''

''A tidy room. An uncluttered bathroom. Going to
bed on time without being reminded...''

Lydia smiled. She removed her hand from his arm

rather quickly, as though she'd forgotten it was there. "Listen, you don't have to stick with me—"

"But I want to stick with you."

"You do?" She seemed surprised. "There's no need. In fact, if you're bored with this whole thing, you could duck out for a little while. Amber seems quite comfortable here."

"You trying to get rid of me?"

"No, of course not!" She colored. "It's just that I—I understand if you're not that interested. These people mean nothing to you—"

"Introduce me to more," he said, reaching for her hand. He tucked it under his elbow again. "That way, they'll mean something to me. Besides—"

"Besides what?"

"I need a dance partner. In addition to my daughter, that is. And Mary, of course. And maybe even little Lissy, if she's agreeable. The rules say I should dance with the one who brung me," he said, in a mock Irish brogue. He gave her a slight bow. "That would be you, my dear Lydia."

SAM WASN'T PLAYING FAIR. He was being far too attentive. Far too much like a real date. Didn't he realize she'd only invited him for the sake of his daughter?

This was a big mistake. She hadn't actually secured the job yet and she needed that job badly. Sam seemed to be implying it was a done deal but she wasn't going to feel secure until she had a signed contract in her hands and a deposit in the bank. She'd already told the film people she'd have a final answer for them on the second, right after the holiday.

Now, he was acting like they were old friends instead of business associates. He was acting like he was her date. How much was plain reflex—good old Sam Pereira automatically working his masculine magic with any and all women—and how much was intended? She couldn't tell. He was too smooth, too practised, too…too charming. And too handsome by far in his charcoal-gray suit and tie. The truth was, it wasn't just Sam she was worried about—it was her own memories. Since she'd met him again, those memories had zinged to sudden and unexpected life.

Charlotte pounced on her the minute she returned from the ladies'.

"Lydia! Is that the man Zoey's been telling me about?" she whispered, pulling Lydia behind a potted palm—a *ficus benjamina,* actually.

"And what's Zoey been saying? Don't tell me, I can guess. Yes, that's Amber's father—she's the little girl who's never been to a wedding. Yes, I'm going to be doing some work for him this month," she said, then added, "probably."

"Oh?" Charlotte's blue eyes danced. Honestly! Between them, Zoey and Charlotte would have her married, if not to Sam, then to the next waiter who walked through. "Zoey tells me he was your first crush—"

"Couldn't have been," Lydia interjected. "I was fifteen. That man over there—isn't he trying to catch your attention?"

Charlotte looked. It turned out to be someone from catering wondering if they could set up the buffet. Charlotte left with him to discuss various details.

The band had finished tuning up discreetly on the dais and were playing light chamber music.

Sam appeared at her elbow. "This isn't dance music, but it's walking-around music. Can I get you a drink?"

There was nothing to do but agree. Sam plucked a glass of champagne from a passing waiter's tray and handed it to her with a smile. She found herself having not only a drink with Sam, but lining up at the buffet with Sam, sitting at a table with Sam, as well as Charlotte's sister, Laurel, and her husband, Frank, and watching Sam's naturally gregarious personality work its charm on them. And, finally, after the bride and groom's dance, she found herself dancing with Sam.

He was a good dancer, too. Well, had she thought for a moment that he wouldn't be?

"You look gorgeous, Lydia. I've been meaning to tell you," he said, when they'd been on the dance floor for a few minutes.

"Oh?" She angled her head to gaze up at him. He

was awfully close. "You look very nice yourself," she said lightly. *Keep it casual.* "I've never seen you all dressed up."

"Of course, since we've just met again. It's been a long time." He grinned at her and she felt her heart give a little hiccup, just the way it had when she was fifteen and he'd deigned to glance at her across her mother's kitchen. "Too long. I remember you used to have braids."

She rolled her eyes. "Yes. And I remember *you* used to have a motorcycle."

"Still do."

"You do?" She stumbled a little and he steadied her. "I thought lawyers drove BMWs."

"Some do," he said easily. "I drive a Harley. And an old Land Rover, which Amber and I use for fishing trips and grocery-shopping and stuff like that. I don't own a car—"

"You don't?" Lydia was feeling rather like an echo. "Well, how do you—you know, get around?"

"Motorcycle. Or transit. Or I take a cab." He grinned. "Believe me, it's manageable."

She nodded. Cars could be nothing but trouble. Hers always were. Necessary but expensive nuisances.

"Sam?"

"Yes, Lydia?" He looked down at her and Lydia realized she liked the way he said her name. He drew out the syllables: Ly-di-a. She felt impatient with herself for noticing.

Business. "I just wanted to say that if we sign the contract on Thursday morning, I can start immediately. I've checked with the cleaners and they'll be available. Also, I'm going to be moving over to Charlotte's house while they're on their honeymoon and—"

"House-sitting?" He frowned.

"Not really. I'm subletting my loft to a movie company for six weeks. I'll be going to my mother's after Charlotte and Liam get back...." She wished she hadn't told him; it sounded so stupid and complicated.

"But you can still do my place?"

"Oh, yes! It's a challenge and I'm looking forward to it. Very much."

"I never thought I'd say this, Lydia, but you know what?"

She looked up and met his eyes. *Big mistake.* "What?"

"So am I."

CHAPTER SEVEN

LYDIA DIDN'T SLEEP a wink. It was nearly half past one by the time she got home, snagging a ride with Charlotte's sister and her husband. She hadn't dared take the minivan for fear she'd have a breakdown, although the mechanic didn't seem to think the van's problem was something that would suddenly render it inoperable. She didn't trust it, though; the ping-ping sound from the engine was noticeably worse.

Cabs had been impossible, even at the hotel, which made her think of Sam and Amber—as if she'd forgotten about Sam Pereira for one single second during the entire evening. She was relieved that they'd left around eleven o'clock, with Sam carrying a very weary and very happy little girl out to the taxi.

His early departure had spared her the embarrassment of possibly having to kiss him at midnight, during the usual round of smooching nonsense. Everybody did it, casually and otherwise, and it would've been very obvious if she'd avoided him during the general "Auld Lang Syne."

If anyone here knew how she'd once dreamed of kissing Sam Pereira—and more! Luckily, no one did.

As she tossed and turned, she alternated between hashing over each and every detail of Charlotte's wedding and thinking about her upcoming job on Parry Street. They hadn't talked about a timetable. His house was going to take a month if she accomplished everything he wanted. Perhaps longer.

Then there was her move to Charlotte's place tomorrow. She had the place for three weeks—and then what? Her mother's, as she'd mentioned to Sam? Or maybe she could bunk in with Zoey, who was agreeable. She knew that Cameron and his daughter were returning to British Columbia in a few days and would come back for the wedding in February. But could she stand to live with someone so caught up in wedding plans and so happy—even if that someone was one of her best friends?

Right now, Lydia felt a little sensitive on the topic. The sudden good fortune of her friends had brought home to her just how thin her own prospects were. No date since September—and that had been with a man who traveled with circuses.

Also bouncing around in her mind was the immediate problem of what to take to Charlotte's, what to store in her basement locker and what to leave for the movie people. Also, what to do with Charlie. He'd be okay at Charlotte's but her mother didn't like birds. The Wolverine people wanted the key to the loft by Friday.

Wise or imprudent, she was committed.

Her mind whirled. What clothing should she pack? Jeans, some skirts and sweaters, a couple of the loose, easy dresses she favored for at-home wear and two tunics and sets of leggings, plus aprons, for her working uniform. Somehow Lydia couldn't see herself spending every day in the Domestica outfit. If it seemed acceptable to wear street clothes at Sam's house, she would. She couldn't forget he was working out of a home office and would be more or less on the premises. Just how informal was the situation? Did he have an assistant or secretary? He must, but there'd been no mention of one....

New Year's Day turned out to be rather depressing. The weather had grown colder and a thick gray cloud hung over the city. Her apartment was a mess due to her packing, with some things going into boxes for storage, others into suitcases. No one called, except her mother. Of course, Charlotte and Liam were flying to Jamaica on their honeymoon and Zoey was busy with her cowboy and his daughter. Who else would call?

Unfair as she knew it was and much as she felt thrilled for them both, she couldn't help contrasting Zoey and Charlotte's newfound happiness with her own boring, same-old existence. Here it was, a brand-new year, and she was still scrabbling for work, as always, still shopping for bargains, still nursing elderly vehicles along with regular injections of cash. As for men—Lydia didn't know what it was about her that attracted such...*unusual* people. Zoey would've said *oddballs*. The circus trainer and the would-be boy musician weren't the only two. There was the park ranger who'd preferred bears and the gay client who'd wanted to hire her as a surrogate mom. Lydia couldn't wait to finish *that* job. It was a stint she'd done in Ottawa, when she'd first gotten the idea for Domestica. Face it, *unusual* people found her, no matter where she went.

But this was the time of year to look on the bright side of life, which she normally did. She lived in a wonderful new loft that she couldn't wait to start decorating, and, on the money front, she'd had some stunning luck. The film people had offered a pile of money to use her place for six weeks as a location, and Candace Downing, whom she'd never even met before last Wednesday, had tossed a fabulous job right into her lap.

The fact was, this new year was looking a lot better than many others had.

At five o'clock she drove to her mother's house. She took her time, avoiding the thoroughfares, and the minivan responded willingly, if noisily—*touch wood*. It had to last at least until she got the first installment of the loft money. After that, she could take the TTC, the city's transit system, for a while.

"Lydia!" Her mother always hugged her, enveloping her in a cloud of scent. Today, Marcia seemed to be wearing that Elizabeth Taylor perfume, which she'd been stuck on for some years. "How nice of you to come early! How was Charlotte's wedding? Lovely, I'm sure." Her mother looked excited. "I've got someone I want you to meet," she whispered.

She took Lydia's hand and dragged her into the living room, which, since her father had decamped, had been done over several times. Gone were the traditional furniture, the florals, the hardwood floors that Lydia and Steve had grown up with. Marcia Lane had reinvented herself several times since her divorce. The at-home mom who'd baked cookies and volunteered at the library now sold real estate and favored hot pink everywhere.

"I'd like you to meet Ray! Ray, this is my daughter, Lydia. Do you know she was on television last week?"

Ray Birch was fifteen years younger than her mother—which Lydia knew, although she'd never met him. Tall and reed-thin, he had a receding hairline and an overbite unhappily topped with a bristly brown moustache, which he'd probably grown to disguise it. He eyed her with an alarming avidity, although her mother didn't seem to notice. Lydia shook his hand briefly and hoped she wouldn't have to touch him again before the evening was over.

Dinner at her mother's house was always an adventure. When Lydia and Steve were growing up, Marcia had been a good, if predictable cook, who relied heavily on recipes torn out of magazines. Now she just threw anything together and sometimes the results were sublime but often they were not.

"Would you like a drink, dear?" At Lydia's nod, Marcia rushed off to the kitchen, returning in less than a minute with a glass of white wine.

"Thanks, Mom." Her mother winced slightly. She'd told Lydia she'd rather her children called her "Marcia," now that they were all grown up. Steve did but Lydia never could.

"So, you were on TV, were you?" Ray said. "What program? Anything I might've seen?"

"Oh, you know—the one where that Candace person tells about what's coming up in town," Marcia interjected. "It's on Wednesday afternoon."

"Ah. 'What's New with Candy Lou'?" Ray took a long drink of whatever it was he had in the tall glass. "Never watched the thing." He shook his head, clearly waiting for Lydia to elaborate.

"Mom, you'll never guess who Candace Downing was married to." Lydia took a sip of wine.

"Who?"

"Steve's friend, Sam. Remember Sam Pereira?"

"Do I? My goodness, Sam Pereira," Marcia said, shaking her head and smiling. "That was one very handsome and precocious boy. What in the world happened to him? Gigolo on a cruise ship, I would've thought…."

"Mother!" Lydia was genuinely shocked. "He's

a lawyer. Used to be with some big downtown firm, but he has his own practice now.''

"Hmmm. I'd have expected him to end up on the opposite side of the law," Marcia ventured. "A lawyer? Really?"

"Yes, a lawyer," Lydia said firmly. "He's got a little girl and they live out on Parry Street near High Park in a big old Victorian. As a matter of fact, I had dinner there the other night because I'm going to be doing some work for him—"

"Oh, Lydia!" Her mother practically screamed. "*Or*ganizing him?"

"I guess so. His household's absolutely chaotic."

"Organizing him? What's that?" Ray looked rather skeptical. "Is that what you do, Lydia?"

"Yes, she shows people how to iron things and wax floors and all that sort of stuff," Marcia mumbled hastily. "Domestic arts, it's supposed to be called. Sounds terribly old-fashioned, doesn't it?"

Marcia had that worried expression on her face. Lydia had seen it before whenever her mother tried to explain exactly what her daughter did for a living. Lydia knew she would've preferred to be able to say that her daughter worked in a bank or was a teacher or even pumped gas at a minimart.

"Domestic *arts?*" Ray took another gulp of his drink. "Drudgery sounds more like it." He had a hee-haw laugh.

Lydia ignored him. "Luckily I can stay at Charlotte's for a few weeks, Mom, while they're on their honeymoon so I won't need to move in here right away. Maybe not at all. Everything's working out perfectly so far.''

"That's nice," her mother said, giving her an exaggerated wink across Ray's chair. Lydia was quite sure Marcia was as relieved as she was that she wouldn't be moving in immediately. "There may be possibilities with Sam Pereira, dear. I wouldn't overlook them, if I were you. You *did* say he was divorced, didn't you?" She added, glancing at Ray, "I do worry. She never seems to meet any decent men…."

"Well!" Ray stood up. Lydia was rather relieved to see that he had no apparent interest in her love life. "I'm quite sure that casserole is done." He rubbed his hands together. "Why don't we all sit at the table. Marcia? Lydia?"

It turned out that Ray had spent the afternoon in the kitchen and was a passable chef. They had a tasty seafood casserole, shrimp and crab in a creamy mushroom sauce, with a green salad, fiddleheads—frozen, no doubt—and a rice pilaf, followed by some kind of cherry dessert and a plate of Marcia's leftover Christmas baking.

Lydia wasn't sure if Ray was living there these days or not; her mother hadn't said.

"Happy New Year's, Mother—and Ray!" she said diplomatically, holding high the glass of ice wine Ray had thoughtfully poured with their dessert and coffee.

"Happy New Year to all," Marcia said, looking sentimental and raising her own glass. "Maybe even wedding bells this year? Hmm, Lydia?"

For someone who didn't seem to have put a lot of store in her own marriage, Marcia was awfully obsessed with her daughter's prospects—or lack of them. Lydia didn't think she wanted to answer that particular question but smiled politely anyway. There was no point in disagreeing.

Marcia wasn't finished. "My sincerest wish for you, Lydia darling, is that you'll find a man this year, someone you can love and respect. Handsome and sexy doesn't hurt, either, just like my Ray here," she finished, giggling as the boyfriend leaned over, pinched her cheek gently and called her something in a low voice. Lydia swore she heard "bunnikins."

"Oh, Ray!"

Lydia left early. She had a headache.

BY NOON the next day, Lydia had finished packing all the boxes she wanted to store in the basement, mostly personal things, clothes she wasn't going to take with her and the antique Balmoral crystal goblets she'd been given by Marcia's maiden aunt, Lydia Trimball, who lived in Ottawa and for whom Lydia was named. She was very fond of her great-aunt Trimball and knew that Marcia fully expected Lydia to inherit everything the old lady owned when she died. Lydia herself didn't expect that; she'd had many interesting conversations with her great-aunt over the years and had jotted down many recipes from her collection that went back to the mid-1800s. That was legacy enough for her. In fact, Lydia's idea for Domestica had come directly from her great-aunt, who'd lamented many times that "girls today" were terrible housekeepers. It had made Lydia wonder what a "housekeeper" was, what made a good one and why "girls today" were so bad at it.

The movie people would be packing up all the rest of her belongings but the goblets were irreplaceable, and she didn't want to risk having them broken.

She loaded up everything she wanted to take, including Charlie, and set off for the Harbourfront apartment tower where Charlotte had bought a condo overlooking Lake Ontario. The difference between her and Charlotte was that Charlotte had money, she decided as she pushed the button for the twenty-first floor. And connections. Charlotte had always had plenty of good-looking and eligible boyfriends but had she ended up with one? No, she'd had to traipse out to the wilds of Prince Edward Island and look up her first love, Liam Connery, who turned out to be the man of her dreams, after all. So much for money greasing the wheels of romance. There went *that* theory.

An hour later, Lydia was settled in. She dug

CHAPTER EIGHT

SAM STARED at his desk but he didn't see the satin finish, the deep cherry stain, the meticulous crafts-manship. One of his clients had made him the desk in lieu of payment. He loved that desk, just like he loved the guy who'd made it. Larry Massullo, former mentor, worn-out addle-brained boxer, the guy he was trying to defend on assault charges now. A guy who would step around a fly if it landed on the side-walk in front of him.

Sam didn't see the desk because all he was aware of was the uproar in his house. He could hear the vacuums, the other machines, the clattering up and down the stairs—what had happened to the carpet that was supposed to be there? Had they taken it *off?* That was perfectly good carpet, what the hell was Lydia Lane *doing?*

He'd been wondering what he'd gotten into ever since he'd answered the door at half-past seven this morning. He had on an old pair of sweatpants and had barely poured his first cup of coffee. There she was, looking sweet and scrubbed and wide-awake. Before he could offer her a cup, and then maybe take

off and get dressed—although he kind of liked the
way she stared at his bare chest, which he caught her
doing when she didn't think he was looking—there
was another knock on the door. A whole damn van
full of people! The cleaners she'd ordered up. All
cheerful and raring to go. Right behind that, another
van.

He was glad she'd called yesterday and suggested
Amber sleep over at Tania's because she intended to
get an early start. Early start! This was criminal.

"I suggested you leave for the weekend," she reminded him, as she followed him into the kitchen.
"I told you this phase of the job can be difficult for
clients to handle." The cleaning crew spread out in
all directions and two men began hauling equipment
into his house—industrial-sized vacuum cleaners,
buckets, mops, brooms, things in bottles and boxes.

"I've got work to do today," he grumbled. "And
it's not the weekend." It was Thursday.

"You wanted to get started, remember?" She
smiled, one eyebrow arched. She produced a docu-
ment. "Here's the contract. The crew doesn't work
on Saturday or Sunday unless you want to pay overtime. Don't worry, this will all be finished by tomorrow evening. Then you'll have the weekend to
yourself. Monday I'll do some measuring and list all
the stuff you need and Tuesday I have another job
I'm obligated to—"

"Another job?" He glanced at the contract with a

practised eye. Simple, straightforward, and the estimate was what they'd discussed. He signed in the two places indicated and handed it back to her. "I'll give you a deposit when I go into my office. Listen, I thought you'd be here the whole time. What's this 'other job' stuff?"

And what the hell was she wearing? Black leggings and a weird-looking tunic. Big, lots of pockets. Her company name on the back. He hoped she wasn't planning to wear that thing around his place for the next few weeks. In that tunic she looked like a—a radish just out of jail. Never mind the outfit—*she* looked fantastic. Bright eyes. Clear skin. Shining hair, pulled up loosely on top, as seemed to be her habit.

"I have an ongoing job I'm committed to, a personal chef-and-shopping service for Griff Daniels—"

"Not the point guard on the Raptors Griff Daniels!"

"The same. So, today and tomorrow will be rather hectic," she said. "I'm sorry about that, but it can't be helped. You *did* want to get started—"

"Do you go to his place for that—that personal chef thing?"

"Of course. Now, if you'll excuse me—" Off she'd gone. To rip his house apart.

Well, as she said, the sooner they started, the sooner they'd finish. He'd been thinking about her off and on—mostly on—since the wedding. The truth was, he *did* want her to complete this job in a hurry because he was interested in starting something else with her. They'd gotten along terrifically at the wedding, he thought. He'd decided he wanted to get to know her better, and he couldn't do that while she was working for him. He'd defended enough cases that involved the boss "taking liberties," as Darlene, his secretary, put it. Now he found out that Lydia was working for some sex-crazed athlete, too!

"Darlene!" He rarely used the phone to call her in the next room, although she told him he should since it was more "professional."

"Yes?" She poked her head around the corner of his office door. Darlene was a former stripper who'd taken a course to become a legal secretary with some of the money he'd won for her in a faulty breast implant case. Then he'd had to hire her—what other law office was going to hire a stripper-turned-legal secretary? He'd always speculated that she'd used the rest of the settlement on new, improved implants. These one were like giant hot water bottles down her shirt. She had to have the biggest bra of any legal assistant in town and never hesitated to display her assets.

"Harmless amusement" was what she termed it when he tried to diplomatically advise her that some of his clients might be offended by her low-cut blouses and miniscule skirts.

"Don't worry, they won't be," she'd reassured him. "I've got the legs for it and up here—" she'd looked down at her ample cleavage and giggled "—the women are either jealous about it or they're cool and the guys love to sneak a peek. It's harmless amusement."

No one, he'd informed her, had to *sneak* a peek.

"Can you get me the transcripts from that hearing just before Christmas? If they're available yet." Sam rubbed his face with both hands. He had a plea hearing tomorrow morning for Larry. *Not guilty.* "And is there any coffee left? I'm scared to go into my own house."

"I'll make some tea," she said. "What's going on, anyway?" Her eyes rolled toward the ceiling.

"Commercial cleaners. Complete overhaul by a professional organizer. Candace found someone. She had her on her show last week."

"Oh? Good for your ex." Darlene never called Candace by her name; she was always "your ex." "By the way, Larry wants to come by this afternoon to talk about tomorrow. Are you gonna be here or you meeting Avie?"

"He had to cancel. I can see Larry this afternoon after I pick up the girls." He and Barbara Jackson took turns walking Tania and Amber home from school. Today the girls were at a day camp at the community center.

Larry Massullo had been a welterweight champ in

his day, which was several decades ago. He'd worked at Guido's Gym when Sam and Steve were teenagers, and the old boxer had taken the boys under his wing and taught them everything he knew. Sam had never forgotten him, even when Larry lost his job at the athletic club and ended up next to homeless, endlessly walking the streets of Toronto, sitting in parks with cronies talking about his glory days, eking out a living with handouts and welfare. He spent the nights at a tiny house in the east end, owned by his widowed sister. Thank God for Alma, or he'd be sleeping in culverts. He had a trade—cabinet-making—but no one wanted to hire a broken-down alcoholic ex-boxer who was over sixty years old.

Now Larry had been charged with assault in a street fight. He told Sam he'd only pushed a guy who'd been harrassing a woman waiting at a bus stop—a woman who'd later disappeared. Several other youths had been involved, all friends of the young man who'd fallen and injured his head on the curb, according to Larry. They all swore Larry had beat up their friend. Because he was an ex-boxer and because he had a list of misdemeanors that went back to his early drinking days, the cops took the allegations seriously. The injured man had been removed by ambulance, and then, instead of hauling everyone else off to jail to spend the night and sort it out in the morning, they'd charged Larry with assault. In Sam's view, they'd given too much credence to the version of events provided by the young tough's pals. That, plus Larry's history, had been the determining factor in his arrest.

If, in the end, Sam failed to get the charges dropped and his old friend went to jail...

Sam didn't want to think about it. He had to find that witness, the woman at the bus stop.

"Sam?"

"Yeah," he called back.

"Your ex is here. Shall I go let her in?"

LYDIA DIDN'T HEAR the doorbell. One of the cleaners came running up to her in the second-floor bathroom to say someone was at the door. Lydia was busy trying to decide about the grout in the tile that surrounded the tub. Bleach it? Or just clean it thoroughly and recommend that Sam have it replaced soon? Grout didn't last forever.

"Okay, you go ahead and get the door, Esmeralda. I'll be right down." The woman hurried away with her cleaning rag in her hand, muttering something in Spanish.

"Ben?" Lydia called out the bathroom door.

"Here, ma'am." A thin black man appeared and she gave him the list she'd prepared. Ben was in charge of the bathroom, sanitizing it from ceiling to floor.

Lydia hurried downstairs. The house was in an uproar. She loved it. The endless, centuries-old battle of the housekeeper against the germs and dust and mildew that endangered the health and well-being of her family. This wasn't *her* family, of course, but Lydia felt the thrill all the same. The hum of activity, the whir of vacuuming and the chatter of the crew. The smell of coffee brewing downstairs. The scent of orange oil, a vital ingredient in the nature-based cleaner she preferred, and of lavender and beeswax in the furniture polish—she loved it all. If it wasn't winter, she'd have a crew outside washing windows, too—really make Sam's house sparkle. That would have to wait for spring.

Sam was nowhere to be seen. Probably in his office, which, he'd warned her, was strictly off-limits. No cleaners allowed. Lydia hadn't been in his office yet, nor had she met his secretary. She'd only seen Sam briefly that morning. He'd seemed rather baffled when the first van of cleaners drove up, followed a few minutes later by another van.

"Who the hell are these people?" he'd grumbled when the doorbell rang the first time. Had she awakened him? No, it was seven-thirty and he already had a pot of coffee on. But he wore nothing more than a pair of gray sweatpants and the view was...distracting.

"The cleaners. Remember?" She tried to keep her eyes away from his bare torso. He looked as fit and muscular as he'd probably ever been. "I told you they'd be here this morning."

Frowning, he went briefly upstairs, coming back dressed in jeans and a T-shirt, then disappeared grumpily into his office.

She glanced at her watch. Nearly noon. The cleaners had already dusted and washed walls in the upstairs bedrooms and were taking down the drapes on all the windows. By tomorrow evening the whole place would gleam. Fortunately, most of the house had hardwood floors, so area rugs could be sent out and the problem of drying steam-cleaned carpets in the middle of winter could be avoided. With luck, they'd get the upstairs floors washed and waxed before the workers went home today.

She went down the stairs, which were bare, to the main floor. The stairs carpet had been folded, ready to be taken out for cleaning, and the old-fashioned carpet rods were neatly piled beneath a nearby window.

"Candace!"

The television host was wearing a light-blue parka and knee-length fashion boots. "Wow!" Her eyes shone as she surveyed the entrance hall. "Didn't I just meet you a week ago?" She smiled. "You've been busy!"

"Thanks to you." Lydia pinned up a tendril of hair on her neck. Her elastic was falling out. "You sold Sam on the idea and he wanted to get started right away. Which is great for me."

"His mother and dad are away. He probably wants

to show his mother he can handle things on his own," she whispered to Lydia. "He'll probably try and take all the credit for this. So, where is Sam, anyway?"

"In his office, I think," Lydia said. "I haven't seen him since I first got here. Actually—" she laughed "—I don't even know where his office is."

"I'll show you." Candace wiped her boots on the mat Lydia had put down so the cleaners, who were coming and going, wouldn't bring in any more snow and grit than necessary. The entire hall, of course, would be cleaned eventually and the bulging hall closet was the first item she wanted to organize. She'd do that next week. "I've come to take Sam to lunch. You, too, if you want."

Lydia shook her head. "Thank you, but I couldn't leave. Besides—"

The door was opened by a statuesque woman wearing a very short skirt and a tight sweater with a plunging neckline. "Hi, Darlene—is Sam in?"

"He is. I'll see if he's free." *This* was his secretary?

When she left, Candace turned to Lydia. "His assistant," she whispered. "A former stripper Sam felt sorry for and hired. That's exactly the kind of thing I was telling you about. Did you see the way she *dresses?*"

"Candace!" Sam was at the door. Lydia couldn't help noticing how his eyes lit up when he saw them.

"And Lydia! Good, you two know each other, of course. What can I do for you, Candace? Did we have a meeting?" He frowned.

"No. Lunch." She looked from Sam to Lydia. "I want to take you both out to lunch. Discuss a few things—"

"Not me, Candace," Lydia repeated. "I've got too much to do here." She gave up on her topknot and pulled out the three remaining pins. To her embarrassment, Sam's gaze fastened on her hair, which had fallen to her shoulders. "You two go ahead," she muttered.

"I, uh, I guess that would be okay," Sam said, returning his attention to Candace. "Darlene? I'm going out for an hour or so. Call me if anything urgent comes up."

He went back inside and Candace grinned, giving Lydia a thumbs-up. "I'll call you later," she whispered urgently.

What was *that* all about?

Sam reappeared, wearing his jacket. "Come on, Lydia. You can leave this hellhole for an hour or so. Take a break."

"I can't," she said firmly. "Thanks, anyway."

His face clouded. "Listen, when will they be done in here? This place is a disaster—"

"It was a disaster *before,* Sam," Candace interjected, with a tiny giggle. "Remember?"

"Never mind that. This is worse. Should I stay at a hotel or something?"

"The crew will be leaving about six. If you want to book into a hotel, go ahead. Your bedroom should be habitable by then, but—" She shrugged.

"I know, I know," he interrupted with a grimace. "This phase is the one where I'm supposed to go skiing or fly to Montreal for a few days."

They walked back to the entrance of the house proper—Lydia knew the office must have a separate entrance, too—and Sam held the door for Candace. "Sure you don't want to join us?"

"Definitely not. Have a good lunch."

She closed the door behind them. *Interesting.* They seemed easy with each other, comfortable. Which was lucky for Amber. A difficult divorce could be so hard on the children involved. She wondered what they had to discuss....

Someone called from upstairs. "Miss?"

Lydia shook her head. She had more to worry about today than Sam and his ex getting together over lunch. "I'll be right there!"

WHAM!

The following Tuesday, Sam smashed the ball into the end of the court on a return from Avie's serve. It felt good after nearly a week without strenuous exercise to put his focus into smacking a rubber ball around the squash court.

Sam kept up the volley, then Avie lunged for the last return and missed. He grinned as he walked toward Sam, one hand extended. "Set point. Good game. One of these days I'm going to beat you, you sonuvabitch."

Sam grinned back. "You do that, Av."

They walked toward the exit, leaving the court for the next set of players. Avie wiped his forehead with the towel looped in the waistband of his shorts. "So, did you enjoy the fireworks?"

"Fireworks?" Sam held open the door to the locker room for his friend.

"New Year's Eve. You and Amber."

"Oh, yeah." He paused. "Didn't go. We went to a wedding instead."

"Wedding!" Avie gave him a surprised look. Sam had talked to Avie Berkowitz once or twice since they'd last played, but he supposed he hadn't mentioned the wedding. "Who got married? Anybody I know?"

"Nobody *I* know. I got invited by Lydia Lane, Steve's sister—"

"The organizer person you were telling me about?"

"Yeah. She was over for dinner a week ago Friday to have a look at my place and Amber was whining about never getting to see a bride. So she invited us."

"Dinner at your place already?"

Sam nodded and ran his hand through his hair.

"The usual Friday thing. I wanted her to meet Amber. Man, Avie! You should *see* my place. I'm wondering if I haven't gotten into something a little deeper than I expected."

"What do you mean?" Avie wiped the back of his neck and tossed the towel onto the bench in front of their lockers.

"A bunch of cleaning people came over Thursday and turned my house inside out. Two vans full. My head's still spinning. I spent the night on my sister's Hide-A-Bed and they were gone by Friday evening, but—hell!" Sam shook his head. "I can't find *anything*."

"You couldn't find anything before," Avie pointed out. "This is supposed to improve things. What's she like? Now that you've got her in your house."

"Very competent. Very organized."

"No, I mean, personally."

"Very competent. Very organized." Sam turned on the shower and prepared to strip. "She's a babe, Avie. I wish she wasn't working for me so I could really get to know her."

"Hey, all the better that she's working for you. She's right there, man, under your nose!" Avie stepped up to the shower next to Sam's. "I thought you might've had her in the sack already—"

"Berkowitz," Sam said, ducking under the hot spray. "You've got a filthy mind."

"I know." He heard Avie laugh in the stall next door. "Listen, is she going to stay at your place, like a housekeeper?"

"No." Candace had suggested the same thing when they'd gone for lunch. She thought Lydia should live in, thought she'd be a good influence on their daughter. "She's staying at a friend's condo, the one who got married. They're on their honeymoon, so she's there while some movie company uses her place for a location. I don't know all the details—it's complicated."

He soaped his chest and shoulders. The hot water felt good. He'd spent the morning lifting weights at Guido's, after he'd dropped Tania and Amber at school, and he was sore and stiff.

"You figure she remembers you? The crush, all that?"

"Nope." Sam poured shampoo into his palm. "Not a bit."

"Hey, what did I tell you!"

"Okay, you were right." Sam rinsed and turned off the shower. "She and Amber liked each other. That's important."

"Yeah. I guess Amber's back in school this week. How's she doing with the karaoke?" Avie had given her the set for Christmas. "It's a while since I've seen the kid. How about I come over on Friday, catch the Leafs' game on TV?"

"Sure." He and Avie went to a few Leafs' home

games every winter. Sometimes they took Amber, but she got bored pretty quickly. Sam stepped out of the shower and caught the towel Avie threw him.

"You think this house makeover will be done by the time your folks get back?"

Sam shrugged. "I don't know. There's a lot to do—hey, don't laugh!"

"I'm not laughing," Avie lied, holding up both hands, his eyes round and serious. "Can you imagine your mother's surprise? Hell, she's been on your case longer than Candace has."

He hadn't thought of that. Avie was right. His mother would be thrilled. She'd think she was coming home to the usual major disaster—even worse now that his last housekeeper had left. But his folks were coming back in less than two weeks, which wasn't enough time for Lydia to work her magic over his entire house. She'd estimated about a month for the basics, barring any unexpected complications. Plus she had other stuff on the go, like that Daniels guy.

Maybe if she lived in... He could pay her overtime, get the job done faster; it was an idea. Sam reached for his own towel. "So, what's happening with the date you had for New Year's, the brainy babe from Accounting?"

Avie snapped the towel at him and missed. "History. I've moved on. I'm seeing someone in Sales, now. She likes hockey. Maybe I'll bring her over on Friday. Huh?''

"Sure, Av. You do what you like.'' Sam grinned. "You know what's on the menu.''

"Yeah!'' Avie pulled on his shirt and started working on the buttons. "Take-out chicken and cole-slaw and make 'n' bake dinner rolls. Hey, this Lydia going to teach you how to cook, too? How about I bring something for dessert? I can do *that*.''

CHAPTER NINE

SAM WAS JUST GETTING Amber settled down to her breakfast—a glass of chocolate milk and a personal-sized pizza, Hawaiian, of course—when the doorbell chimed.

"Hi!" Lydia stood on his doorstep, her breath billowing frost in the cold air. The weather had turned again, and Toronto was in a deep freeze.

"Hi, yourself. This is getting to be a habit." He held the door wide. "Come in."

"Who's that, Daddy?" Amber called from the kitchen.

Lydia paused, one foot inside the door. "Oops. Am I too early? I forgot all about school. Why don't I go around the corner and have a coffee and come back in half an hour?"

"Don't be silly. We're just having breakfast and then I'm taking the girls to school. My day." Sam was amazed at how pleased he was to see Lydia again. He *couldn't* have missed her; he hardly knew her. And, considering the hell she'd put him through last week, he should've been grateful for the peace and quiet of the last few days. *Five* days today, since the cleaning crew had left Friday evening. Not that he was counting. She'd been here Monday, apparently, but he hadn't seen her.

Then yesterday? Oh, yeah.

"How'd it go with Griff Daniels?" he asked as he led the way to the kitchen. "The professional basketball player who can't cook or shop?"

"Hi, Lydia!" Amber crammed pizza into her mouth and chewed quickly. Her hair was combed—just. She wore a pair of red pants today and a yellow sweater.

"Oh, fine." Lydia smiled at him, then patted his daughter's head. She wasn't going to say any more about Daniels; he could see that. "When you're finished, would you like me to brush your hair, Amber?"

Amber nodded, her expression one of triumph as she glanced at him. Her hair was a running battle between them. He wanted her to get a short cut that would be easy to take care of, and she wanted to grow it long like her friend Tania, who had the most ridiculous braids.... "Can you do braids?"

"I can try." Lydia said with a mischievous grin. "Can't your daddy do braids?"

"I think he can. But he won't even try." Amber shot him a mutinous look. She was half-right. He probably could do braids if he put his mind to it, but what was wrong with a simple, straightforward ponytail?

"Coffee, Lydia?"

"Yes, please." She took a stool at the breakfast bar, next to his daughter. He'd noticed that Lydia's hair was down today, not loose, but in some kind of low style, caught at her nape with a ribbon. He was fascinated with her hair. Soft, tawny, the color of wheat. The other day, when she'd casually released her hair and shaken it out, the day Candace was over, he'd amazed himself with his instant, visceral reaction. He couldn't tear his eyes away.

Today she had on that dumb uniform again. "Listen, what's with the—you know, the outfit?" he asked as he operated the espresso machine. He placed the cup in front of her with a flourish.

"Thank you. Outfit? You mean this?" She glanced down at her striped tunic and leggings. "I wear this on most of my jobs. People generally like it. They think it looks more professional."

"I don't—not that you don't look good in anything you choose to wear, but—" He raised his eyebrows. "Feel free to wear regular clothes. Please. I practice law in jeans and a T-shirt. Do you think I care about what looks professional?"

She smiled and shook her head. "I was hoping you'd say that."

"Good. What's on the agenda for today?" Last Friday, before she left, she'd asked him to keep a few hours open today and tomorrow.

"Your hall closet," she said firmly. "I was hoping

you'd be able to spend some time with me either this morning or this afternoon."

"Morning might work." He hadn't checked his agenda, but he knew he didn't have any hearings or court. "Why do you need me?"

"Your closet is bursting at the seams and you'll need to make some keep-or-toss decisions. I figure if we do that first, every time you start to wonder why you ever got yourself into this, I can show you the hall closet and you'll be reminded what a difference organization can make to your life."

"Will you clean up my room, too?" Amber asked.

"No, I won't clean up your room, Amber, but—" the girl looked crestfallen "—I'll show you how to clean up your own room...and something even better."

"What's that?" Amber asked eagerly. Sam checked the clock on the wall. Ten minutes and they had to be out of here.

"I'll show you how to keep it clean so it never gets messy again. Unless you really, really *want* it to get messy. Which is different, right?"

"Yeah!" His daughter covered her mouth with her hand.

Lydia turned to him. "How about Friday, after school, for Amber's room? Or Thursday?"

"Thursday Amber's got her homework group and I play squash," Sam said. "Friday's best. If you get it done, you can show Avie, hon. He's coming for your special dinner Friday night.''

"Yippee!''

"And this morning's fine for me,'' he said to Lydia. He was looking forward to spending a few hours alone with her, hall closet or no hall closet. "In fact, I think I've got most of the day free.''

"Dad, I can't finish this.'' Amber pushed away the last third of her pizza. He scooped up the uneaten portion and dropped it in the trash, then set her plate and glass in the sink, along with some other dirty dishes he hadn't gotten to yet.

"Sam?''

He whirled. "Hmm?''

"Is this a good time for a little housekeeping lesson?''

He bowed low. "But, of course, madam!''

Amber giggled.

"You could save time and energy by reducing how often you handle dishes. Instead of putting them in the sink or on the counter to be stacked in the dishwasher later, why not put them directly in the dishwasher and close the door? That way, they're out of sight and they're also where they should be when the time comes to wash them. Saves time, saves energy, clean kitchen counter.''

"Ah!'' He grinned at her. "A no-brainer. But, madam, what is one to do with the dishes that are already *in* the dishwasher? The *clean* dishes?''

Amber giggled again and looked to Lydia for her reaction. Lydia laughed. "Oh, I see. Not so simple, after all. We have a two-part lesson coming up."

"Later. I've got to get this kid to school. Can you do her hair in under three minutes—" he glanced at his watch "—because Tania Jackson's supposed to be here in three minutes and she is never late."

WHEN HE GOT BACK, he could hardly open the front door.

"Wait!" Lydia yelled when he pushed against whatever was obstructing it. "I need to move something."

He closed the door again, listened to some shuffling sounds, then pushed it open when he heard her call out "okay!"

"Holy cow!" He was stunned. "All *that* was in the closet?"

"More. There's tons more." Lydia stood in a sea of coats, boots, running shoes, track shoes, umbrellas, mitts, hats, tennis racquets, squash racquets—

"Hey, I haven't seen that Wilson racquet for a long time," he said, brightening. "I wondered where it was."

"Believe me, Sam, there's a lot more you'll wonder about before this morning is over." She indicated some empty cardboard boxes at the end of the hall. "See those? Those are vital to our plans. Like I said,

I need you here so you can make the decisions. It's your stuff.''

"What do we do with the boxes?" Sam was intrigued, in spite of himself. He took off his jacket, wasn't sure for a few seconds where to put it, then threw it onto the nearby pile of coats. She laughed out loud. He felt terrific.

"We label them. I call it the Four G's of organizing. *Good, Give Away, Garbage* and *Goes Somewhere Else.*" She took a black marker from one of the pockets of her tunic, bent down by the first box and began printing in large letters: G-O-O-D.

"Got another pen?"

She handed him another marker and he started writing *Garbage* on one of the boxes, then *Goes Somewhere Else* on another.

She finished the fourth box with *Give Away.* "We'll be able to use these boxes in every room as we go through the house."

"Okay. Now what?" He was getting the picture.

"First of all, we have to settle on goals. *Your* goals." She sounded so serious. "Tell me what would make this closet perfect for you."

"Perfect? Let's see. I don't care about wrinkles but I'd like to be able to find things easily."

"Easy access. We can do that. You can decide to put all your outerwear in this closet, or only the in-season stuff. If you want everything here, we'll have to find other storage for the sports equipment and the—uh, the fishing rod—''

"You found a *fishing rod* in there?''

"It's on the top shelf at the back. I couldn't reach it but it's definitely there.''

Sam made his way over the piles of stuff to the closet to have a look for himself. She stood on her tiptoes beside him with a flashlight she'd produced from somewhere. Probably one of the pockets in that radish suit. "See?''

"Son of a gun!'' He reached up and pulled out a fly fishing rod his uncle had given him years ago. It wasn't that great for fishing, but it had sentimental value. "Uncle Manny's fishing rod!''

"Sam?'' She had her hands on her hips.

"What?''

"Please put the fishing rod down. The biggest danger when you set out to organize is getting sidetracked. Put it down somewhere and we'll deal with it when we get the boxes going.''

"Yes, ma'am.'' He leaned the rod against the wall, by the bottom of the stairs.

"So, do you want all your outerwear in this closet or just seasonal clothes and maybe the other items you use all the time?''

Sam pondered. He didn't have a clue what she was talking about, although he did recognize that a fishing rod probably didn't belong in the hall closet. "Tell you what—you decide. You're the expert.''

"You're the one who lives here. The whole house has to be organized with *your* needs in mind, yours and Amber's, or it won't work. You can't keep up someone else's system—it has to mean something to *you*. Luckily," she said, wading over the pile of coats, "it's fairly easy to see who belongs to what, since there's only one large man and one small child in this house."

So far.

She turned to face him. "I'd suggest seasonal. You can always bring out other clothes from storage as you need them, and that's a good excuse to go through your closet regularly—"

"Go through it regularly?" Sam's brow furrowed. He thought they were just doing this once. "Aren't closets just…closets? You put stuff in and it stays there, doesn't it?"

"It doesn't hurt to vacuum the corners once or twice a year. Or wipe off the shelves." She gave him a severe look. He'd seen that expression on his mother's face when she opened the vegetable drawer in his refrigerator and found—oh, a cucumber he'd forgotten about or a bunch of carrots that had dehydrated in the months they'd been there.

"Sounds like a lot of work," he muttered.

"Believe me, once you're used to keeping things up, it's not going to be a big deal to take out some clothes once or twice a year and put other ones in.

I'll even write it on your calendar for you, as a reminder.''

"Fine. Okay, just tell me what to do, Lydia, and I'll do it.''

The next two hours were actually enjoyable. Lydia was tireless. She'd pull something out of his closet and he'd say, Good or Goes Somewhere Else and she'd say, Give Away or Garbage and he'd protest that no, no, the football shoes with the four missing cleats were still good. Then she'd ask him if he played football and he'd say, no, but he might someday. An Old Guys League.

She'd look at him skeptically and hand it to him to be placed in the right box—Garbage. When she realized that a fair number of items they'd designated as Garbage were going into Good or Goes Somewhere Else, she traded places with him.

"This jacket?'' She held up a brown windbreaker. He'd never liked the pockets in it. They were too small.

"Good.''

"Sam?'' He loved that warning, no-nonsense look of hers when she didn't believe him. "When's the last time you wore this? The truth.''

He thought hard. "I can't remember.''

"More than a year?''

"Maybe.''

"Okay. Give away.'' She bypassed him and fired

it into the box that was designated for the neighbor-hood thrift store.

"Hey, wait a minute! That jacket's still good. Maybe I'll wear it when we go fishing this summer."

"And maybe you won't. If you haven't worn it for a year, get rid of it. Listen, Sam, the very fact that it's still good means somebody else is going to get some wear out of it. Isn't that a lot better than letting it sit in the back of your closet, taking up space?"

When she put it like that, when she looked so adorably serious, so incredibly *interested* in all his old junk, how could he not agree? And it was true; everything she said made perfect sense.

They talked about other things, too. Steve. The old neighborhood. Why she'd started Domestica. It turned out some old aunt of hers was behind it all. *Thank you, Great-aunt Lydia.* She mentioned she'd had some unusual jobs and they talked a little about that.

Sam had something else on his mind. And it just wasn't going away. He wondered if she'd think he was being too nosy....

"Lydia?"

"Hmm?" She looked up from where she was sort-ing mitts and gloves. Anything unmatched went into the Garbage box; anything clearly too small for Am-ber—and, amazingly, there were all kinds of tiny mittens on one of the shelves—went into Give Away.

"I'm curious about one thing. You don't have to answer if you don't want—"

"I know that, Sam," she said serenely. This was exactly the kind of calm competence that had appealed to him when he'd seen her on Candace's show.

"This Daniels guy, he's got quite a reputation in the media—he ever put the make on you?"

"The *make* on me? You mean, asked me out?"

"Yeah." Although he was thinking more along the lines of caught her in the kitchen and kissed the daylights out of her—

"No. Of course not. He's a professional." Her eyes danced but he realized she wasn't saying anything more.

"Fine, fine. I just wondered—"

"Of course, he's not often there. I have a key. He's usually in training or at a team meeting or something."

Sam felt an odd sense of relief. He had no idea why. "What exactly do you do for him?"

"Shop for groceries. Do up a weekly menu. Prepare freezer meals." She shrugged. "Sometimes I cater, if he's entertaining."

"You're not offended, that I asked?"

"Of course not. This pair of sneakers." She held up a small pair of green running shoes. "Amber still wear them?"

"No. Too small."

She tossed them into the Give Away box.

"But you must get lots of guys who, you know—*do* put the make on you," he persisted. "Or proposition you in some way. You're a very attractive woman."

"You mean like the guy who asked me if I'd mind having his baby because he didn't want to bother getting involved with a woman?"

"You're kidding!" He stood and stared at her, appalled.

"No." She sorted through some scarves that were huddled on the floor. "He was totally serious. He thought since I wasn't married it might not be a problem for me."

"He wanted you to have *sex* with him?"

"That's the usual idea, isn't it?" she asked matter-of-factly. "But, no, he was gay. I believe he was thinking of the turkey baster method—"

"Lydia!" Sam didn't think he was shockable, but he *was* shocked.

"I also had a client who wanted me to pretend I was his girlfriend because his mother was coming to visit for the weekend and she didn't believe he had one. Which he didn't."

"You do it?" Sam wanted to laugh.

"Poor man." She threw a torn and decrepit baseball cap into Garbage. "He was desperate. I said sure, two days only and no kissing. I figured I was doing him enough of a favor."

Sam started to laugh. Then she started to laugh, too. "You took a big chance." He glanced at his watch. "He sounds like a weirdo."

She shook her head, still smiling. "Not really. I just felt sorry for him."

"Shall I make us some tea or coffee? Milk? Hot chocolate?" It was nearly half-past ten and they'd done a lot. The closet was nearly empty now and the boxes were overflowing.

"We're not done, Sam," she said sternly.

"I know. Ten minutes. Coffee break."

Lydia disappeared in the direction of the bathroom and Sam went toward the kitchen, humming the old Van Morrison tune, "Brown-eyed Girl." Now, if only he had some Sara Lee cake in the freezer, they could have a snack, too. Sit down at his breakfast table, across from each other, talk, share a few more laughs. *Like a real couple.*

But it was just wishful thinking.

He studied the pathetic contents of his freezer looking for a cake among the heavily frosted half-bags of pyrogies and the gummy Popsicle wrappers frozen to the bottom. Damn! He'd forgotten to put a Sara Lee cake on his grocery list last week....

CHAPTER TEN

LYDIA MET ZOEY for dinner at one of the new hot restaurants in town, Paladin's Landing.

Zoey's treat. She'd finished working on the current manuscript of her thriller-mystery writer, Jamie Chinchilla, and had sent it off to New York. That, Zoey said emphatically, was reason to celebrate.

"Besides," she said after they'd settled in on a leather banquette near the window, "I haven't seen you since the wedding. That's ages!"

"It's been a busy time," Lydia admitted. "Heard anything from Charlotte?" The last few months, she'd found herself in the role of friend-in-the-middle, passing on greetings and news from Zoey to Charlotte and vice versa. Now, with Zoey in town, things were different.

"Oh, Lydia!" Zoey accepted a menu from a waiter. "Who sends postcards on their *honeymoon?*"

True. Lydia studied the menu, which seemed to be a compendium of last year's fresh 'n' local and this year's ethnic-reinterpreted. "Speaking of honeymoons, where are you and Cam going?"

"Would you believe British Columbia?" Zoey

made a face but Lydia could see that she didn't really care *where* she went for her honeymoon. "Maybe a week up at Whistler skiing and then he says he has to get back to his cows. His daughter's going to stay with my friend Elizabeth and her family in Stoney Creek while we're away." Zoey leaned forward. "It's weird getting used to figuring a child into all my plans—our plans," she corrected herself.

"She's a delightful child," Lydia said. She remembered Lissy well from the wedding. Amber had spent the entire evening with Lissy and with Mary Macdonald, the little girl from Prince Edward Island.

"She is." Zoey smiled fondly. Lydia had a good feeling about Zoey's new role as an instant mother. Although her friend had always claimed she didn't think much about marriage and children, Lydia had always suspected she was as interested in a family as most women.

"You might be having a baby soon yourself."

She expected a protest from Zoey, but instead she got a dreamy look. "Maybe." And a happy sigh. "I'm going to have the tuna with pineapple salsa. What about you?"

"The Moroccan ragout."

"Beef?"

"Hey, red meat's back," Lydia said with a smile. "Besides, don't forget what business your Cam is in. Where would he be if nobody ate beef?"

"Good point."

They gave the waiter their order and Zoey continued, eyes alight. "Okay, tell me all about your new
job."

"It's going well. I was there today and finished up
his hall closet, which I'd started yesterday, and I got
the linen closet sorted out and his bedroom—"

"His bedroom! Was he in it?" Zoey winked and
prepared to dig into the salad the waiter had just
brought her.

"I wish you'd realize this is just another job to
me," Lydia complained. "There's nothing special
about it."

"Oh, yes there is! It's a big job, the kind you told
me you were dying to try." Her friend looked her
squarely in the eyes. "And your client's also your
first crush."

"Oh, Zoey, will you give it a rest? I was fifteen,
for Pete's sake! All he knows is that I was Steve's
little sister. And that I had braids—he mentioned
those. Other than that, he barely knew I was alive."

"That was then," Zoey said, undismayed. "So,
tell me what you did with his bedroom. I'm curious."

"Well, one good thing about this job is that he's
pretty well given me a blank check. Within reason,
of course," she added hastily. "He's told me to buy
whatever I need. So I've bought him all new towels,
in two colors, dark green for him and yellow for
Amber, so he can keep them straight and in separate

laundry loads. You should've seen his old ones! I gave them to the Humane Society to use as bedding for the animals."

Zoey's laughter rang out. Lydia looked around. "It's true! They do use old towels and stuff for bedding."

"Trust you to know."

"I kept a few of the all-cotton ones to tear up for rags. You can always use good rags."

"I'll take your word for it. What else?"

Their soup had arrived, cream of pumpkin for her and mushroom in a clear broth for Zoey. Lydia tasted hers before answering. "Mmm. I pulled everything out of the linen closet and ended up buying a set of new sheets for each of them, white—"

"White?"

"Well, I like white. And I didn't know what he'd like. He's got a lot of that horrible department store so-called masculine stuff, you know, black and navy in little squares and stripes, half polyester, half cotton?" She made a face. "It's just one set. I got a yellow set for Amber's bed, plus some other things. Dustproof mattress and pillow covers—"

"You *are* thorough."

"Of course I am. It's my job. I haven't talked to Sam about tossing the old ones. I don't know if I dare, since he hates to throw anything out."

"So do most people who get themselves into that situation," Zoey said dryly.

"Except socks. He has no socks that I've seen, anyway."

"No socks?" This information halted Zoey, spoon halfway between bowl and mouth. "No *socks?*"

"I think he buys new ones all the time. Think of the expense! I can't believe anyone could be so hopeless with a washing machine," she said with a shudder. "But, actually I can—you should've seen the towels."

"I have a theory about that, Lydia. I think it's a 'man's man' thing."

"A 'man's man' thing?"

"Yes." Zoey lightly touched Lydia's arm. "You know how paranoid guys are about anyone thinking they're gay or girly?" she said in a low voice. "Hearty-ho-ho handshakes and everything?"

Lydia nodded, frowning. "Yeah, I guess so."

"Well, *that's* why they throw in jeans and underwear and socks and T-shirts and whatever else is in the laundry basket. It's to show how manly they are. They think only women and gay guys are fussy about laundry."

"They do?" Lydia laughed. "That's the weirdest thing I ever heard."

"Trust me." Zoey returned her attention to her soup. "They think if they do a good job of laundry people will think they're wussy."

"Or maybe they just don't care if their T-shirts get gray."

"Well, I suppose that *could* be it," Zoey admitted. "But I like my theory better."

Their main courses arrived and the two women ate in silence, except for brief murmurs of appreciation. Lydia was exhausted. Sam had been in court all day, according to Darlene, and she'd only seen him once, just before she left at quarter to four. She'd knocked on his office door and Darlene had ushered her into Sam's office, half of what had once been a formal living room in the old house, she suspected. He was on the phone, looking fabulous in a dark blue suit, crisp tie and pristine white shirt—probably new. He'd held his hand over the receiver while she told him she was leaving early. She reminded him that she'd promised to help Amber with her room, so she was stopping work temporarily on the upstairs linen closet, his bedroom and the spare rooms. In case he wondered at the shambles.

He'd given her his sexy smile and waved her away. "Anything you want to do, Lydia, is fine with me. See you tomorrow."

Darlene had ushered her out. "Today's his squash day," she'd said. "Then he picks up his daughter from her homework group. Then, of course, he has to come home and make supper for the two of them."

"Oh." Lydia didn't know what else of import could be said on the subject.

AT THE END OF THE MEAL, Lydia slipped out to go to the ladies' room while Zoey perused the dessert menu. The restaurant was laid out on several levels, each designed for privacy.

"Lydia!" she heard as she made her way along one of the upper levels. "Lydia!"

"Candace! How nice to see you." Candace was sitting at a table with a handsome man who looked vaguely familiar.

"I went to your place to chat yesterday—you didn't tell me you had movie people there. Where are you staying? At Sam's? This is my friend, Kip Russell." She smiled adoringly at her companion and he shifted forward to take Lydia's hand. "Kip, this is Lydia Lane. She's doing some work for my ex."

"How do you do?" he said formally. Ah, Kip Russell. Lydia recognized the name as that of a well-known architect in the city.

Candace patted the chair next to her. "Are you here alone? Sit down!"

"I'm with my friend Zoey—"

"Go get her and have coffee with us. I've been dying to talk to you."

What about? Lydia wondered as she continued to their banquette. Zoey was happy to accept the invitation and told the waiter to bring the bill to their new table.

Lydia introduced Zoey to Candace, who completed the introductions, snuggling closer to her companion. The two women sat down and Candace quickly waved over a waiter.

"Coffee? Dessert? We were thinking of having the *zabaglione,* weren't we, Kip?" Her companion gave her a high-voltage smile and nodded. Candace practically chirped.

Zoey decided on the same and Lydia refused anything but coffee. She watched her companions as Candace ordered. Kip Russell was a very handsome man—and so was Sam. Candace obviously liked her men decorative. But what a difference! Sam gave her goose bumps, even hauling old sports equipment out of a closet, while this man, dressed to kill, with undeniable charm and handsome as sin, left her cold.

"Lydia! *Are* you at Sam's now?" Her blue eyes were unabashedly curious. "It makes sense to be on the spot, don't you think—"

"No, I'm at a friend's apartment," Lydia broke in. "She's away on her honeymoon, so I'm there until they get back."

"Then what?" Candace stared. "How long have the movie people got your place? That's so exciting! Just think, your apartment's going to be in a *movie!*"

"Then, I think I'll be moving over to my mother's. Or to Zoey's, if she'll have me...."

"Don't be silly! You know I will. I could use your help anyway with the rest of the wedding details." She slid her eyes to the talk-show host and waggled her left hand with its modest-sized solitaire in front of her.

"Oh!" Candace squealed. "Another wedding." Zoey explained about her trip out West and how she'd ended up with her first love's brother, rancher Cameron Donnelly, and how their friend Charlotte, who was even now on her honeymoon, had ended up with the man who'd been *her* first love.

"That's so romantic! Isn't it, Kip? Wouldn't that make a great story for my show—searching for first loves?"

Kip shrugged but he didn't disagree. Diplomatic man, Lydia thought. The topic had nothing to do with what was happening in the city, the premise of Candace's talk show, but what did that matter? She hadn't been hired for her news judgment, obviously.

"And you'll never guess...." Zoey leaned toward Candace confidentially and Lydia prepared to kick her under the table. "Lydia had a crush on *your* ex way back in high school—ouch!" Zoey grinned. "Didn't she tell you?" Lydia hadn't kicked her very hard.

"That is in-cre-di-ble!" Candace's blue eyes were huge. "Oh, that is *so* incredible and to think I got the two of you together! You were on *my* show—"

"Hold it, please!" Lydia held up both hands and looked to Kip, who seemed to be the only other sensible human being at their table, for support. "I'm doing a job for the man. I'm organizing his house. I'm not *marrying* him.''

"Yet," Zoey said, with a wink. "Look at me and Charlotte. We thought the same thing. *Now* look at us.''

"Oh, Zoe! You're totally hopeless. Candace, did you know that Zoey edits Jamie Chinchilla—''

"The mystery writer?'' Candace practically screamed. "Oh, my goodness. Wouldn't *that* be a good topic for my show!''

"And Kip—'' Lydia turned her attention to the architect. "Didn't you design the extension on the Hubbard Community Centre, the day-care wing?''

Mercifully, Candace's date came to Lydia's rescue and began discoursing on urban planning, City Hall, neighborhoods and the challenges involved in designing modern day care centers.

Lydia was less pleased to see Candace and Zoey, heads together, talking animatedly and exchanging meaningful glances across the table, smiling every time they looked Lydia's way. Those two were cut from the same cloth.

Matchmakers! With only her to practice on.

SAM NOTICED THAT something had been done to his bedroom. He ran up to change out of his suit and tie before rushing off to meet Avie and then pick up Amber from her homework group. The mothers of four of Amber's friends had gotten together and organized the rotating after-school group, which meant every fifth time it was Sam's turn.

The large Turkish carpet, which had been taken out last week to be cleaned, was back and positioned squarely on the recently polished hardwood floor. His bed sported a new bedskirt, he noticed, a square-cornered black affair, which gave the impression that the bed was floating off the floor. There were also two extra pillows at the headboard. It looked very inviting.

But he didn't realize until he showered that night—fluffy new towels, he noted with approval—and crawled into his bed that it was altogether *different*. Different sheets, different feeling somehow.

—*a properly made bed contributes to a good night's sleep*—

He remembered what Lydia had said on Candace's show. *A properly made bed.* He wriggled his shoulders around, settling into the comfort of the mattress. He didn't recall his bed being this soft and at the same time firm and supportive. Nice new sheets, too. Cool and welcoming.

Hadn't Lydia said she preferred white? Now, he told himself with a grimace, if only she was here to share these brand-new sheets with him...

The extra pillows were a good idea. Easier to sit up and read in bed—why hadn't he thought of that? He arranged them to his satisfaction and started looking through a brief, which involved a longtime client who said he'd been roughed up in the police station when he was hauled in on a drunk and disorderly charge.

The house was very quiet. Amber had gone to bed three hours ago, and Sam had watched an Aussie rules football game on the sports channel. He should've been doing some work, but he felt restless. Once he went out to the hall closet and opened the doors just to gaze at the miracle that had been wrought.

His jackets and coats hung on one side. Amber's hung on the other. Three neatly labeled baskets under Amber's side contained "mitts and scarves," "hats" and "school stuff." Amber was supposed to put anything to do with school in that basket, so Sam would be able to take a look at it. No more hunting for permission slips, field trip schedules, fund-raiser events. No more calls from the teacher wondering about the report card that hadn't been signed and returned. At least, that was the idea.

"We can adjust this system if you find it doesn't work for you," Lydia had said. "We'll give it a try for two weeks."

Just two weeks? Would she be gone by then?

On the other side, in two stacked baskets and also neatly labeled, were his things: "gloves and scarves," "sports," which contained ski goggles, headbands, sunscreen, sunglasses and various other items. Beside that was a basket labeled "gym clothes." On the inside of the door she'd attached a white plastic basket labeled "mail." Also on the door was a brass motorcycle-shaped key caddy with several brass pegs for keys. Hanging on their own hooks on the wall of the closet were two racquets, one squash, one tennis. On the shelf was his motorcycle helmet. On the floor, a plastic mat for boots and a shoe rack for shoes.

A miracle, all right. Sam's mind kept wandering from the brief. He couldn't concentrate on his client's woes or what the chances might be of getting him off this time.

All he could think about was his bed, which was so comfortable—and so large with just him in it. He really did wish Lydia there with him. And it wasn't just because he wanted to have sex with her, which he did.

He was tired of sleeping alone. He was tired of one-night stands. He was tired of having girlfriends, getting them and keeping them—at his age? He considered the women he'd dated in the past three months as potential marriage prospects. Miranda? No way. She wasn't interested in marriage. Bethany? Too cold. He'd thought she was cool and sophisticated but she'd turned out to be cool and self-absorbed. She'd been a challenge for a while, but the challenge was over. Sylvia, the physical trainer? Too buff and boring. She lived to count calories and work out.

He wanted someone to put his arms around, to cuddle with, to laugh over the events of the day—every day. And every night. Someone who put him first in her life. Who put his daughter first.

He wanted to be in love. He wanted to be married. True, his marriage to Candace hadn't worked out, but surely there was a second chance for him. There had to be.

He didn't know why he thought of Lydia. Hell, he'd only known her for two weeks! And she probably had lots of guys interested in her. Probably serious ones, too.

The motorcycle key caddy kept drifting into his mind. She hadn't mentioned it. She could've bought anything—a cat, a house, a pewter thing that spelled out K-E-Y-S. But she'd gone out of her way to find something that had meaning for him.

He had a great life—a wonderful family, a terrific daughter, all kinds of friends, a thriving law practice. He owned the house he'd always wanted. Almost all his dreams had come true.

But somehow, Lydia being in his house, doing the things she did, so serenely, so happily—with such grace and generosity—had reminded him of what he *didn't* have.

And the feeling just wasn't going away.

CHAPTER ELEVEN

THE MORNING AFTER the meal at Paladin's, Lydia went to Sam's house at nine. About ten o'clock she heard sounds from the kitchen and came down expecting to see him. Instead, there was a hunched-over, elderly man, making something in the microwave.

"Hello, miss. I'm Larry Massullo," he said. His eyes were blue and vacant-looking. This was the boxer Sam had told her about. "You must be Lydia. Sam told me to come over and get something to eat," he explained.

Lydia left him alone and when she returned twenty minutes later, he was gone. So this was the sort of thing Candace had been worrying about. The old fellow seemed harmless enough, but why hadn't Sam or Darlene mentioned he was coming into the house? She supposed it happened fairly often.

She left at noon to run her errands, locking the house securely behind her. If Sam wanted to let someone in his house, he'd have to unlock the doors himself. The measurements she'd taken in Amber's room meant she'd be able to buy everything ahead of time to ensure that the cleanup was as painless and efficient as possible.

Wasn't that the key to developing new, better habits? Instant rewards. Like the hall closet, which she'd seen Sam admire more than once. There was nothing like running into a major glitch—like no storage boxes for toys—to halt a room cleanup. A quick, visual inventory of the room and its contents helped her decide what was needed.

Lydia hummed as she strolled up and down the aisles of Ikea, filling her shopping cart. This was fun. This was playing house, grown-up style. And she was getting paid for it.

She saw a clock that would be suitable for the upstairs bathroom and put it in her cart. Unobtrusive, but still a way of reminding Amber how much time she had to do her hair, brush her teeth—whatever— before bedtime or school. Generally, Lydia didn't approve of clocks in bathrooms, which were supposed to be places for privacy and relaxation, where time didn't matter. If you were up to your chin in a tub, surrounded by bubbles and essential oils, nothing like a glance at a clock to bring stress roaring back again. But, temporarily, until the girl learned to manage time a little better, it couldn't hurt. Thus a fairly cheap model...

She loaded her purchases into the back of the minivan, said her usual prayer to the automotive and mechanical gods and set off for Parry Street. Her plan was to get back in plenty of time to unload her goods and finish up the linen closet before Amber came home from school.

The minivan stalled at the corner of Bloor and Bathurst, which gave Lydia momentary heart failure, but it started again when she turned the key. She frowned as she continued. What was *that* all about? The engine noises were constant. A hideously expensive valve job would eventually be necessary, according to the mechanic, but he'd said nothing about the vehicle stalling.

It stalled again at the following light and Lydia panicked a little. After several tries, the van started, and she began to think maybe she should simply head in the direction of her garage. If it conked out completely, she'd rather be close to her mechanic, who wasn't all that far away, than halfway to Sam's house. But when she reached the next light, Bloor and Christie, the van stalled again. She was in the outside lane of traffic, thank heaven, and as the van coasted, she wrestled it toward the side of the road, looking desperately for a service station.

No such luck. The minivan coasted to a stop at the side of the street and went no farther. No amount of banging the steering wheel, yelling or twisting the key in the ignition brought it to life again.

She put on her hazard lights—at least she remembered to do that—and gripped the wheel tightly. Now what? She wanted to cry. A knock at her window had her turning to see a cab driver who'd stopped to see if he could help. "You want a boost, lady? You want me to call somebody?"

"Thanks, anyway," she said, managing a smile. Her last one of the day, she was sure. "I'll call a tow truck."

With a wave, the cabbie got back in his vehicle and roared off. Traffic swerved or stopped behind her. A few cars honked, then angrily pulled out when they realized she wasn't going anywhere.

This was horrible. And what about poor Amber? She'd have to cancel. Her van was full of stuff for the girl's room, too.

Lydia got out her cell phone with a sigh. She knew the minivan was on its last legs, but why couldn't it have waited until she'd finished the job before it died?

"SAM?" He glanced toward the open doorway. Darlene was wearing a tight lime green T-shirt today and a black leather skirt the size of a postage stamp. "Your organizer on line one."

Sam snatched up the receiver. "Lydia?" She'd never called him before.

"Hello, Sam? I'm sorry to bother you—"

"No problem. What's up?" He could hear traffic noises in the background. "Where are you?"

"I'm at the corner of Bloor and Christie. My van broke down and—"

"Your *van* broke down?" Actually, he'd been wondering when that might happen. Her van was at least a dozen years old and he knew what a valve job sounded like when he heard one. "Have you called a tow truck?"

"Not yet. It just quit a couple of minutes ago." She sounded worn out. "I'm going to call one now, but I thought I'd tell you I've got a bunch of stuff in the back of the van that I bought for Amber's room. Storage items. I feel terrible. She was looking forward to this afternoon and—"

"It's not your fault. Bloor and Christie? Stay right there. I'm coming to get you." The tremble in her voice went straight to his heart. She was trying to be tough but this breakdown was obviously a complication she didn't need. He could empathize.

"Darlene?" Sam stood up and gathered some papers. "Type these out for me and get hold of the coroner's office, will you, please? There's a report on Hubert Diamond that I want." Diamond was another of Sam's clients. Could you call someone a client if he never paid? Sam had done a few things for him pro bono over the years, including a will, and now he was dead, found frozen behind a Dumpster.

Poor bastard. Sam wanted to see the coroner's report before he got in touch with the family. Sam had always wondered why Diamond's brother and sister, living in a small town near Owen Sound, hadn't taken him in when he lost his job ten years ago and started living on the streets. Now poor old Hubert had died and left his meager estate to them. There was irony for you.

Human nature was a mystery. An endless, complex, fascinating mystery. Sam was no crusader; he just liked to make sure the law worked for the poor as well as the rich, the way it was supposed to. If that meant he'd never make the kind of money some lawyers made, well, how many steaks could he eat in a day? How many Porsches could he drive at once?

The phone rang again and Darlene put it straight through.

"Sam? Don't hang up on me like that." Lydia had a little more starch in her voice now and he smiled, glad to hear it.

"I said I'm coming to get you. I'll be there in ten or fifteen minutes. I'll get Amber's stuff from you, see what I can do to help—"

"Okay," she said stiffly. "I—I want you to know I appreciate it. Thanks."

Sam hung up for the second time and shook his head. He walked through to the reception area. "Darlene, I just have a meeting scheduled for this afternoon, don't I? With the crown counsel in the Atkins case?"

She checked her agenda and nodded.

"Cancel it."

"Mr. Pereira!"

She only called him that when she didn't approve of what he was doing. He grabbed his jacket, threw her a thumbs-up and left, leaving her staring open-mouthed in astonishment.

SAM ARRIVED AT THE CORNER of Bloor and Christie in record time. The Land Rover was no Porsche, but traffic tended to make way for it. The number of dings on the bumpers and side panels clearly indicated that its owner wasn't at all car-proud. Sensible drivers gave it as wide a margin as possible.

Which suited Sam just fine.

There was a knot of three or four men standing with Lydia—the damsel in distress—when he arrived and found a parking spot for the Land Rover in the diner parking lot just ahead of where she'd stalled.

"Sam!" Lydia wore mitts and a scarf and the tip of her nose was red. She took a step toward him.

"Hey!" Sam caught the attention of the men with her, who were about to disband at his arrival, and called them over. "Lydia, you get in and steer. Hey, guys, let's push it off the street over here to the parking lot, okay?"

They all cheerfully lent a shoulder and a few minutes later, continued on their way with waves and smiles. One of them, obviously Italian, blew Lydia a kiss, which she didn't seem to notice—but which made Sam bristle.

"Sam!" Lydia repeated as she got out of the van. She hurried toward him and he had a hard time not reaching out and putting his arms around her. She looked thoroughly rattled.

"You call a tow truck?"

"Yes. Right after I talked to you. They said they'd be right here."

"You got a regular garage?"

"Yes."

"Good." He gazed down at her. "How about I move the Land Rover next to your van and we transfer all the stuff you bought, okay?"

She glanced doubtfully at his vehicle. "Sure."

They moved over boxes and bags and even a small wooden bookshelf that Lydia told him was for the collection Amber kept in her bedroom. When the van was empty, he slammed the side door shut and held out his hand. "Keys."

"Keys?"

"You go sit in the Land Rover and warm up, and I'll deal with the driver when he gets here." He pointed at the nearby diner. "I'll bring you a coffee. What's your garage?"

"Wallace Motors. On Sherbourne."

"You've dealt with him before?"

"Yes. Lots of times, unfortunately." She smiled and he could have kissed her. A woman with a sense of humor!

"Yeah, well, that's partly why I don't have a fancy car. Too much aggravation—"

"*That's* not aggravation?" She pointed to the Land Rover. He could see her point. It wasn't the showiest of vehicles.

"Nope. First of all, nothing ever goes wrong. But if it does, I fix it myself. Same with the Harley. Little hobby of mine."

"I know," she said softly.

"You do?"

"I remember you used to work in a garage. After high school, somewhere in the neighborhood."

"That's right. George Dack's place." He held the door for her and, when she got in, he closed it and walked toward the restaurant, pleased that she remembered anything at all about him, other than that he was a friend of Steve's. He brought her a coffee, thinking her eyes were a little too bright and her face a little too pale.

Just then the tow truck arrived and Sam spent a few minutes helping him hook up. He told the driver to take the minivan to Lydia's garage, giving him a credit card number in case she didn't have towing coverage with her insurance or her motor association membership. After that, he got on his cell and called Wallace Motors to say it was on its way and they were not to do any repairs until they'd talked to Ms. Lane. She'd call tomorrow. They weren't open Saturday? Okay, she'd call Monday. He gave them his phone number.

When he got into the Land Rover, he saw that she'd finished her coffee and set the empty cardboard container on the floor, in among the rest of the debris he'd been meaning to shovel out for the past couple of trips. "When you go to the garage I'll go with you, okay?" He stuck the key in the ignition. "Just to make sure you're not getting ripped off—Lydia?" He glanced her way, then let go of the key and turned to stare at her. "You're crying."

"No, I'm not!" she said fiercely. "I *was* crying, but I stopped." She wiped her nose with a tissue. "A few minutes ago."

He'd never been so happy the Land Rover had out-of-date bench seats. He slid toward her and drew her into his arms. "Oh, Lydia! Everything's going to work out. Don't cry, honey."

"I'm not," she said weakly and he felt her collapse against him, her shoulders shaking. "A-and I don't think you should be calling me that."

"Sorry." He grinned, glad she couldn't see him. "Don't worry, it's not just you, I call all women who cry on my shoulder 'honey.' What's the matter? Is it the van? They can fix it, whatever's wrong."

"I know," she said, her voice muffled against his jacket. He held her tighter, glad of the chance to get so close to her. *Finally.* He wished she wasn't wearing a woolly hat; he would've liked to touch her hair.

"I know all that." She pulled away from him slightly. Tears trembled in her eyelashes.

"Then what?"

"Oh, a bunch of things." She pulled away from him completely then and gave him a severe look as though to say, *how did that happen?* She dug through her bag for a fresh tissue.

Sam slid back to his side of the bench seat and turned the key in the ignition. As always, the Land Rover roared to lusty life.

"Like what?" he persisted.

"Like, I'm spoiling everything for Amber—"

"She'll get over it. You can do her room next week. Besides, it's hardly your fault your van broke down, is it?"

"It is. I should've gotten it fixed ages ago. I—" She stopped and blew her nose again. "And this is the absolute worst time! I have to move from Charlotte's place next week, either to my mother's or Zoey's, and I need that stupid van."

"You could move in with us." Candace had suggested that very thing last week. At the time, he'd let the comment go in one ear and out the other, like he did with most things Candace said. "Why not? You're working there. It would be a lot more convenient. You'd be just like a live-in housekeeper—"

"I'm *not* a housekeeper. At least not the kind you mean."

"I know, I know." She seemed sensitive on that

issue. "You'd be just like a live-in organizer." He caught a slight smile. "Hell, it'd be simpler all around. No more commuting—"

"I'd have to take the subway now," she said doubtfully.

"Yeah, just think how long that would be." He could see she was wavering. The more he thought about it, the better the idea got. "And then there's all the stuff you cart back and forth," he added for good measure.

"I don't think it would be the right thing to do," she said stiffly. "In the circumstances."

"What circumstances? Sure, you're not a house-keeper, but what's the difference? We've had lots of live-in housekeepers, nannies, you-name-it and we've got the perfect setup."

"Where?"

"Third floor. I don't think you've gone up there, have you? Two rooms plus a bathroom, totally private. Everything you need."

She didn't say anything for a few minutes.

"To tell you, the truth, I've been thinking of ask-ing you about this anyway," he said. "I'd like to surprise my mother when she gets home next week. Have the whole downstairs done, maybe. I'd be happy to pay you overtime. And that way, I could help you on the weekends, too, instead of just knock-ing off until Monday." How was he doing? He cast her a surreptitious look. "You probably want to get the job done faster, too. What do you say?"

When she remained silent, Sam threw all caution to the winds. "Hell, let's go back to your friend's place and pick up your things now. You'll be settled right in by the time I get Amber from school. There's plenty of room for all your stuff—how much do you have?"

"I have a bird."

"A bird? We've got lots of room for a bird!"

CHAPTER TWELVE

AS SAM HAD FORECAST, Amber was delighted that Lydia had moved into the housekeeper's quarters on the third floor. Zoey, when Lydia called to say she wouldn't need to impose on her hospitality next week, had been extremely upbeat and cheerful, which made Lydia a little curious.

Her mother's reaction was plainer. "Oh, Lydia! That's perfect. You can be right there on the spot, show him what a great housekeeper you are and cook and iron and do all those things you're so good at and—who knows?"

Lydia knew exactly what her mother was saying with her coy "who knows?" but she wasn't going to acknowledge it. She was tired of reminding people, especially her mother and Zoey, that she was a professional like any other professional and she had a job to do. Just because her line of work happened to involve the traditional homemaking and domestic skills so many people lacked these days, that didn't make it any less professional.

She did a good job for decent pay and she *wasn't* in this business because she wanted to snag a husband with her recipe for chocolate chip cookies or her ability to iron a shirt.

So far, today had been pretty much a disaster. Lydia couldn't help wondering whether she'd made the right decision in moving to Parry Street. Decision? Sam had decided; she'd just followed along. But they were both adults, and if things didn't work out the way she thought they should—she'd move out again. Big deal.

Her real concern, which she hated to admit even to herself, was the increased proximity to Sam Pereira. She'd never been immune to his charms— in fact, quite the opposite. And with the exception of the few minutes in the Land Rover when he'd put his arm around her, something she was sure he would've done with *any* woman who was bawling her eyes out, Sam seemed as oblivious to her now as he'd been when she was fifteen. That was to be expected, of course.

If only she could have said the same! When she was with him, every single cell of her body was on full alert. So far, she hadn't seen that much of him— strictly nine-to-five, weekends off. She'd be seeing much more of Sam now.

She'd fallen for the tough teenager with the sensitive heart and it would be easy to love the warm, caring man he'd become. He was compassionate and committed to justice, as his law practice proved. He was a rescuer; look how he'd dropped everything to help her today. She'd have to be very careful not to misinterpret any interest he might seem to have in her as personal.

"Can I invite my friend Tania over to help us?" Amber asked, practically dancing with excitement when she saw the new bookshelf and the boxes and bins that Lydia had purchased for her room. "Please? I *want* her to help us!"

"I'm sure that would be all right," Lydia said. "Do you think you should ask your dad first?" Sam had carried her bags to the third floor, dumped them there and left. She thought he'd gone back to his office before he collected the girls from school, but she didn't know for sure. Charlie, who'd seemed surprised to see her in the middle of the day—if a bird could seem surprised—was chirping happily in his cage on top of the dresser.

Lydia glanced around at her new quarters, which consisted of a small bedroom, a sitting area and her own private bathroom—perfect accommodations, really. And Sam was right; she'd finish the job a lot more quickly if she was on the premises.

"No," the little girl answered earnestly. "He'll let me, Lydia. I know he will. He lets me do everything I want."

Somehow, Lydia didn't quite believe that.

Tania Jackson arrived, accompanied by her cat, Punch, which Lydia hadn't seen yet. Amber explained that Punch was "almost" her cat, too, and sometimes he even slept on her bed. Punch was a very large, orange, scruffy part-Persian with bulging amber eyes and a stare that could stop an elephant. He was a most unpleasant-looking creature, but the two girls obviously adored him. Lydia suspected that was because he let them dress him up in doll clothes and push him around in a baby carriage.

Thank heaven Charlie was safe on the third floor! If Lydia had known there was a cat around, even occasionally, she would've taken the bird to her mother's.

Organizing Amber's room was not as difficult as Lydia had expected. The girls were enthusiastic about clearing out the closet and under the bed, and then, when everything was in the middle of the floor, they were only too happy to help sort, which they caught on to very quickly. Tania picked out all the Lego blocks, for instance, and put them in the plastic box Lydia had designated. Clothes that Amber said she didn't wear because she didn't like them anymore or because they were too small, Lydia put to one side in the Give Away box. Into the same box went toys that no longer held interest. Other children would be pleased to have them, a concept Amber immediately grasped, unlike her father who was stuck on the idea that something still "perfectly good" should be kept in storage. Damaged toys, single socks, last year's crumpled Hallowe'en mask, combs with teeth missing, broken crayons and used coloring books went into Garbage.

While Tania and Lydia hung Amber's clothes neatly in the closet, which now had plenty of room, Amber sat at her small table, printing out labels for her new boxes and bins. The storage containers, all with lids and stackable, were given designated places in the different activity areas they'd blocked out in the room: play area, schoolwork area and sleeping area. *A place for everything and everything in its place,* as the girls chanted delightedly.

There was a light knock at the door and Sam poked his head in. "How're you girls doing in here?"

"Daddy! Daddy!" Amber flew to her father, who scooped her up and gave her a big hug. "Look how nice my room is now and Lydia showed me where to put everything. I even have a shoe rack!"

"Lydia's very talented," Sam agreed, a comment directed as much at her as at his daughter, Lydia thought.

She watched from her position, cross-legged on the floor. She and Tania were putting together a simple farmyard animal puzzle to see if all the pieces were there before putting it into the Give Away box.

"And, Daddy, I want Lydia to help me make supper tonight for Uncle Avie. I want her to help me make chili. Tania knows how to make chili—her mom showed her how."

Tania glanced up, holding the puzzle piece she'd just located. "I *do* know how," she whispered loudly to Lydia, who smiled.

"You'll have to ask nicely," Sam told his daughter. "That's not really part of Lydia's job here, honey, teaching you to cook."

"*Will* you, Lydia?" Amber called to her. "Pleeease!"

"Of course," Lydia said quietly. "If you want me to." Sam's gaze caught hers over his daughter's head. His eyes were warm, appreciative…and more.

"What about this piece, Tania?" Lydia quickly averted her own eyes. "Where does it go?"

It wasn't going to be easy, this not taking things personally. Sam Pereira was a *very* personal kind of man.

SAM OPENED THE DOOR at precisely six o'clock to welcome Avie and his friend to his new, improved house. He felt like showing off already and the place wasn't even finished. The oak floors gleamed, and a new carpet runner had been laid in the hall. At Lydia's suggestion, he'd put some classical music on at low volume and started a fire in the family room fireplace—which no longer smoked.

Avie bore flowers and a large string-wrapped cardboard box from a Bloor Street bakery. He stamped the snow from his boots and stepped inside. Sam pointed to the vinyl mat to one side of the door, specifically for winter boots.

Avie raised his eyebrows and grinned. "Sam, this is Sharon Boler. She's a Sabres fan." Sharon was a thin, intense woman with the kind of designer glasses favored by the arts community.

"How do you do?" she said, taking Sam's hand in a brief, firm grip. She bent to remove her boots and left them standing neatly on the vinyl mat.

"Come in, come in," Sam said, taking the flowers from Avie. "This is a Leafs household, but I guess we'll let you in since you're a friend of Avie's." He set the flowers down on the hall table, an addition that had been recommended by Lydia. He'd quickly discovered how handy it was to have a horizontal surface to put things on near the front door. The marble-topped hall table, Lydia had pointed out, even had two shallow drawers for extra keys, mail and bus fare. "Coats?"

Sharon handed him hers and Av whistled when Sam opened the hall closet door. "Will you look at that!" Sharon stared at him, as though wondering what the big deal was. Clearly, she was the type of woman whose own closets were perfectly organized.

"Yeah," Sam said with real satisfaction, glancing at the closet from top to bottom, as he never tired of doing. "Looks good, huh? And that's not all, Av. She's living here now so—you know, so we can move things along a little faster. As a matter of fact, she sent me out for groceries earlier and she's helping Amber with the meal even as we speak.''

"You mean I'm not getting take-out chicken and mushy coleslaw and Pillsbury biscuits?'' Avie wailed, causing his date to give him another odd look. "And I came all this way—''

"Shut up,'' Sam said cheerfully. He smiled at Sharon and picked up the flowers. "Don't mind him.''

"I won't,'' she said, with a thin smile for Avie, who took her hand as they followed Sam into the kitchen.

Sam performed the introductions. Lydia smiled shyly and took the flowers Avie had brought, then busied herself with cutting the stems and sorting through them before arranging them in a vase. She looked fantastic in a long patterned skirt and a sweater that draped softly, showing her curves to advantage. He couldn't believe his luck in getting her to move into his house. All kinds of possibilities had suddenly opened up, although he knew he was going to have to play it extremely cool with her. For some reason he hadn't figured out yet, she didn't seem to trust him.

His daughter was in overdrive, bouncing around the kitchen in an apron concocted out of a towel and a safety pin. She immediately launched into telling her "uncle" Avie and his date how she'd chopped all the onions with a special little knife and she hadn't cut herself once even though they'd made her cry. She explained how she'd opened the can of tomatoes and dumped them in the pan after Lydia did the meat and how she'd put the beans in herself and now she could make chili just like Tania and—

"Hold on, honey!" Sam held up his hands. "Let me get a glass of wine for our guests, and you and Lydia can keep on with whatever you're doing in here. It smells great, doesn't it, Av?"

Avie sniffed the air appreciatively and rubbed his belly and Amber laughed.

"Glass of wine for you, Lydia?" Sam asked as he opened the fridge.

"Later, maybe," she said, still smiling. "Amber and I have a few things to finish up." She handed the vase of flowers to Avie. "Could you put these on the sideboard for me? Thanks!"

Sam saw his friend take the flowers and give him a tiny thumbs-up as he carried the vase to the dining room. Amber had set the table, with Lydia's guidance, and there was a checked tablecloth she'd found somewhere, as well as folded napkins, water glasses, dessert forks—everything. Nothing plastic, nothing straight out of a carton, nothing mismatched.

He poured the wine, handing one glass to Sharon and taking his and Avie's through to the family room. There were flowers on the mantel that Lydia had arranged earlier. They'd been on the grocery list she'd given him.

"Can I help you with anything?" he heard Sharon ask as he left the kitchen.

"Thank you very much," he heard his daughter say airily, "but we've got everything under control in here, don't we, Lydia?"

Sharon came into the family room with Avie, shaking her head. "Quite the kid you've got there, Sam. How old is she?"

"Eight."

"Are Lydia and you, uh—" She looked at him, shaking her hand this way and that. *Lovers. Involved. Seeing each other.*

"No." Sam bent to poke at the fire. *Not yet.* "She's doing some work for me, organizing my house, stuff like that. We're just...just friends."

"Friends, huh?" Avie shot him a quick grin, which he ignored.

"Say, Av, did I mention one of Lydia's clients is Griff Daniels—"

"The *Raptors* Griff Daniels?" Sharon asked.

"None other."

"No kidding!" Avie looked properly impressed. "What's she do for him?"

"Groceries. Menus. Personal chef service." Sam held up his glass. "Cheers. To good friends."

"I'll drink to that," Avie said, giving him a wink that was totally inappropriate, in Sam's opinion. "To *friends!*"

"I KNEW A Jill Berkowitz at school," Lydia said, wiping her mouth with her napkin. Amber was still basking in all the compliments she'd received on her meal. "Is she related?"

"That's my youngest sister," Avie said. "She's married, lives in Brampton. I guess you two lost contact, huh?"

"Yes." Lydia had been surprised to hear that Avie was a friend of Sam's from high school days and that he knew her brother, as well. "We weren't really close. I was in a few classes with her, that's all."

"How are your mother and dad?" Avie asked. "Sam tells me they're divorced."

Lydia smiled and played with her coffee spoon. "They're fine. Dad lives in Albany and he's remarried, and Mom's still in the house I grew up in, although she's completely redecorated it. Several times. She sells real estate now and has a boyfriend. He's fifteen years younger than she is." Lydia glanced from Sam to his guests and shrugged.

"Lucky girl!" Sharon said with a grin.

"What do you mean?" Avie sounded shocked.

"She gets someone who appreciates her, um, experience, and he gets someone who…appreciates his, uh, energy," she said, with a quick look at Amber, who seemed oblivious to the adult conversation. She was humming happily and drawing patterns in the small amount of coleslaw remaining on her plate.

"What's in that box you brought for dessert, Uncle Avie?" she asked suddenly.

"Why don't you go see, honey? Let me know if you approve."

Amber hurried out of the room.

"Energy?" Avie asked, immediately turning back to Sharon.

"I was thinking more along the lines of—well, endurance." She laughed and Avie once again pretended to be shocked. Sam caught Lydia's eye and she blushed. She tried hard not to, but it was impossible.

"Enough of that, you two," Sam said. "That's Lydia's mother you're talking about."

"Sorry!" Sharon leaned across the table and winked at her. "I still say, good for your mom!"

"That's okay. Hey, we've had a few laughs over it ourselves. Mom's become very modern since she and Dad split up. She doesn't even want me to call her 'Mom' anymore. She'd rather I called her Marcia—which I just can't. She's horrified at what I do for a living, too—thinks I'm letting down the side somehow."

"What exactly is that?" Sharon asked.

"I do all the things women used to do in the home, only I charge for it," Lydia said. "I teach people the lost skills involved in keeping a house. Homemaking, or domestic arts, as I call it."

"People like me," Sam broke in. "People who are—"

"Hopeless!" Avie offered.

"Like Sam," she agreed lightly, looking down at her spoon, "who is actually not hopeless at all." When she glanced up, he was staring at her, and there was something in the heat of his gaze that went straight to her head. Perhaps she'd had one glass of wine too many.

"Lydia's been teaching me everything she knows," Sam said gallantly. "When she's finished with me, I'm going to make some woman a hell of a husband, right, Avie?"

"You said it." Avie wore a strange expression. Lydia couldn't keep up with the shots tossed back and forth between him and Sam.

"It's a beautiful, beautiful *cake*," Amber said, coming to the door, her eyes shining. "A chocolate cake."

"I'll help you serve it," Lydia said, getting to her feet and collecting several plates and glasses to take back to the kitchen. *Husband?* Sam was thinking of getting married again? Candace hadn't mentioned that. Did he have someone in mind?

"I'll help," Sharon said and began to collect the rest of the plates.

Sam stood. "Coffee, anyone? That's *my* domestic specialty."

CHAPTER THIRTEEN

AFTER DESSERT and coffee, Lydia pleaded a headache and escaped upstairs. She knew Avie and Sam and Sharon intended to watch a hockey game on television, but that was the last thing she wanted to do.

Besides, she wasn't quite sure of her place in the household. Sam was very generous, but did he really expect her to be part of the family now? They hadn't talked about that. This evening had been unusual because Amber had asked her to help prepare their regular Friday evening meal. Even if things hadn't turned out as well as they had, she'd have been happy to do it. Amber was so enthralled with the simplest events in the kitchen. She'd watched in awe as Lydia quickly whipped up a batch of baking powder biscuits.

"Don't you have to look at something in a book?" the girl had asked.

"A recipe?"

Amber nodded. "Tania's mom always has a recipe in a book."

"I don't need one when it's something I know as well as this," Lydia said, allowing the girl to knead and turn the biscuit dough on the floured counter. She'd had to send Sam out for every single ingredient of their meal, even flour and baking powder. A large grocery-shopping trip to buy basics was a definite priority for this household.

Of course, the biscuits and the chili had received raves at the table. Lydia had expected nothing less and reminded herself that this was a very appreciative audience. A dad who couldn't cook. A guest who'd expected mushy salad and takeout. A guest's date who...well, she had no idea what Sharon Boler had expected.

Lydia got into her nightgown and bathrobe. The bathroom window overlooked the side of the house, and from the sitting room and bedroom windows she could see the backyard, white with snow and silent at this time of year, with a big, bare maple near the back.

She brushed her teeth and washed her face, then brushed out her hair and put it in a loose braid for sleeping. There were a few paperbacks and some magazines on a low shelf and, looking for something to read in bed, she found a *Canadian Geographic* with killer whales on the cover. It was just after nine, but she was unusually tired. No wonder, considering the events of the day. Her plan was to get up early and begin work on the Pereira kitchen. At least the oven didn't need cleaning, as she'd been astonished to discover when she put the biscuits in to bake. Probably because it had never been used...

Charlie chirped his, "hey, look at me" whistle and she unlatched the door of his cage. She often let him out at home to get some exercise and amuse himself. After flying around the room a few times, he landed on the pillow beside her and began to groom his feathers.

Later, she heard Charlie's loud "watch out" alarm call and realized she must've dozed off. She forced her eyes open. Goodness! It was nearly ten o'clock and she'd forgotten to put the bird back. She pushed off the covers and was about to stand when she heard a soft knock on the door to the sitting room.

"Lydia! Are you awake?"

Sam! She scooped up Charlie and returned him to his cage, then reached for her robe, tying it as she went to the door. "Yes?"

"Oh, damn, you went to bed already. I'm sorry, I hope I didn't wake you—" Sam was standing on the dimly-lit low-ceilinged landing.

"Come in." She held the door a little wider and Sam stepped into the room. She shook her head. "No, I don't think I was really asleep. Is there a problem?"

"No. No problem. I just wondered—you know, how you were." His dark eyes searched hers. For some reason, he did seem worried.

"How I *was?*" What was he talking about? Or was she still half asleep?

"You said you had a headache. I thought—"

"Oh, that!" Lydia put one hand to her head and smiled. "I'm fine. Actually, it was just an excuse, more or less, to come upstairs—"

"I thought so." He was so close, so concerned...so handsome. "I wondered if everything was all right, if Avie or I said something that might've upset you, talking about your mother that way or—"

"Oh, Sam!" She managed a laugh, tired as she was. "Nothing like that at all. I was just really exhausted and, well—it was *your* dinner party, wasn't it?" She searched his expression. "I was kind of a third wheel."

He reached out and took her hands. "I can't thank you enough for what you did with Amber. She was so happy. When I put her to bed, she couldn't stop telling me how you taught her to make real biscuits. Apparently she's now one up on Tania Jackson."

"Really?" Lydia smiled. "She's just at the age where she's keen to learn that kind of thing."

"And she's never had the chance." Sam let go of her hands, which was a relief. "Poor kid. I'm hopeless at this stuff and Candace has never done anything the slightest bit domestic with her. I don't think *shopping* counts."

"Don't knock it. Learning how to shop wisely is a valuable skill in our consumer world."

"Come on, you know what I mean. There's my mother, of course, but—" He gave her a probing glance. "Listen, on another subject, I have a huge favor to ask of you."

"What's that? Do you want to sit down?" she asked rather formally.

"No, no, I'm leaving in a minute. The favor? Well, you know my parents are in Portugal and they're coming back on Friday—"

"So soon? I won't be finished yet, and I know you wanted to have everything done—"

"Never mind that. My sister's having a big welcome-home get-together for them and I was wondering if—well, if you'd come with me and Amber."

"To your parents' homecoming? Sam, I'm hardly a family friend," she began. "I'm not even sure I ever *met* your parents."

"You're our friend, mine and Amber's," he said firmly. "We want you to be. While you're here. Maybe even—even after that. Why not?" He studied her face, then her braid, and stretched out one hand. "Braids again, huh?" He grinned. "No, really, we'd be honored if you'd come with us. Of course, if you have something else to do next Friday or you don't want to, that's fine."

"I'd like to come," she said. Now that she thought

about it, yes, she'd like to attend a Pereira family gathering....

"You would?" He looked pleased. Surprised and pleased. He took her hands again and squeezed them gently. "Great. I'll tell Amber in the morning."

"Was this her idea?" Of course. Amber wanted her along.

"No, as a matter of fact, it wasn't," he said slowly, his eyes warm on hers, "It was mine. I have my reasons—which I'll tell you about later."

Sam turned to the door. "Well, sorry for bothering you. I hope it wasn't too boring for you tonight. Avie can be a pain—"

"Oh, not at all! I enjoyed myself. It's just that I'm not a hockey fan and I really wasn't sure if I should stay downstairs after dinner. I'm not exactly a member of the family."

"Consider yourself a member of the family, Lydia. Please. You know we're not formal and I'd like to think you feel comfortable with us. Totally comfortable." He bowed. "My home is your home. Okay?"

"Okay." Lydia laughed, closing the door behind him. She covered Charlie's cage and he made small sleepy sounds, the kind he made when he was settling down.

So, she'd just accepted an invitation to a Pereira gathering of the clan. Curiosity? Maybe...

SAM WOKE UP at half past eight. He'd slept well, as he had ever since Lydia had transformed his bed.

When he got out of the shower, the phone rang. Jessica Smythe, reminding him about the gallery opening she'd invited him to. Damn, that was tonight. He'd forgotten; she'd asked him more than a month ago. Jessica was someone he'd always liked. She was bright, breezy and good-looking.

Now, though, the thought of spending several hours at a gallery, followed by a tête-à-tête dinner, even with a beautiful woman like Jessica, was a nuisance. But he could hardly get out of it at the last minute, could he?

Sam headed downstairs, remembering to put on a T-shirt over his sweatpants. He'd liked the way Lydia had eyed him the last time, but now that she was actually living in his house, he thought he should be a little more circumspect.

"Good morning." Sam paused at the door to the kitchen, which resembled a disaster zone. Lydia was on a step stool, peering into an upper cupboard. Cracker packages, dry cereal, can openers, chopsticks, bags of raisins and dried apricots he hadn't seen for months, plastic spoons and forks, boxes of spaghetti, tins filled with all kinds of things from sardines to evaporated milk, plant food, a package of drinking straws—every surface in the kitchen was covered. She was in the process of reaching for a blender on the top shelf of the cupboard. *A blender?* Where had that come from?

"Good morning." She looked down at him.

"You're up early."

"Six." She looked a little tired. Her hair was in a loose ponytail, delightfully mussed, with the elastic sliding out. "I couldn't sleep."

"I slept like a baby. I don't know what you did to that bed, but I sure sleep well these days. Here, hand me that." He took the blender from her. "I have no idea where I got this."

"Probably another wedding present."

"Maybe." He held out his hand and helped her down. "Where's the Give Away box?"

She laughed. "I'm glad to hear you say that. I thought you'd tell me you might want to make daquiris someday, so no sense getting rid of it...."

"I hate daquiris." He set the device on the stove; there was no more room on any counter.

"Breakfast?" It felt strange having her in the kitchen like this, first thing in the morning. Strange but nice.

"Haven't got around to it yet."

"I suppose Amber's gone next door. Did you see her leave?"

"Yes. She said she was going to watch her program with Tania."

"Barbara's turn," Sam told her, waving a frying

pan he'd pulled out of a lower cupboard. "I skip a turn because they went away skiing last Saturday."

"Amber mentioned the chili again," Lydia said, smiling. "I'm afraid you're going to be getting chili every Friday night for the foreseeable future."

Sam grinned. "No, we're not. You're going to teach her how to make a few other things and you're going to teach me how to cook, too."

"I am?"

"Don't look so surprised, Lydia." He placed the frying pan on a front burner, transferring the blender to the floor, and pulled some bread out of another cupboard for toast. Since she'd told him the fridge was the wrong place, he hadn't put bread in there once. "It's part of the Domestica full-service package, you told me yourself. When you get all the organizing done, I need you to stay on for the same stuff that Daniels guy gets—shopping, cooking, putting things in the freezer."

"We'll see." She smiled enigmatically. "The first problem is getting rid of all this. You don't mind if I throw most of it in the trash?"

He shook his head.

"Then I'll wash out the cupboards and put back what we can. Replace what needs replacing. Organize things. Your kitchen is an utter mess, no logic to anything. Crackers stuffed into cupboards with mixing bowls. Canned goods in with the plates and bowls."

"I know that."

"There are all kinds of supplies you don't even have—"

"Like what?"

"Like flour. Salt. Baking soda. Some basic spices—"

"I've got spices!"

"I don't call one tin of paprika and one ancient jar of Chinese five-spice powder basic spices! Its best-before date, by the way, was two years ago. Basic spices I call things like pepper, oregano, nutmeg—"

"Okay." She was so attractive when she lectured him. "Good point."

"Can you do a big shopping trip either this morning or this afternoon?"

"With you?"

She nodded. He'd find time, he decided. He dug in the fridge, looking for a package of ham or bacon. Voilà! "Amber wants to go skating today before Candace picks her up. Why don't you come with us?"

Lydia hesitated, then shook her head. "I'd rather get this done, Sam. Plus, I have no skates here. They're in storage at my loft."

"We could go get them. Or you could rent a pair. Now, breakfast. How about coffee to start?"

"Coffee would be very nice." She returned to

making notes on a piece of paper—the grocery list, he assumed.

Sam ground the beans and transferred the coffee to the espresso machine, thinking. She was so cautious, so determined to be professional at all times. "Tell you what..."

"What?" She looked up.

"I'll go shopping with you and help you get this organized this morning, and you'll go skating with us this afternoon. Deal?" He knew he had no grounds whatsoever for negotiation. If she didn't want to go skating, he'd still have to go to the grocery store.

"Okay. Deal."

Which told him she *was* interested. She didn't want to accept a simple, straightforward invitation, that was all. Why? Maybe because of what she'd told him about not knowing where she fit into his household.

He supposed she was right—it was a little confusing. On the one hand, she was working for him. She *was* Domestica. On the other, he wanted a relationship with her that had nothing to do with Domestica. Ethically, he should wait until the job was done, then ask her out. He'd defended enough clients whose bosses had put the make on them to know better.

Not that he was trying to put the make on Lydia. Not exactly. The hell with surprising his parents. *Be honest.* He wanted to get this project finished for one reason: so he could start another one. Lydia Lane.

"Let's have breakfast. How about if I fry the bacon and you make some eggs? Scrambled, boiled, fried, I don't care."

"Sounds like a plan."

CHAPTER FOURTEEN

"SKATING! THAT SOUNDS like fun." Zoey was in the small but extremely well-planned kitchen of her apartment, putting together a snack for their mid-afternoon tea. "Where did you go?"

Lydia had taken the transit system to her mother's in the morning for church, something she did fairly regularly. Ray never accompanied them; in fact, Lydia wondered if Ray even knew her mother went to church. Probably Marcia's little secret. As children, Lydia and Steve had attended Sunday school at an Anglican church, but since Marcia's divorce, she'd sampled churches the way she sampled home-decor styles. Marcia currently attended a Unitarian service in Cabbagetown.

Then Lydia had taken a cab to Zoey's to try on her bridesmaid's dress, which had been delivered there the day before.

"The Sanford Community Center. It would've been nice to go to High Park, but I had to rent skates." Lydia picked up one of the dresses. "Do you really think this color's going to show up?" The dresses were a pale ice-blue, almost white.

"Who cares? They're gorgeous. Hey, don't forget, I'm the bride," Zoey joked. "I'm the one who's supposed to stand out, not you guys."

"Right." The dresses were really quite lovely, raw silk trimmed with satin, with a high waistline designed to accommodate Charlotte's growing pregnancy. She'd be four months along by the time of Zoey's wedding.

Zoey brought out the tray with crackers and a few bakery goodies, a teapot and two teacups. She poured and handed one to Lydia. "How are things on Parry Street?"

"Fine." Lydia took a sip of the steaming Earl Grey. "I've only been living there for two days. I helped Sam's daughter with dinner on Friday, which was fun. We made chili and biscuits together. Then yesterday, I spent most of the day doing his kitchen, which was an absolute mess. You have no idea. In the afternoon we went skating."

"What about last night?" Zoey eyed her over the cup.

"Nothing. Sam had a date and I worked on the—"

"A date!" Zoey's teacup rattled as she set it down. "Is he *seeing* someone?"

Lydia shrugged. "I really don't know. This is the first time I've heard anything about a woman in his life, but he doesn't tell me everything. For heaven's sake, Zoey, I just *work* for him! He's a single, attractive guy—of *course* he has women in his life."

She wasn't going to tell her friend how she'd lain awake the night before, straining to hear sounds that would indicate Sam was back. She'd heard him come in around one. By himself? She couldn't tell. Lydia preferred to think she couldn't sleep because she was a little nervous being all alone in a strange place.

"Oh, well." Zoey gestured in an offhand way. "So much for that. I've been hoping something would happen between you and Sam, but you know very well that I wouldn't want you to get involved with anyone who wasn't right for you. If he has a girlfriend—" She made a face. "I just got excited when I found out he was your first love—"

"He *wasn't* my first love! I keep telling you that."

"Whatever." Zoey offered her the plate of snacks. "You have to admit, though, you've felt a little— oh, a little *something* since you've seen him, haven't you? I did when I saw Cam's brother again, who was *my* first love. Of course those feelings can be quite deceptive—look what happened to me!"

Lydia sighed and reached for another macaroon. "It's true. Being around Sam has definitely brought back some of the old pitter-patter, you know what I mean?"

Zoey laughed. "You bet I know what you mean."

"But I'm not fifteen anymore. I can put it in perspective."

"I know you can, Lyd. If things don't work out over at his place, you know you can move in here for a while. I admit I was pushing for romance because I just want everyone to be as happy as Cam and I are, especially my best friends. Plus, of course, Candace was so keen on the two of you hitting it off—''

"She was?" Hitting it off? Candace had told Lydia she wanted her to organize Sam's household and maybe provide a little positive influence for their daughter....

"Oh, yes! She was hoping that, you know, something would spark between you and Sam. The night we met at the restaurant? That's what we were talking about."

If Candace had told Zoey, a complete stranger, her secret agenda for her ex, she'd probably also told her ex. Maybe that day she'd shown up to take him for lunch. Which meant that Sam might think Lydia was in his house for reasons that had nothing to do with cleaning his cupboards. How embarrassing.

But he'd had to talk her into moving in. It had hardly been *her* idea....

Lydia shook her head. Life was getting too confusing.

SAM MET AVIE at the club. He'd spent most of the day in court and, luckily, didn't have to go home to pick up Amber in between. Barbara Jackson was taking the girls directly from school to their homework group at another kid's house.

He was still wearing a jacket and tie when he walked into the locker room. Avie was already dressed in his whites.

"Playing lawyer today?" Avie aimed the handle of his racquet at him and pretended to fire it. "Pow! Another law man bites the dust."

"Yeah. Sorry I'm late, Av." Sam shrugged out of his suit jacket and flung it on the bench. He suddenly remembered. Picking it up, he slid it onto the hanger inside his locker. He was learning. Slowly, but he was learning. "Traffic was tied up."

"You drive?"

"Cab."

Avie bounced the squash ball on the tiled floor with his racquet. "Great to see the sprout the other day. Who knows, with a little help from your Lydia, she might even turn into a cook one day."

"Not *my* Lydia, Av—"

"Jeez, Sam, if it was me, I'd've married her by now. I don't know what's holding you back."

Sam straightened, one leg in his gym shorts. "Holding me back? I've only known her since just before New Year's—"

"She's a babe, Sam! You said so yourself. And look at her—she's got your house so shipshape already I wondered if I was at the right address. Seriously! Hall closet cleared out, flowers on the mantel, a tablecloth—I mean, what more could you ask for? Teaching the kid to make biscuits on top of it? Hell,

I've never *eaten* homemade biscuits before! I didn't even know you could make 'em at home. Yup, she's marriage material all right.''

"Haven't you forgotten a little matter of being in love?'' Sam was thoroughly ticked with his friend. Maybe because he was already in a foul mood, thinking about Lydia spending the entire morning at Griff Daniels's place. "How about that, Av—how about being in *love?* That count?''

"Yeah,'' Avie admitted. "There's that. But I figure, that's the kind of thing that just happens. You know—first comes sex, then comes love. Sometimes. Hell, you gotta try and manage these things. If it happens with the wrong gal, look at the trouble you can get into.''

"Candace.''

"Did *I* say the wicked witch's name? The trick is to make sure it happens with the right one this time. Besides, didn't Lydia have a big crush on you once? Work on her a little. It could happen again.''

Avie had a point; look at Candace. He must've thought he was in love when they got married—he honestly couldn't remember—and now he could barely spend ten minutes in her company without yawning. How the hell were you supposed to know about these things?

On the squash court, Sam was merciless. He smashed his returns, served flawlessly, kept Avie darting and jumping until he begged for mercy. Sam took pity on him and called their third match at 11 instead of 15.

"Holy cow," Avie panted when they came off the court. "You mad at me or something?"

"No. Why would I be mad at you? You're my best friend."

"You're mad 'cause I said if it had been me, I'd have married her already," Avie said with certainty.

"Oh, yeah, that." Sam grinned and tapped Avie on the back of the head with his racquet. "Hey, buddy, I'm a lawyer, remember? I can't start romancing an employee, even if I'm interested. Which I am, by the way, so hands off. Anyway, you've got your hands full with Sharon...."

"You can say that again," Avie returned with a lewd wink.

"Employer-employee relationships are not ethical, not smart and could possibly be a ticket to harassment charges, which means I'd get tossed out of the bar association and then how would I make a living, pay my mortgage, put food on the table for my kid—"

"Sam, Sam, Sam!" Avie shook his head, reaching up to wipe his neck with the towel. "I always took you for a smart guy, but, jeez, I don't know—"

"What you talking about?"

"She's not *working* for you. She's an independent contractor. You hired her company, not her. Right?"

"ALWAYS MAKE SURE your wash water is hot and your dish towels are clean. Linen is best for glassware and—Sam, are you listening?"

Lydia took a step back. The wash water was definitely hot; steam billowed up around Sam's face. Probably too hot. She was giving him a lesson on washing dishes by hand. The dishwasher was working fine, but she thought he should know the principles behind washing dishes properly. There *were* principles; you didn't just wash whatever you happened to grab first.

"I'm listening. Hot water, right? Detergent. First glasses, then cutlery." Sam pulled his hands from the sink. "Man, that's hot! Then plates and stuff, right?"

"Right. And do you remember why that order is important, Mr. Pereira?"

"Yes, I do, Ms. Domestica. It's because glasses are the cleanest and you shouldn't get any grease on them or they'll look ugly. And we can't drink out of ugly glasses, no, no, no!"

"Sam," she said, trying to keep from smiling. "Are you teasing me?"

"Absolutely not!" He gingerly immersed one hand in the water. "Ouch! This is going to need some cold." He turned on the faucet.

"Not too much," she warned.

"—and cutlery comes next, because it's the second cleanest and then dishes and then pots and pans because they're the dirtiest," he finished in a singsong voice, grinning at her. It was *very* hard not to smile back.

"I know it seems very basic, Sam, but that's why I'm here. You've never actually learned the basics. Laundry, dishes, making a bed properly..."

"Right." Sam began to wash the glasses they'd used for the evening meal, slowly and carefully, his hands looking overlarge for the job. "I wish we'd get to the bed part soon."

She ignored him. "Now rinse." He obediently put the glass into the next sink, which was filled with hot water.

"Now drain." He put the glass carefully on the drain board.

"If we were really worried about germs, which we're not since we all know each other and usually it's just you and Amber, so you already share the family germs—"

"Family germs!" He gave her a look of mock horror.

"Yes, every family gets used to each other's germs," she continued. "As I was saying, if you really wanted to keep things sterile, you'd put a drop of bleach in this rinse water and then rinse in clear water a second time. And you'd let the dishes air dry. But I'm going to dry them because—"

"Because?"

"Just because!" she said, polishing a wineglass and holding it up to the light. "I think they look nicer dried and put away immediately." She glanced at him quickly. "Now that you actually *have* a designated cupboard for your wineglasses."

The kitchen organization was finished and Lydia was proud of her work. The cupboards were temporarily labeled until Sam and Amber learned what was behind each door. Spices were together, baking supplies together, wineglasses in one cupboard, drinking glasses and mugs in another.

"Lydia," Sam began after he'd washed a few more glasses. "What do you think about getting married?"

Fortunately Lydia put the wineglass she'd just dried on the shelf or she would've dropped it. *"Married?"*

"Yeah, you know—" He shrugged with apparent nonchalance. "Love and marriage, one girl, one guy, children, all that stuff."

"Is this a proposal?" she shot back, mainly because she couldn't think of what else to say. She laughed, to show she was just kidding.

He watched her thoughtfully, which sent Lydia's heartbeat up a notch, then slowly tipped the meal's allotment of cutlery into the soapy water. "Nah. I was just wondering if you get any pressure about marriage from other people."

"You mean friends, family?"

He nodded.

"I suppose I get my share. Any woman my age does. Do you?"

"I've already been married."

"Oh, sorry!" She felt silly; how could she have forgotten about Candace?

"The pressure's worse now."

"Why's that?"

"Because I'm a marrying kind of guy," he said, turning to her. "I like the idea of being married. I *want* to be married. Not to Candace, though. My friends know that. But they think I screwed up once, so I can't be trusted to figure things out the second time. They're always trying to introduce me to women they consider likely prospects."

"Why—" Lydia began. She frowned. "Is there a point to this? I mean, why are you asking—"

"For instance," he interrupted her. "My friend Avie thinks I should marry you."

"Me?" she squawked.

He caught her gaze and held it, hands suspended over the sink. "Yeah." He waved one soapy hand. "Avie's—well, he's just Avie. He was very impressed with you the other night. Okay, never mind him. But it made me think. Why *aren't* you married? You're a very attractive, talented, appealing woman. I wondered if you've got something against the state of matrimony."

"Nothing against it," she returned lightly. *Just never been asked by the right man.*

"Good. Glad to hear it."

Lydia plucked another glass from the drainboard. She felt very brave. "Funny you should mention this, because a lot of people seem to think I should marry you...."

"What?" His shock wasn't very flattering. Lydia was glad, though, that he'd reacted so strongly. It underlined their just-friends relationship, in case she happened to think there was more to it. Not that she thought any such thing...

"Yeah." She laughed. "Let's see—my friend, Zoey—"

"Zoey?" he repeated, shaking his head. "That clarifies something for me."

"What?" Lydia put the glass on the shelf and picked up a handful of forks to dry.

"I thought she was really giving me the once-over at the wedding. I couldn't figure it out. Here she was engaged to this guy who's obviously crazy about her." He turned to her and smiled. "So, she was checking me out for you!"

"Maybe. I have no idea. And the bride, too. Charlotte cornered me and gave me unwanted advice about my matrimonial prospects, much of it to do with you being single."

"No kidding!" He looked pleased.

"And my mother's been pushing me to, you know, take an interest in you—"

"Your mother! Why would she be pushing you to get married?"

"She thinks—well, it's true—that I've been involved with a fair number of rather *unusual* men...."

"Losers?"

"That's putting it a bit too harshly. Mother's worried about me, I guess. She doesn't understand how I'll ever meet anyone suitable doing other people's housework, which is how she sees Domestica.''

''Mothers are mothers.'' Sam dried his hands after letting the water drain out of the sink. ''Hey, maybe we should give it some thought, huh?''

''Give what some thought?''

''Marriage. If everybody else thinks we'd make a good pair, maybe we should consider it.'' He leaned toward her, smiling. ''Maybe they're right.''

''Oh, Sam. I don't mind if you're an idiot sometimes, but please don't be a *complete* idiot. I couldn't stand it.''

''Okay.'' He flicked the towel at her, then went to hang it up. She heard the phone ring and he disappeared around the corner to answer it, still clutching the towel.

What a conversation!

When she'd moved in, there hadn't been a dish towel or kitchen towel in the entire Pereira household. They'd relied on paper towels for everything that involved wiping. Now there was a neatly ironed drawerful of dish towels and a supply of paper napkins for use at the table. Paper napkins were appropriate for this household, she'd decided. Good-quality ones. Sometimes tradition had to bow to convenience.

She was definitely making progress, though. Sam was even getting the hang of doing laundry. Doing a "white" load was obvious enough now—white was white—but he still seemed confused about "light" and "dark" loads. Jeans and pajamas didn't go into the same loads, even if they were both blue, she kept telling him.

Sam returned to the kitchen, frowning. He hung the tea towel on the rack she'd installed inside a cupboard door.

"Problems?"

"I've got to go out. I'll see if Sandy's available to sit with Amber—"

"I'm here. I can stay with her." Amber was upstairs doing her homework.

"That's not your job, Lydia." Sam's face was grim.

"Is it Larry?" She knew he was worried about the old boxer.

He nodded. "That was Alma. She says he hasn't come home for two days. She doesn't know where he is."

"You go, then. I'll call Sandy, if you insist. But it's not necessary. Amber doesn't need taking care of, she just needs someone in the house and—"

"I insist. You're not a baby-sitter here. Or is that a Domestica specialty, too?"

"Yes," she said. "Tonight it is."

CHAPTER FIFTEEN

"I'LL MAKE A THERMOS of hot chocolate," Lydia suggested quickly. "And how about some sandwiches?" She put her hand on his arm. "When you find him, he might be hungry."

"Or worse," Sam said. "Thanks. I appreciate the offer. After what happened to Hubert last week—"

"Hubert?" Lydia got some milk out of the fridge and put a pan on the stove to heat. Hot chocolate was probably more nourishing than coffee.

"Hubert Diamond. Another of my clients," he said. "Froze to death behind a Dumpster. There's too many people like Larry and Hubert. Some of them find shelter on cold nights but—" Sam shrugged. "Guys like Larry have too much pride to ask for help. Sometimes they're just too stupid."

"He was here last week making something to eat," Lydia said. She hadn't mentioned the incident before now.

"Friday?"

"Yes. The day I moved over here. He kind of scared me. I—I didn't know anyone else was in the house," she said, recalling her surprise. She got out some bread and a can of tuna and started to make the sandwiches.

"Damn!" Sam's gaze held hers. "That's my fault. I should've let you know. It's not the first time, of course—"

"I gathered that. He said you told him to."

"I did. He was shaky. I could see he hadn't had a decent meal in a while." Sam shook his head. "I should've read the signs then. Usually his sister Alma takes pretty good care of him, but he's upset about this court case coming up and maybe he's avoiding her. He's ashamed. He's afraid he's going to jail again."

"Is he?"

Sam's expression was resolute. "Not if I can help it." He hurried down the hall and a minute later came back wearing a coat and carrying a small nylon backpack. She handed him the sandwiches and the thermos, and he stowed them in his bag. When he opened it, she could see he had a flashlight in it, as well as a few other things.

"Thanks!" His smile warmed her. "This is great. Now you be sure and call Sandy—"

"Sam." She looked up at him as he pulled on a wool cap. "I meant what I said. I'm a friend of the family, remember? I can baby-sit Amber for you. It's ridiculous to call out a high-school student to baby-sit on a school night when I'm right here." It was Wednesday. "Really."

"You're sure?"

She held his gaze for a fraction of a second too long. "I'm sure."

To her amazement, he moved toward her and pulled her into his arms and hugged her tightly. Then he stepped back. "Thanks, Lydia. I appreciate it."

She followed him into the hall, heart hammering. "Gloves?"

"Yeah, I'd better take gloves," he said, reaching for the basket that contained the gloves and mitts. He put a spare pair in his backpack.

"Got your cell phone? Just in case?"

He patted his pocket and grinned. "Yeah, Ms. Domestica. See you later."

With a whoosh of cold air, he was gone, and Lydia went to the window. It was just after eight o'clock in the middle of winter. The snowfall they'd had that afternoon had spread a blanket of pristine white snow over everything, reflecting the light from streetlamps and porches. It looked lovely. Soft. Deceptive. A death trap if you weren't prepared for it.

She hoped Larry Massullo was okay and that Sam would find him quickly. The thought of Sam being out on the streets all night himself gave her the shivers. She didn't even have his cell phone number if she wanted to call him. That was foolish. But it had to be written down *somewhere*. She'd worry about finding it later.

She went upstairs. Tania and Amber had finished

their homework, which, in third grade, was pretty minimal. "Your dad had to go out for a bit, Amber. I'm baby-sitting."

"Good!" The two girls were happily engaged in playing dress-up with the contents of the trunk Lydia had provided on Sunday, after her visit to Zoey. Zoey was getting rid of things in preparation for her move to British Columbia after the wedding. Two old boas—why in the world had Zoey ever bought those?—a half-dozen pairs of high-heeled sandals and pumps, a couple of skirts. Discarded purses, scarves, jewellery. All grist for the imagination mill.

"Bedtime in half an hour, all right? I'll walk you home, Tania."

The girls nodded. Lydia sat in the small rocking chair in the corner of Amber's bedroom and watched them play, glancing around from time to time and musing about what she'd accomplished. Already, there were dividends. Sam said he noticed Amber wasn't spending as much time staring at the television. Instead she was playing in her room. And, Lydia thought, the reason was that her room was so much more fun to be in. Now she could find things. Now she knew where to put things when she was finished with them. Her bed was clear of toys and clothes. Her homework area was set up with her table, drawers and all her supplies.

Domestic arts. Lydia didn't care what anyone said. The proof of the value of care and orderliness was before her—two happy little girls absorbed in what children loved best: play.

SAM TRUDGED through the snow that had begun to fall again, trying to keep to the path through the park. Where the hell was Larry? He'd been across every inch of this small city park that was a favorite with the old boxer and his cronies. No sign of him and there were few around to ask. Most of the homeless had found places to hunker down out of the bitter wind and swirling snow. Some community centers provided space on the floors on nights like this. And there were the usual angels of mercy: the city hostels, the churches, the Salvation Army.

Sam kept seeing Lydia standing at the window, dark against the cozy glow of the lights inside, as he left the house. It was a powerful image. Hearth, home, his loved ones safe and sound, his children fed—well, one child—his woman waiting for him to return. Lydia was no doubt waiting for his return but she was hardly his woman.

Not yet.

The date he'd had with Jessica, a woman he'd once thought he'd be interested in pursuing, had set him straight in the clearest possible way. It wasn't Jessica he wanted. Or Miranda or Delores or any of the rest. It was Lydia Lane. Steve's kid sister. Marcia and Hank Lane's daughter. The little girl with the honey-colored braids, all grown-up now. The woman who barely remembered him yet, at the same time, seemed wary of him. Why?

The question was driving him crazy. Had Candace said anything to set Lydia against him? Not likely. Probably the other way around. Candace was always pushing him to get married again and, in fact, the day they'd had lunch, she'd suggested Lydia would be a good candidate. He hadn't known Lydia a week yet, not counting when they were kids. Candace desperately wanted him to marry someone who'd be a good stepmother for Amber, which would take some of the pressure off her. Sad, but true.

What sort of mother would Lydia make? She was thoughtful, kind, patient, sensitive. Yeah, she'd be a good mother; Sam had no doubt of that whatsoever. But he also realized there was no point even thinking about it. He wasn't looking for a mother for his daughter. He was looking for a wife.

And right now, damn it, he was looking for Larry Massullo. He ducked into the brightly lit doorway of a smoke-shop near the bus station. "You see Larry today?" he asked Walter Long, the proprietor, a short, burly ex-cop.

"Nope." Walter came from behind the counter to peer out the window at the snow. "What, he's missing?"

"Alma says he hasn't shown up for the past two nights."

Walter shrugged. "Poor bastard."

"If you see him, put him in a cab and send him to my place, eh? I'll pay you for the taxi."

"Sure thing. Good luck, Sam."

Sam stepped back into the darkness.

He could understand the pull of the streets. There'd been a time in his life when he'd lived practically the way Larry did now, roaming from here to there, making a few dollars where he could, going home to sleep, or to a girlfriend's. The temptations of drugs and booze and women had surrounded him, and he'd sampled his share, much to his parents' despair at the time. They'd wanted him to settle down, get a real job, maybe in one of the trades. But he hadn't given his future much thought until the time he'd seen a friend, an over-the-hill prostitute named Vicky, beaten almost unconscious by her pimp. Sam had dragged her, bleeding, back to her rooming house and begged her to go to the police. He'd offered to stand up for her, to be a witness if she went to court.

She'd refused. He'd pleaded and she'd finally laughed in his face. "You think the law's there for people like me, Sam? Grow up!" All he could do was tend her wounds and think about what she'd said.

That was when he'd made up his mind to study the law. He had the brains, he knew that, and he could get the money. He'd never regretted his decision until he'd found himself saddled with a wife, a baby and a seventy-hour week in a law firm he hated—getting businessmen out of trouble they'd created for themselves, whether with the government or through bad business deals.

He'd quit. Candace had left—although he realized now it was no loss. He still had his daughter and was spending time with her, working out of a home office, being the kind of father he wanted to be. And he still had plenty of corporate clients who'd followed him to his own practice, enough to pay the bills. A third of his time went to people like Larry. And Hubert. And Darlene, before she'd lucked out with her implant suit and financed an education for herself. Darlene had actually been able to pay his fees with her settlement. That didn't happen too often.

"You seen Larry Massullo?" he asked a panhandler at the entrance to the Queen Street subway station.

"Yeah, saw him earlier, over by the soup van at that little park near Bathurst."

"When?" Sam tossed him five dollars.

"Five, six o'clock."

"Thanks, pal." Sam hurried off. It was nearly ten now.

The park was shadowy but because of this snow, brighter than usual lit by yellow-orange light from the street. Sam checked the benches along the north side. No one out in this cold. To the east was an alley that ran behind a row of old buildings. Heat ducts vented into the alley drew regulars to the warm air. Sam knew there were territorial rights that went with certain warm air ducts, like the ones at the subway stations. He didn't know if that was the case here.

He started down the alley. Several bundles, looking like so much newspaper put out for recycling, turned out to be men and women, wrapped in blankets and sleeping bags, spending the night in the open. Some folks didn't like the shelters, wouldn't go there, refused to follow the rules some shelters required. There were as many feeble-minded and mentally ill people living on the streets these days as economically deprived. He shone the flashlight he'd brought on a few faces, bringing curses. He apologized, hurrying on his way.

No Larry. At the end of the alley, on the park side, was a huge spruce tree. Sam shone his flashlight under the branches, on the bare ground beneath, sheltered from the winter's snow.

"Hey, Larry!" He saw his old friend leaning against a pack of some kind, along with two other men, like a trio of discarded garden elves. One was lying down, apparently asleep.

"Huh?" The vacant face turned toward the light.

"It's Sam, Larry. Get your sorry butt out of there, old man! I'm taking you home." He shoved the bag of sandwiches and the thermos under the spruce tree. He'd leave the food for the other two.

Larry was cold and stiff and smelled of urine and liquor. Had he spent the previous night there, too? Sam had no idea, and there was no point in talking to Larry now. He flagged a cab on Queen and ten minutes later was half-walking, half-carrying Larry up the snowy steps of his house on Parry Street.

"Wha'?"

"Shh, Larry! Everybody's asleep. Let me get you up the stairs and into the shower. You can stay here tonight and talk to Alma in the morning."

"O-kay, boss," Larry mumbled. "Oooo-kay."

Sam got him into a warm shower and collected a bathrobe from his own bedroom for the derelict man. He dropped the entire lot of Larry's clothes, including his wool socks and running shoes, into the washing machine, setting the level on "full" and the program on "heavy duty." He dumped in plenty of detergent and added a dollop of bleach. Lydia would forgive him for not separating the lights from the darks this time.

When he got back to the bathroom, Larry was sitting down in the shower stall, almost asleep. Sam shook him, and the old man finally stood up so Sam could wrap a towel around him and get him into one of the guest bedrooms. Lydia had worked her magic here, too. Larry slipped naked, with Sam's help, under tulip-pink sheets in a room smelling faintly of lavender and beeswax. He was out, as they said, like a light, and Sam was glad the old man was so dazed that he wouldn't remember a thing in the morning. The humiliation of being stripped and bathed by someone who'd years ago been his student would have been too much for a once-strong, still-proud man.

What to do with him tomorrow? He'd worry about that when the time came. Sam threw his bathrobe over the end of the bed and put a T-shirt and boxer shorts on the small table.

Was Lydia still up? Had she heard them come in? Sam transferred Larry's clean clothes to the dryer, including his running shoes, then made his way quietly up the stairs to the third floor. He ought to let her know there was someone else in the house, in case Larry surprised her in the morning.

There was a light under the door.

Sam rapped softly and the door was immediately flung open.

"Sam!" She was in her dressing gown, hair tumbling to her shoulders and beyond. He'd only seen it loose once before. "Did you find him?"

"Yes, I found him," Sam said, wondering why his heart was racing. Probably the events of the last few hours. "He was sleeping under a tree and—"

"A tree!" She put one hand to her mouth. He heard a loud chirp somewhere in the background and glanced over her shoulder.

"Yeah." Sam managed a smile. "Larry and two other bums. I brought him back here and put him to bed in one of the guest rooms. I wanted to tell you in case you saw him in the morning, so he didn't scare you."

She shook her head from side to side. "I can't believe it. I'm so glad you found him. I was so worried that—oh!"

There was a swoosh of wings and something flew out of her sitting area and into the hallway. Sam ducked.

"Charlie!" She made a swipe in the air as the bird went by. "Oh, come back here, you silly bird!"

Charlie squawked again and Sam felt something land on his shoulder. He resisted his immediate instinct to shake it off. He knew it was only her little bird.

"Hold still, Sam," she whispered, coming closer, her eye on his shoulder. She reached out slowly and the bird hopped up Sam's shoulder, toward his neck. *Nice move, bird.* He wanted to grin. She was just inches away.

"Oh!" She sounded completely exasperated. He watched as her face got closer and closer. Her lips were parted, her eyes shining....

"What kind of bird is it?" he asked. He might as well be conversational, although these were the oddest circumstances of any conversation he'd ever had. The bird hopped onto his head. He grinned.

"It's a lovebird," she said. "Stupid thing!"

"A lovebird? Aren't there supposed to be two of them?"

"Yes and no. Sometimes." Her eyes were on Charlie, who was preparing, Sam had a feeling, to hop to his other shoulder. "It's kind of complicated—" She reached out both arms, as though to capture the bird in her hands, and Sam moved half a step forward.

It was nothing at all to put his arms around her. To forget about that incredibly clever bird on his shoulder and just think about the beautiful woman in his arms.

"It's always kind of complicated," he murmured against her cheek. Her forehead, her nose. "Isn't it?"

He lowered his mouth to hers. He felt her surprise, then the instant softening of her lips as she accepted his kiss. As she stepped into it, moved even closer to him. As she wrapped her arms around him. The hell with Charlie. Sam felt the bird leave his shoulder, fly off, into the sitting area.

As she sighed.

And kissed him back. As though she'd been waiting for this as long as he had. Two weeks? No, he thought it must've been years. Years and years and years.

CHAPTER SIXTEEN

LYDIA WOKE AT EIGHT, later than usual, and stared straight up at the ceiling. He'd kissed her. She could feel his hands framing her cheeks as he smiled at her, his face just inches away—and then he'd disappeared down the stairs.

Leaving her to a restless night, dreaming the feverish dreams of her fifteen-year-old self. Those dreams and memories were very much a part of her, she realized, overlaid with all the other years and all that other experience.

Inside, we're always fifteen, aren't we? The insecurity, the vulnerability, the yearning. The hope. Great-aunt Lydia had told her that very thing once, when Lydia had asked if she minded getting old. Her mother's aunt had looked at her seriously and said, no, she never thought about all the years that had passed or felt any different than she had when she was fifteen—until she looked into a mirror and saw an old woman staring back at her.

If that was true, would Lydia always carry this tiny, intensely burning flame for her first love deep inside? Sam Pereira. The hot, tough, devil-may-care boy on the motorcycle. The young man who'd been so distant from her schoolgirl world that he'd barely known she was alive. Who'd considered her, perhaps, just part of the furniture in the Lane household.

And now, for some reason, he'd kissed her. Lydia chalked it up to the odd circumstances, the late hour, the unusual emotions of the evening. Sam searching for his old friend, finding him, bringing him safely back to his home, coming upstairs to tell her...

And then there was Charlie. If Charlie hadn't flown out into the hallway, would she have ended up in Sam's arms? Even for a brief, off-balance moment?

No, it was happenstance. Sam was probably as embarrassed about it as she was—or as she would've been if she didn't carry a torch for him in her heart. She wasn't embarrassed. For her, the kiss had seemed terribly romantic. For him, probably just one of those unpredictable things...

Lydia pushed back the covers and put her feet over the side of the bed. Good thing she was going out with Tag Blanshard this evening. He'd called yesterday, after Sam had left, to tell her he was back from Germany and would like to see her again, if she was free.

She *was* free. She was always free. They were going skating at Nathan Phillips Square and then he was taking her to dinner somewhere so they'd have a chance to talk. Catch up on each other's lives. He'd missed her, he said. Lydia tried to picture him in her mind. Short blond hair, muscular and fit, cheerful, good sense of humor. Age? Early thirties. It had been quite a few months since she'd last seen him and a lot had happened.

She had a shower in her tiny bathroom and dressed quickly in a skirt and sweater. She secured her hair in a twist and slipped on flat shoes. As she opened the door, Charlie squawked. His night cover was still on. She whipped it off and smiled at his morning antics. He stretched his wings and she swore that if birds could yawn, he yawned. Then he fluffed up his feathers and tucked his tiny head back on his shoulder, prepared to snooze a bit longer.

Lydia had grown very fond of the blue-and-green lovebird, given to her by an early client who was leaving the country. She'd taken the bird reluctantly, but in the end, had been glad she did. The lovebird, a species that was a small cousin in the parrot family, was good company, took little care and could be very entertaining when he wanted to be.

She thought of Sam kissing her with Charlie perched on his shoulder. Yes…entertaining, all right.

Larry Massullo was sitting at the kitchen table, wearing a bathrobe she'd seen in Sam's closet. When she came in, he was staring at his large, bony hands, clasped in front of him on the table.

"Good morning, Larry." She glanced at the wall

clock. Sam had obviously gone to take Amber and Tania to school. "Have you had breakfast?"

Larry raised teary pale-blue eyes. "I'm much obliged, ma'am, to have a place to stay last night—"

"Please don't mention it. It's Sam's house and he tells me you're old friends. You're very welcome to stay."

"I've caused people a lot of grief, ma'am, including Sam. He's the best man in the world, ma'am." He nodded solemnly, his eyes never leaving hers. "The best man in the world."

"So, how about some breakfast?" Lydia continued brightly. And where were Larry's clothes? "Do you remember what you were wearing when you arrived last night? I'll see if I can find your things."

Larry looked down at the robe he had on in surprise. "I believe I was wearing jeans, ma'am. Jeans and a shirt. And shoes. Shoes with laces."

There were no clothes in the washing machine, but Lydia pulled out quite a cornucopia from the dryer, including two T-shirts of a motley gray color, a long-sleeved flannel shirt, a fleece vest, long underwear with the knees out, jeans, two pairs of linty, wool socks and…and a pair of canvas running shoes!

She smiled, shaking her head. Maybe Zoey had a point with her theory about men and laundry. She folded the clothes and carried them out to the man who was still sitting there, staring at his hands, his eyes full of tears.

"Here they are, Larry," she said, giving him the pile. "Why don't you go back upstairs and get dressed? And while you're doing that, I'll make a nice breakfast for the two of us. Okay? How about that?"

Larry gave her a tremulous smile, then left the kitchen carrying his belongings.

Poor old guy, Lydia thought as she got out a frying pan. He looked to be about sixty-five or so, definitely much the worse for wear, thanks to booze and hard living. She didn't suppose all the blows he'd taken to the head as a younger man and a boxer had helped any....

She put the pan on the stove and opened the fridge. Let's see—ham, a cheese and spinach omelette, fried potatoes, orange juice, plenty of toast and jam... At least she'd be sending him out wherever he was going, or wherever Sam was taking him, with a full stomach.

SAM KICKED THE SNOW OFF his boots and went through his front door to one of the most heavenly smells known to a hungry man—breakfast. And a good breakfast, too. None of this muffin and coffee business, or a bowl of granola with skim milk.

He heard the sound of laughter.

When he entered the kitchen, he found Lydia and Larry sitting at the table, finishing their meal like a couple of old pals. She glanced at him over her shoulder as she went to the counter for the coffeepot. "Had breakfast? There's plenty."

Gorgeous, competent, a woman who took things in stride.

And Larry. He looked like another man. His eyes were clear and shining. They'd obviously been having a good laugh over something. Larry wore the clothes Sam had washed for him, everything but the running shoes, which were sitting neatly by the door that led to the hallway.

Lydia could be cool and composed. So could he. *Nothing ventured, nothing gained.* He walked up to her, dropped a kiss on the back of her neck and said, "Yeah, breakfast sounds good." He rubbed his hands together and grinned as she whirled toward him. He was gratified to see the flush spread across her face. "Sleep well, honey?" he murmured.

"Not well at all," she said ominously. "And please don't 'honey' me."

"Hey," Larry said, gazing from Lydia to Sam. "Are you two—?"

"No," she said firmly, "we're not. Sam's just being silly. More coffee, Larry?"

He pushed his mug toward her, his expression confused. "Sure." He looked up at Sam. "You better listen to the lady, Sam. If you know what's good for you."

"I do," Sam returned, holding out another cup for her to fill. "I always listen to her. Speaking of ladies,

Larry, what are you going to say to your sister? She's very worried about you.''

Larry looked down at his coffee cup.

''She's been taking care of you all these years, Larry. I think she deserves better than this.''

''Omelette?'' Lydia asked softly.

''Yes, please. Larry?''

''I'll talk to her, Sam. I promise I won't leave anymore. I'll tell her I'm sorry—'' The big man's eyes filled with tears again.

''Never mind, Larry. You just stay on the straight and narrow until this case is over. I'm going to get you off. Trust me. There's no way they can make that story stick. Listen, do you want me to lend you a razor after breakfast?''

''Sure, Sam. I could use a shave.'' Larry nodded, his grizzled face full of trust, and Sam felt his heart contract. How could he make promises like that— that he'd get him off? Who could tell what a judge might do? But if he didn't manage to keep his old friend out of jail, at least this time, he'd never forgive himself.

He walked to the stove, where Lydia was busy with a small frying pan, some butter, some other ingredients and a couple of eggs.

''Lesson?''

''What kind? Manners, ethics, omelette?''

''Lydia, I'm sorry about last night. I know I

shouldn't have, but—" He grinned. She didn't really look mad.

"But what?"

"You were so damned tempting. So beautiful. Ready for bed—"

"I was dressed. I was wearing a bathrobe."

"And you were reaching out to me—"

"I was trying to grab Charlie." She turned up the heat under the pan.

"Charlie?" He frowned, pretending mystification.

"The bird on your shoulder!" She gestured toward the pan. "So, omelette lesson? Never mind what happened. Just forget it. I have."

Which was a bit of a blow. But surely she didn't mean it. "Okay. What do I do?"

"Watch me and pay attention."

"Yes, ma'am!" Sam stepped closer to the counter, where Lydia was breaking two eggs into a small bowl.

"Two eggs is perfect for an omelette. One's not enough and three's a little too much." She met his eyes and he nodded. "Use free-range eggs. They're more expensive but they're much tastier. And you don't want to support an industry that keeps hens in tiny cages just so you can save a dollar or two."

She looked at him severely and he shook his head and put his hand on his heart. "No, ma'am. Especially since I've met a bird myself. Charlie."

Lydia stifled a grin—he could tell—and walked to

the sink. "Now, put in about as much water as will fit in one half of the eggshell." She filled part of the shell she'd just broken, dumping it in with the eggs.

"Why is that, ma'am? If I may ask."

"The water provides a little burst of steam to the eggs, makes them lighter. I add a pinch of salt—" she demonstrated "—although some cooks say not to because it toughens the eggs."

"No salt?"

"They add it later, after the egg's started cooking." She went back to the stove. "Meanwhile, of course, you've had your pan heating on medium-high heat."

"Of course."

She glanced at him, the smile hovering on her lips. "If you don't want things to stick to a pan when you're frying, always wait until the pan heats up, then add the butter or oil or fat. That's a tip for everything, not just omelettes. Here—" she handed him the bowl with the eggs and water "—give this a stir with a fork. Not too much, though."

Sam did as he was told while Lydia put a dollop of butter in the pan. It sizzled immediately and she swirled it around.

"Watch out. It's getting brown." He felt quite pleased with himself for noticing and pointing out to her what was clearly a mistake.

"You want it to get a little brown," she said. "It's

what the French call *à la noisette,* the color of hazelnuts. That's when the pan's ready. Okay, in it goes!''

"Ah. I see."

Lydia shook the pan while the egg mixture bubbled and steamed alarmingly. She ran the fork through the top of the mixture, disturbing it a little, letting the raw part run under, then shook some more. "This shouldn't take more than a minute or two," she said. "Then you can add your other ingredients. Grated cheese, salsa, sour cream, spinach, whatever kind of omelette you're making. Put them on top and leave it another thirty seconds or so, while the cheese melts and the filling gets hot."

Sam watched Lydia slide his finished omelette—spinach and cheese—onto a plate. Perfect! "You are an extremely talented woman, Lydia Lane," he said as he accepted it from her.

"It's all in the technique," she said modestly.

"I'm impressed. I am going to practice this, with your help, until I get it right. I promise. I'm going to be a new man when you get through with me. Larry, you want some?"

Sam sat down at the table with the old boxer, who refused, opting for another piece of toast instead. "Lydia?" He waved at her chair and she came and sat down, bringing her coffee cup with her.

"This is wonderful!" It was—moist and succulent, the best omelette he'd ever eaten. Bar none.

"So," he said, after a few more bites. "Are you

interested in coming to Amber's skating practice tonight? You're welcome to join us.'' This was the first step—okay, maybe the second—on a path that Sam had mapped out last night. After he'd kissed her. After she'd kissed him back. *Thank you, Charlie.*

She shook her head. ''Sorry. I've got a date.''

''A date!'' He was stunned.

''Yes, a date, Sam. You know, where a man and a woman go out, have some fun, maybe dinner, a movie…''

''Who?'' He couldn't prevent himself from blurting out the question, even though it was none of his business whatsoever. A date!

''Someone I used to see. He's been out of the country for a few months and now he's back. He called yesterday.'' She obviously wasn't planning to tell him who this guy was. So he was going to stick around, see for himself. Surely Mr. Back-in-the-country would show up before Amber's practice was scheduled. He consoled himself with the fact that he had dibs on her for the next night.

''You haven't forgotten about my parents' homecoming tomorrow?''

''I haven't forgotten, Sam,'' she said quietly. ''What time?''

''My sister would like us to pick them up at the airport. We'd have to leave here about three. That okay with you?''

She caught his gaze and held it. He felt something

turn over and over inside him, and it wasn't the omelette. A challenge? If so, it was subtle as hell. He had the distinct feeling that she was stepping up to the line somehow. Date or no date.

"That's fine with me," she said, finishing her coffee and pushing back her chair. "I'm looking forward to it. Very much."

TAG BLANSHARD SHOWED UP on the dot of five.

"Lydia!" He hugged her immediately and swung her off her feet. "How're you doing? I missed you, babe!"

Lydia felt a little embarrassed. They hadn't been *that* close, even though they'd gone out half a dozen times. She noticed Sam hovering near the entrance to the kitchen, looking quite grim.

What was *that* all about?

"Sam, I'd like you to meet Tag Blanshard." She smiled up at Tag, who seemed quite surprised to see Sam there. What, did he think she lived in this house on her own? "Tag, Sam Pereira. He's not exactly my boss," she said, laughing, "but I'm doing some work for him this month."

She watched the two men shake hands, bonecrushers, she was sure. She was reminded of Zoey's comment about the hearty handshakes some men favored. That was definitely the case here.

"Tag works in a circus," she said, watching

Sam's reaction, adding for Tag's benefit, "and Sam's a lawyer."

"So, where are you two off to?" Sam said, ignoring her comment about Tag's occupation, which most people found interesting. How many people did you meet who worked in a circus?

"Skating," Tag said, looking completely comfortable and unaware of the tension Lydia felt darting around the foyer. Sam, she sensed, was positively steaming. "Then dinner at a new restaurant a friend told me about. We've got a lot to catch up on. You ready, Lydia?"

"Yes. I'll have to rent skates, I'm afraid," she confessed. "Mine are in storage."

"Fine." Tag put his hand on her elbow and held the door for her.

"Have a good time," Sam said as they went down the steps. Lydia risked a glance. She half expected him to demand when she'd be in. He didn't, but he watched them all the way to Tag's vehicle, a rental SUV, before closing the door.

Skating was fun. Tag was very athletic and knew plenty of stunts, which impressed other skaters. He liked to get laughs from the crowd and was very good at it. Probably why he was in the circus business, she thought.

They ate at a Mexican restaurant, which was all right although terribly noisy. Tag regaled her with stories about the circus's German engagement, so she didn't have to contribute much to the conversation.

That was lucky, because she didn't have a whole lot to say. She kept thinking about Sam. Sam and Amber. Amber's skating practice. Sam's face when she left. Sam kissing her last night. What it all meant.

In a way, she was very glad Tag Blanshard had shown up when he had. Sam had probably thought she had no social life at all, at least judging by the evidence since she'd been at his place. Not far from the truth, really.

But if she was so glad to see Tag, who was a pleasant and attractive man, why couldn't she get Sam Pereira out of her head?

CHAPTER SEVENTEEN

A *CIRCUS* GUY? She had to be out of her mind! What was he, a trapeze artist? A *clown?* The guy who picked up elephant plops?

Through the window in the family room, Sam watched her leave with this Tag character. What kind of name was Tag, anyway?

There she went. Skating, a little dinner, a little dancing, who knew what else. How could he stop her? He couldn't. He'd always figured she had her own life, with lots of guys in it, and here was the evidence. This one happened to work in a circus. She had a client who'd wanted her to have his baby with a turkey baster. Then there was the loser who wanted her to be his pretend girlfriend for the weekend.

She was surrounded by weirdos. And there wasn't a damn thing he could do about it.

Except marry her.

The idea had occurred to him. Quite often lately. And it scared him silly. He hadn't done very well with his first effort at marriage. How could he be sure things would work out with a second attempt?

''Dad?''

"Yes, honey?" He turned to go back into the kitchen, where Amber was just finishing up a card she was making for his parents. As Avie always said, first comes sex, then comes love—sometimes—and then comes marriage—maybe. He'd hadn't even gotten to the first item on the list and he was thinking about the third.

"Isn't my card nice?" She had paint and glue and crayons and scraps of paper all over the kitchen table. "Lydia helped me make it. She's going to help me make all my Valentines this year, too."

"It's great, honey."

"How do you spell 'welcome'?"

Sam spelled it out for her and admired her card and retrieved her skates from the garage and phoned for a pizza—Hawaiian—to be delivered for their dinner. And all the while he kept thinking *circus* guy? Come on!

LYDIA TOOK THE SUBWAY to Sherbourne and then a bus and picked up her minivan at ten the next morning. It had needed the valve job, nearly a thousand bucks, and a carburetor something-or-other, another three hundred. Luckily, she had the money from Sam's deposit and the up-front money the movie people had paid her. Her mortgage payment wasn't due for another two weeks, and by then the movie people would have given her the rest of the money for the loft, plus, of course, she had regular money dribbling in from her gig with Daniels. Most of her business was word-of-mouth. She'd been hoping to cash in from the exposure on Candace's show but so far it hadn't happened. Wrong time of year. She still hadn't heard whether the movie people were going to be needing her loft for the full six weeks, or if they'd be finished earlier. Either way, they paid her for six.

The car repairs had cut drastically into her decorating budget, which had been the whole reason for renting out the loft but—oh, well. She was probably getting off cheap and now she had a vehicle that ran like a charm. She also had a few other leads to follow up. Zoey had told her about a couple who wanted an overhaul done at their summer cottage near Kingston, a possible two-week job for early spring, and one happy customer often led to another one. She might even end up with some new customers among the people Sam knew who were impressed with what she'd done at his place.

She was meeting Zoey for lunch at half-past eleven at a popular delicatessen on Yonge Street, near St. Lawrence Market. She was early. She selected a table near the window, and as she waited for Zoey, she indulged in one of her favorite pastimes, watching people go by. Why did the couples stand out? The men and women who walked by hand-in-hand, talking and laughing, carrying shopping bags, books from the library, large backpacks. Her date with Tag had been...well, less than thrilling. And she actually used to like him quite a lot. Well, before he left for Germany.

"Hi! Sorry, I'm late." Zoey slid into her side of the booth. "Yes, coffee, please," she said to the waitress who appeared.

"You, ma'am?"

"Tea, please." The waitress hurried off after slapping two large, plastic-laminated menus down in front of them. "I can't stay long, Zoey. I've got to get back and get ready for the big Pereira event."

"Oh, yes, that's today, isn't it? Should be fun. Lots of almond cakes and espresso. And port wine." Zoey winked. "Don't you think it's *amazing* that he asked you? Not because it's you, of course—" she leaned forward and patted Lydia's hand "—just because it seems kind of private. A family thing."

"You're right. I've wondered myself. He did say he had his reasons, which he's never explained."

"Probably wants you there to beat off all the women his family's trying to match him up with."

"You think so?" Lydia stared at her friend. "Zoey, where do you come up with these scenarios?"

"Lydia, you're too soft-hearted. You don't realize that a guy like that, single, successful, not to mention *gorgeous*—remember, I've seen him—is going to be considered a huge catch. The family has a stake in this. There's a granddaughter to consider and he's already screwed up the first marriage, right?'' She wrinkled her nose and tapped her menu with one forefinger. ''Of *course,* they want a say in who gets him.''

''Zoey, you're nuts.'' Lydia shook her head. ''This isn't some romantic plot in a book by Jamie Chinchilla, you know. Honestly! Okay—'' she put her menu down ''—I'm having the calamari wrap.''

But she wondered. Sam T. Pereira had always been incredibly attractive to women. Every girl she'd known in high school had a crush on him. She was no exception.

''Tell me this, Lydia.'' Zoey's eyes were intense. ''You've been living in the same house with him for a week. Do you *like* him? You know what I mean.''

Lydia looked down, played with her teaspoon for a few seconds. ''Yes,'' she said softly. If she couldn't tell her best friends, who could she tell? ''I think I do. I—I'm definitely attracted.'' She looked up again. ''In fact, *quite* attracted. I don't know how much is the old crush and how much is—you know, *now.* Us as grown-ups.''

''I'm probably the last person to ask, considering my paved-with-good-intentions romance record—''

''Zoe, I'm not asking—''

''—but my advice is, go for it. What have you got to lose?''

''Dignity, self-respect, professionalism—''

''Oh, Lydia! If you think there's something there,

grab him before someone else does. If it turns out you were wrong, well, fine. No hard feelings. You both move on. Someone else gets a crack at him. The calamari wrap? That sounds good.''

SAM TOOK THE SECOND EXIT off the 401 to Lester B. Pearson Airport. The car he was driving—his dad's—was a ten-year-old Buick. It still smelled new. As part of a plan carefully orchestrated by his sisters, Sam had picked up his parents' car at their house and was meeting them at the airport. Then he'd drive everyone to his sister Teresa's and—surprise!—big party. Later, he and Lydia and Amber would take a cab home. That way, he could have a glass or two of *vinho* if he wanted.

"Are we almost at the airport, Daddy? I can't wait to see Nana and Papa! Do you think they brought me anything?"

Sam smiled in the rearview mirror. "I'm sure they did. Not long now. Ten minutes maybe." His daughter was practically bouncing around in the car. Lydia Lane, who sat beside him in the passenger seat, was quiet. Sam glanced at her quickly. He still couldn't get over how good she looked. After he'd brought the car to Parry Street and gone over to the Jacksons' to collect Amber, he'd called upstairs to tell Lydia he was ready. It was three-thirty already and his parents' plane was due in an hour.

He'd been nervous. He hadn't seen Lydia since the

evening before, when Tag Blanshard had shown up
at the door. She'd come in around midnight; he knew
that because he'd been awake, reading a brief, and
happened to notice the time.

Yeah, sure, Sam.

When she came down the stairs she took his breath
away. A white, figure-hugging top in some soft material, a short black skirt that showed her long legs
to perfection, knee-length boots. At the bottom of the
stairs, she put on a saucy red cap and a navy coat,
which she'd carried down on her arm, looking at him
all the while and not saying a word. Then she took
some red leather gloves out of her pocket and started
to put them on.

''Ready?'' she'd asked when she was finished, and
he'd opened the door and escorted her out, almost
forgetting to lock up. He wondered how his family
was going to react. He loved his parents and sisters
and cousins and aunts and uncles dearly but he knew
how—well, how *territorial* they could be. Showing
up with a woman at a family party like this would
be sending a clear signal: marriage material. And,
even if he thought that might be true now—although
he hadn't really thought it when he'd asked her a
week ago—it was premature for his family to get that
message. If they approved, they'd be all over Lydia.
If they disapproved, they'd be all over her, too. Either way, he'd have to run interference. Stick close
to her. Which suited him fine.

Teresa expected them at six-thirty for a buffet supper for family and friends, and the party would be over—he hoped—by ten.

The airport was busy as usual, and they had to wait nearly forty-five minutes in the arrivals lounge while his parents cleared customs. Sam got Lydia a coffee and wandered around with Amber, checking out the various stores and leafing through magazines. Lydia, he noticed, seemed quite content to simply sit in her uncomfortable plastic chair and look around.

Finally, there they were, loaded down with shopping bags and duty free bags, his father pushing their luggage piled high on a cart.

"Sam!" His mother dropped her bags when she saw him and held her arms wide open. "Amber!"

Amber ran to her grandmother and threw both arms around her neck. "Nana! Here—" She fumbled in her small backpack. "I made you a card. Lydia helped me."

"Lydia?" His mother looked around, then smiled and kissed her granddaughter. "It's beautiful, Amber. Here, let me kiss your father. Oh, Sam, it's so good to see you!"

Sam kissed his mother while Amber was swept up into a big hug by his father. All around them, family groups were doing the same thing, in half a dozen languages. Lydia stood to one side, watching and smiling.

"Mom and Dad, this is Lydia Lane. She's a friend

of mine. You remember Steve Lane? Lydia's his sister." He smiled at Lydia and held out one hand. "My mother, Emilia, and my father, Luis."

"Ah, Miss Lydia Lane," his mother said, taking Lydia's outstretched hand in both of hers. "You are Sam's new girlfriend?"

"Oh, no," Lydia said quickly. "We're just friends, as he says. Plus, I'm doing some work for him." She shot him a glance as if to say, what's this *friends* thing?

His father bowed slightly over her hand as he shook it. "Very pleased to meet you, Miss Lydia Lane. Any friend of our son's is welcome. I remember your brother very well. He played football, yes?"

"That's right."

"Mom, Dad," Sam said, spotting another luggage cart that had been abandoned. "Let's pile all your bags on this and we'll go to the parking area. I brought your car, Dad."

"Oh, did you? Very good!" His father, at least, was being sensible, in Sam's view. His mother couldn't take her eyes off Lydia.

They got in the car with a maximum of difficulty and bother, and in the end, after arguing briefly with his father, Sam drove, with Lydia beside him and his daughter stuffed between his parents in the back seat.

Sam negotiated the exit, stopping to pay the parking fee, and looked over at Lydia. She was still smiling, apparently amused by all the fuss and excitement. He smiled back at her, relieved.

"Not so bad, eh?" He indicated the back seat with a nod. His parents were busy telling Amber what they'd had to eat on the plane and his mother had produced a package of almond candies out of her purse.

"Lovely, I think," she said. She clasped her gloved hands in her lap. "Families are nice."

He wondered if she'd change her mind on that. Before they were even a third of the way to his sister's house, his mother was leaning forward. "Amber tells me you are *living* with them." She glanced from Lydia to him. "How long has *that* been going on?"

"Mother, she's in the housekeeper's suite on the third floor." Sam set his mouth in a grim line. He'd half expected something like this but he'd thought his mother would have the grace to tackle him on the subject privately.

"Since when?"

"One week," Lydia said quietly. Was that all it had been? She didn't seem perturbed by his mother's nosiness.

"Are you married?"

"No."

"Have you ever been married?"

"Mother!"

"No," Lydia replied. She put up a cautionary hand that his mother couldn't see.

"And just what kind of work is it you do?" his mother pressed on.

"I teach people how to organize their homes so they're more pleasant to live in," she said. "Sam here, for instance, needed a lot of work done—"

"Oh, my! I do what I can but he's terrible—" his mother began.

"And you've got your own household to worry about," Lydia said soothingly. "This way, Sam's learning how to do things for himself so he doesn't have to rely on you or anyone else."

"I'll believe it when I see it! If you can change my son's ways, you'll be a miracle worker. I did too much for him as a boy, and he never learned a thing about looking after himself."

"She *is* a miracle worker, Mom. I'm already a changed man." He exchanged a smile with Lydia. "Aren't I?"

"I don't know about that. You do know how to separate laundry into different loads, though. Whites, darks, running shoes."

He laughed out loud and noticed in the rearview mirror that his mother sent him a very knowing look. She stared at her husband, then at Lydia for a long considering moment. Then back at him.

Oh-oh, Sam thought.

HIS SISTER'S HOUSE in Scarborough was large and modern, which was lucky, because by the time they drove up, both sides of the street were lined with cars. A lot of people had been invited to welcome the Pereiras home. Luckily, his parents didn't seem to notice anything amiss.

"Amber," he whispered into his daughter's ear. "You run up to the house and tell Auntie Teresa we're here. Don't say anything to Nana and Papa."

Amber's eyes danced with excitement as she dashed up the front steps.

When they'd parked, his parents wanted to know why they'd stopped at Teresa's before Sam drove them home. Then they wanted to get into the trunk to dig through their packages to find the gifts for Teresa's two girls, which was what they were doing when he told Amber to alert the household.

Everything worked perfectly. The elder Pereiras made their way up the steps, his mother carrying some packages for her grandchildren and his father carrying a big bottle of duty-free port for his son-in-law. Sam followed with Lydia. So far, she'd borne up admirably.

"Thanks for handling my mother so well," he whispered as his mother pushed the doorbell. He and Lydia stood at the bottom of the steps. "She's incorrigible."

"Don't mention it," Lydia whispered back. "I think she's delightful. I wonder how you'd stand up to the kind of second-degree *my* mother would put you through."

''She would?''

Just then, the door was opened by Teresa's youngest daughter, Cecilia, who was Amber's age, and his parents went inside, he and Lydia trailing after them.

''Surprise!'' The lights went on, and the entire living room was jammed with cousins and neighbors and relatives of one sort or another.

His mother was struck speechless.

For once.

CHAPTER EIGHTEEN

"WHO'S THAT MAN OVER there, the one in the orange vest?"

"By the door?" Sam rapidly surveyed the crowded dining room. He still couldn't believe the turnout. Not just family, but friends and neighbors, too. His mother was in her glory, hugging and kissing and crying out with pleasure every time she spotted someone else. They'd been in Portugal for six weeks, but you'd think they'd been gone for a year.

"Yes. He keeps staring at me."

Sam smiled. *Everyone* kept staring at her. Hadn't she noticed? "That's my uncle Manny. My mother's brother. The one who gave me the fishing rod."

"Fishing rod?" She frowned.

Sam touched her elbow and helped direct her through the crowd. "On the top shelf of my hall closet?" he murmured, bending close to her ear.

"Oh, *that* fishing rod."

"And who is this lovely lady you have with you today, Sam?" His uncle took Lydia's hand and smiled.

Today? "This is Lydia Lane—Lydia, my uncle Manny Carvalho. Lydia is a good friend—"

"Ah!" His uncle's eyes lit up.

"—who's doing some work for me," Sam finished.

"And what kind of work is that, miss?"

"She has a company that performs the magic of organizing people's lives," Sam broke in, answering for her. "She's in the process of rearranging my household for me."

"Yes. As a matter of fact, I recently found a fishing rod you'd given Sam some time ago, Mr. Carvalho—"

"My best fly-fishing rod! He *lost* it?" Sam's uncle broke into a torrent of Portuguese.

"No, no, I didn't lose it, I just couldn't find it," Sam said, placating his uncle and trying to distract him with a few queries about ice fishing, which his uncle had tried for the first time that winter. He noticed Lydia was enjoying his discomfiture immensely.

"Where's Amber?" he asked, relieved to be moving away from the group that had suddenly gathered around his uncle to talk about fishing. "This must be a huge bore for you, all these people speaking Portuguese...."

"It's not. I'm enjoying it. And when your uncles and aunts speak Portuguese, I don't have to worry about saying anything, do I? I can just look around.

Amber?'' She accepted the glass of punch he handed her by the buffet. ''I saw her earlier with some other children.''

Sam wanted to go check on his daughter, but he wasn't leaving Lydia to face his relatives alone. He hadn't been wrong about their interest. After the grilling she'd received from his mother on the ride from the airport, he didn't dare—

''Sam!'' It was his sister Teresa. ''Isn't the party going well? I'm so pleased for Mama and Papa. They had a wonderful trip but they're so happy to be home.''

Sam kissed his sister on the cheek. ''Thank you for organizing this. It's a great party.''

''Lydia! I know we met briefly when you came in, but I'm so glad to finally have a chance to talk to you.'' His sister's gaze was riveted on Lydia's face. ''Mama tells me you're living with my brother?''

''Teresa!'' he protested.

''*Living* with him? Goodness, no, not if you mean what I think you mean. I'm just doing some work for Sam. Organizing his house. It's quite a job.''

''I see. Good for you.'' His sister smiled and Sam realized she didn't see at all. She didn't *want* to see; no one did. Which meant, he knew, that they all approved of Lydia—which had to be a good thing in the long run but was very confusing right now.

''Lydia's just a friend, Teresa. Listen, have you

seen Amber?'' Sam took a sip of his drink and
moved a little closer to Lydia. He couldn't believe
his family! For now, he was sticking to the ''good
friend'' story, no matter what they said or thought.

''She's upstairs with the girls. They're fine. Play-
ing with the stuff Mom brought them. Cissie wants
Amber to sleep over.'' His sister smiled again and
put her hand on Lydia's arm. ''Goodbye for now.''
She winked. ''I'm glad you came with Sam today.
I'm sure we'll meet again.''

''You'll have to forgive my relatives,'' he said,
tucking Lydia's hand under his elbow. She didn't
pull away. ''They're incredibly nosy.''

''Understandably.'' She smiled. ''I'm sure they're
just worried that some unsuitable woman might sink
her claws into you. They feel you may need their
protection. At least, that's my friend Zoey's theory.''

''Really? You mentioned it to her?'' He laughed,
pleased that she'd discussed his invitation with one
of her friends. ''She was way off on the laundry theory you told me about but she might have a point
here. Actually, I've got a confession to make.''

''Yes?''

''That *is* partly the reason I asked you to come
with me today.''

''Oh?''

They stopped in an alcove just off the living room
and close to the hall entrance. Someone in the dining
room, probably his uncle Alberto, was starting to

sing a fado, one of the mournful Portuguese folk songs. He heard a few bars on a badly tuned guitar, probably his brother-in-law, Alec O'Neill. Teresa's husband. Things were going to get crazy around here. The noise level had gone up several decibels since they'd arrived an hour and a half ago. What had he been thinking? It wasn't fair to bring Lydia into this wild gathering.

"Lydia—" He put his hand on her shoulder to draw her nearer as someone shoved by. "I feel a little stupid about this now, but one of the reasons I invited you was to deflect not only the unsuitable women your friend Zoey mentioned but the—" he grimaced and glanced around "—extremely *suitable* women my family keeps coming up with."

"To marry, you mean."

"To marry. Yes. Right. They want me to get married again."

"Do you?" She stared at him.

"Want to get married? Of course I do! I just happened to hook up with the wrong woman the first time, that's all."

"So they introduce you to women they think would make good wives—"

"Suitable wives. And suitable stepmothers for Amber." Keeping his gaze on hers, he moved slightly as his cousin Jorge ambled past, a glass in his hand. "For instance, you see that woman over there, the one with the red dress?"

She craned her neck. "The blonde?"

He nodded. "My brother-in-law, Teresa's husband, Alec, works with her. She's in insurance. Very clever woman. He's tried to get us together twice, once at a dinner party here and once with some tickets to a hockey game he was giving away, strings attached."

"She doesn't look the type—hockey, I mean."

He shrugged. "And you see that good-looking tall woman over there in the green sweater?"

"Mmm." She wasn't *that* good-looking....

"She's a widow my sister Maria introduced me to, dropping a lot of heavy hints. A very nice lady but there's just no chemistry. It's embarrassing for both of us."

"I can see that it would be." Her eyes sparkled with amusement.

"So, you can understand the predicament I'm in when I show up at these family gatherings. They look for *suitable* and I look for—"

"Chemistry." She looked highly entertained, which was heartening. Some women might have been offended. "I see. I'm here as a decoy. Just as you presented me to Amber as a 'friend of the family' instead of a business associate, you've brought me here today so you can more or less present me as 'Sam's choice' in women, is that it?"

He paused, a split second too long. "That's it." That was *exactly* it. More, not less.

She immediately looked away. "Well, okay," she said, finally meeting his gaze again. Her cheeks were pink and her eyes were a little wary, the expression he'd seen so often before. "I'll go along with it. But what about the fact that I'm doing some work for you?"

He waved one hand and made a face. "Nobody believes that anyway. Do *you* think they believe it?"

"No." She giggled and took a step forward, so that they were practically touching. He raised his arm to her shoulders and drew her against him. How he wanted to kiss her! "Thanks, Lydia. You're a good sport."

"Hey," she said, a little too brightly. "What are friends for?"

LYDIA WONDERED if she might be drinking too much. It was either the port wine, of which she'd only had a couple of glasses, and one glass of punch—or the sheer headiness of being with Sam. After their little talk in the corner, he'd become extremely attentive. He kept touching her. Either he tucked her hand under his arm, or he placed one arm around her waist as they talked to people, or he had a hand on her shoulder as they moved from one room to another.

He was definitely creating the impression that she was "his woman," all right. Which he'd told her was his aim. But how much was genuine and how much for show? Lydia couldn't help feeling that *some* of it was genuine. Why would she have goose bumps when he looked at her if it wasn't? But then she'd had goose bumps where Sam Pereira was concerned ever since she was a teenager, no matter how she'd tried to convince herself that she'd put him out of her mind for the past thirteen years.

The very thought that his attentiveness might be partly genuine thrilled her. Zoey said she was too cautious. That she had to take more chances, especially with Sam. If she felt there was something between them, according to Zoey, she ought to grab it…and fast.

She got rather daring when Sam left her near the buffet table with strict instructions not to go anywhere while he checked up on Amber. The woman in red, the one from the insurance office, slid close to her, ostensibly to load up on more of the crab-and-artichoke dip.

"How long have you known Sam?" she enquired pleasantly.

Lydia decided to abandon the "just good friends" and "I'm just organizing him" lines. "Thirteen years."

"Oh? So long?"

"Yes. We knew each other ages ago, when I was still in school, but we lost touch. We've just gotten back together since Christmas."

That was appropriately ambiguous—"gotten back together."

"Oh. Isn't that nice?" the woman said, smiling in a friendly fashion, then slithering off.

Slithering? Lydia wondered where the claws had come from. She didn't think she had any, and yet her reaction to the woman Sam had described as one of his family's "picks"—a very pleasant, ordinary, friendly woman—had been visceral. Primitive.

And rather exhilarating.

"Everything okay?" Sam was back, his arm around her shoulders as he leaned closer to hear her response over the music that filled the room. Someone had put on a CD and several people had started to dance.

"Fine."

He took her empty glass and set it on the buffet table behind them. "Dance with me?"

She moved into his open arms. It was a natural thing to do. She caught her foot on something and his arms tightened instantly. "Hey, you all right, Lydia?"

"Perfect," she said, looking into his eyes. A little dizzy, perhaps. Which, under the circumstances, was understandable.

They danced for a few minutes without saying anything. Lydia saw something in Sam's gaze she hadn't noticed before. An intensity. A light that seemed focused entirely on her. She smiled a little. It was very warm in the room. He smiled, too.

The smile turned into a grin and he bent toward

her and whispered in her ear, "Man, you don't know how much I'd like to kiss you right now."

"Sam?" His father bowed ever so slightly, an old-fashioned gesture. "Allow me, son."

Sam stepped aside, his face a mask of surprise that almost made Lydia giggle. She felt fifteen again; she was giggling as though she *was* fifteen again. Luis Pereira, a leaner, shorter, grey-haired version of Sam, was an excellent dancer, better than his son.

"Are you enjoying yourself, Lydia?" He said her name the way Sam did, drawing out the syllables. "I hope so." She could see Sam over his father's shoulder, talking to his mother in the background, sending impatient glances their way.

"Yes, I am. Very much," Lydia said. "It was very kind of Sam to invite me."

"He is a good boy, my son. He works hard for the poor people, did you know that?"

Lydia nodded.

Luis whispered loudly. "He has a soft heart, Lydia."

She smiled, not quite sure what else was expected of her. Probably nothing, because the instant the music stopped and Luis Pereira released her, his son was there taking his place.

"Aha!" He took her smoothly in his arms and segued into the next tune. The CD was some kind of old-fashioned dance mix. "I don't know what got into the old man. Probably checking you out for him-

self. Now,'' he added with satisfaction, ''where were
we?''

Before they'd even gone around the room once,
Sam's brother-in-law had cut in. Then his cousin
Jorge, a large, sloppy man in a cardigan sweater who
wasn't a very good dancer and stepped all over her
feet. She was aching to sit down when Sam rescued
her one more time and whisked her away from the
living room, where most of the action was taking
place, to the more secluded hallway.

''That's better,'' he said, glancing toward the
brightly lit dance area. ''If one more male relative
shows up here and tries to dance with you, I'm going
to punch his lights out.''

''You're not!''

''Well, no. I probably wouldn't.'' He smiled into
her eyes and Lydia felt a familiar ache bubble up
inside her. ''Wasn't I just telling you, before we were
so rudely interrupted, how beautiful you are tonight,
Lydia?''

''No,'' she said breathlessly, ''you weren't.''

''Wasn't I telling you how unbelievable it is that
we've just known each other three weeks? Three
weeks! And that I feel like I've known you forever?''
His voice was rough and Lydia's heart skipped a
beat.

''No,'' she whispered. ''You weren't.''

He gazed deep into her eyes. ''Wasn't I telling you
how much I'd like to kiss you right now?''

"Yes." *Oh, if only this was real.*

"It's true," he muttered, glaring at a cousin who slapped him on the shoulder, saying, "Hey, there! How you doin', pal?" as he passed them in the hall,

"Sam?"

"Yes, Lydia?" He sounded distracted. He'd started to move slowly to the music again. She automatically followed his lead.

"How much of this is real and—and how much of it is just show? You know, for the family?"

He stopped dancing and stared at her. "It's real, Lydia. It's *real.*"

She didn't know where she'd found the nerve. "So, why don't you kiss me then?" she whispered. "If you want to…"

He pulled her against him and next thing she knew, his mouth was on hers and he was kissing her, hard. Setting off a flash fire in her brain. He was kissing her the way she'd dreamed of being kissed— ever since she was fifteen. Only now, she was nearly twenty-eight and he really *was* kissing her, desperately, as if he couldn't ever get enough of her.

And she was kissing him back. With the same hunger, the same need. The other night, when Charlie had flown onto his shoulder—that had just been a teaser. A trial run. A hint of what could happen if he *really* kissed her. Tasting his mouth, feeling the hardness and heat of his body against hers. His hands on her face, her back, her fingers in his hair—

"Oops! Pardon us, folks—"

Lydia sprang back. "Oh!"

Sam swore. "For crying out loud, Jorge, can't you do anything right? Why don't you go through the dining room?"

"Sorry! Sorry!" Jorge held his drink high as he sidled past, accompanied by a young woman with mussed hair and sleepy eyes Lydia didn't think she'd seen before. "'Scuse us!"

Lydia's face was hot. Thank heavens for the dimness in the hallway. What in the world had just *happened?*

"Lydia?" Sam's voice was strained. "You okay?"

"I'm fine." Her own voice was barely audible. "I—I don't know if this is such a good thing—"

"It *is* a good thing! But you're right, it's not something we should—I don't know!" He ran his hands through his hair in a gesture of pure frustration. "Maybe we should get out of here. Go home. I'm sick of stumbling over relatives."

He took her hand and led her back into the crowded living room.

"Oh, Sam! There you are!" Emilia Pereira hurried toward them. "I thought you might have left—"

"We're just leaving, Mom."

"Are you?" Her eyes went from her son to Lydia. "I'm so pleased to meet you, my dear." She took Lydia's hand. "I'm going to come over soon and see what you've done to my son's house. Excuse me for being so nosy in the car on the way here. My granddaughter tells me you helped her make the card she gave us, so sweet, and helped with her room and she can find things in her closet again—'' Sam's mother raised her eyes to the ceiling. ''I can't believe it!''

''Come anytime,'' Lydia said. ''I'm not there on Tuesdays, but almost any other day until I've finished the job is fine.''

''And you cook, too?'' She squeezed Lydia's hand. ''I'm so thrilled for my son to find someone like you, after all this time and we were almost ready to give up on him....''

Lydia looked at Sam, startled, and he raised his eyes to the ceiling in a gesture mimicking his mother's. He still held Lydia's other hand. ''We're going now, Mom. I'll call a cab and then find Teresa and Maria and say goodbye.''

''Oh, Sam!'' She threw her arms around her son and he hugged her, winking at Lydia over his mother's shoulder. ''You are making your mother so *happy!*''

It was snowing when the cab arrived. Sam handed Lydia into the back seat and went around to the other side. He leaned forward to give the driver his address.

''What about Amber?'' Lydia hadn't seen her for most of the evening.

"She's staying over with her cousins," Sam said. "They've got lots to talk about."

Which meant...that just the two of them were going back to the house on Parry Street. Lydia glanced sideways at Sam but he was looking out his window, his head turned away from her.

It seemed so quiet after the noise and bustle of the party, despite the occasional bursts of chatter from the dispatcher. Lydia's head was spinning. She thought Sam's parents must have been gratified to receive such a homecoming from their family and friends.

The silence in the cab was beginning to make her nervous. Neither one of them said a word for most of the trip. When they were about halfway home, Sam reached out and took her hand. He held it for a moment or two before he spoke. "Do you want me to apologize?"

Lydia knew exactly what he was talking about. She looked toward him, seeing him only in the flash of streetlights and passing cars. His expression was usually serious. Subdued. He seemed uncertain, even a little vulnerable.

"No," she said. "I don't want any apologies. Not at all."

CHAPTER NINETEEN

THE SNOW WAS really coming down by the time the cab pulled up at Parry Street. Lydia got out while Sam paid the driver. She raised her face to the dark sky, watching the snow drift toward the earth, then wiped her nose and cheeks where large flakes had landed, melting instantly. The city was always alive, but somehow the thickly falling snow deadened the sound of traffic and distant sirens.

The porch steps had an accumulation of an inch or two, and Lydia heard Sam mutter something about shoveling tomorrow as they walked up to the front door. She had a key in her purse but Sam took his out immediately and unlocked the door, swinging it wide and letting out a great waft of warm house air. The interior was dark but welcoming, smelling of lavender and fresh flowers, lemon oil and floor wax. The shiny brass knocker on the door, bright in the outdoor porch light, was as good a symbol as any of all the changes she'd brought into this household over the past few weeks. She was satisfied that she'd made a difference here, to this family, even though there was still some way to go before she was finished.

Sam flicked on the hall light and she bent to unfasten her boots. "Lydia." She looked up.

"Yes?"

He held out his hand. He hadn't taken off his coat yet, although the closet door was open. A little confused, she gave him her gloved hand and stood, awkwardly easing off her unzipped boot with the toe of her other foot.

His eyes were hot; they had that look again, that intensity she'd glimpsed in the hallway of his sister's house. He stared down at her hand in his and began to ease off her glove, working slowly at loosening the fingers, one by one. Then he took her other hand….

Lydia caught her breath. The sensuality of what he was doing gripped her heart. She cleared her throat, intending to say, "I can do that," but what came out was faint and indistinct. He paid no attention, his entire focus on removing the other glove. Slowly, ever so slowly, he drew it off, then turned and put both gloves on the hall table.

Lydia took the opportunity to catch her breath again and try to gather her skittering thoughts. It was impossible. As soon as she met his eyes, she knew she was lost, totally lost. *She wanted this man.* She'd wanted him all her life, despite what she'd tried to pretend—to herself, to Zoey, to everyone.

Sam bent down on one knee and unzipped the boot she still had on. She closed her eyes as she felt his thumb trace the zipper's path down her calf, felt his fingers slip into the top of the boot to ease it down. She lifted her leg slightly, allowing him to remove her boot. Her breath ached in her throat.

When he stood again, Lydia felt the powerful emotion in his eyes stab straight into her heart.

He moved closer to her and put both hands on the collar of her coat. He unfastened the top button, raised his eyes briefly to hers, then focussed again on what he was doing. Lydia heard his breath, ragged and halting as hers, only inches away.

"Sam!" she whispered. She lifted her arms, put her hands on his coat and tentatively undid the top button. His eyes flew to hers the instant she touched him and he backed her against the window in the foyer and pressed his mouth to hers. Lydia was too stunned to kiss him back; she felt the cold of the window against her head, the sharp ledge of the lower frame pushing into her hip.

His mouth hot on hers…and then nothing as he pulled away and unfastened her second coat button, eyes intent, once again, on his task. Emboldened, she reached out for the second button on his coat, and again, he pressed her against the window and kissed her, this time his mouth moving hungrily over hers.

Lydia abandoned any attempt at thought and gave herself up to the absolute sensuality of the moment.

She trusted him. He wouldn't hurt her, no matter what. Nothing else was important. There was no point in being afraid, wary, no point in trying to figure anything out. The past was past. She wasn't a vulnerable fifteen-year-old anymore to be hurt and rejected by a glance or a careless word. She was a woman, grown and experienced. She wasn't chasing him anymore, begging him to notice her. This was mutual, and it was passion.

She felt Sam's fingers groping at the remaining buttons on her coat, opening them, sliding the garment from her shoulders, without ever breaking the contact of his mouth on hers. Her coat dropped to the floor. His hands were all over her, on her shoulders, her breasts, her ribs, and then he pulled her tight against him, crushing her in his powerful arms. His kiss deepened and deepened again, until she felt she would faint from the pleasure.

He eased his mouth from hers and began kissing her rapidly, lightly…her lips, her chin, her closed eyes. She fumbled for the remaining buttons on his coat and he helped her, shrugging it off to fall in a heap beside hers. He stepped away, taking her with him, his hands on her waist, and balanced awkwardly on first one foot, then the other, kicking off his shoes.

His mouth moved lower, to her jaw, her earlobe,

and she let her head fall back against his arm, offering herself fully to the storm of sensation. His tongue created whorls of fire on her skin. His hands slid under her sweater and she sucked in her breath as he touched the sensitive skin of her ribs, the sides of her breasts. There was no thought of restraint, of hesitation. Her need for him was powerful and unstoppable. It was only a question of how they'd get from the entrance of the house to his room. Or hers. Or to the sofa in the family room. Or they could stay right there, on the floor of the hallway....

He tore open the buttons of her sweater and pushed it from her shoulders, his mouth moving to her breasts. She tore at the buttons on his shirt and he helped her, flinging his shirt on the hall table, and then they were skin to skin.

Lydia tugged at his belt and loosened it. She felt him unzip her skirt and the silky slither as it fell to her feet. He kicked his pants away and she felt the slide of his hand along her hip, to her knees, and then suddenly she was in his arms and he was carrying her toward the stairs.

Carrying her up the stairs in the dark, the only light coming from the streetlights outside, illuminating the snow as it fell, fell, fell—and the flash of fire in his eyes as they passed the uncurtained window on the landing.

Lydia thought she heard a muffled squawk from

upstairs, from her suite on the third floor as he strode down the hall to his bedroom, and then the door slammed behind them.

SAM WOKE SLOWLY. His room was very bright because of the sun's reflection on the new-fallen snow. The windows, of course, were bare. Closing the blinds and drawing the drapes had been the last thing on his mind.

He felt fantastic. Utterly relaxed. Totally content. He turned his head on the pillow. Lydia was sound asleep, her body curved toward him, covered only with the sheet. She was a goddess, a tawny, tousled goddess, one soft, voluptuous breast partly exposed, rising and falling evenly as she breathed. Her hair, her *glorious* hair, loose and flowing on her silky bare shoulders, on the pillow...

Sam couldn't get enough of her. Looking at her, touching her, kissing her, making love to her. He never wanted her to leave his bed or his life—ever.

For a few minutes he indulged himself and studied her, barely breathing for fear of waking her. He glanced at his watch on the bedside table—nearly ten o'clock! It was quiet outside, the snow muffling the usual Saturday-morning sounds, but he could hear a car door slam somewhere, the shouts of children outdoors in the new snow, probably building snowmen, throwing snowballs, doing all the things kids liked to do in winter.

He eased slightly toward the side of the bed. He'd decided to sneak out and surprise her with coffee and breakfast. He'd try one of those omelettes she'd showed him how to make. How hard could it be? And toast—he could handle toast. He'd set the breakfast table with a cloth, if he could find one. Plus, he'd snag some flowers out of the huge bouquet sitting on the mantel in the family room and put them in a vase on the breakfast table. Then, when she got up, delighted to see how competent and talented he was in the kitchen now—as well as everywhere else—he'd ask her to marry him.

Yes, he'd ask her to marry him....

She'd agree, and Amber and his family and even Avie would be so happy at the news. They'd get married and she'd move in permanently and he'd sleep with her every night. He'd get Larry off on the assault charges somehow, and Lydia would have a baby, maybe two or three, little sisters or brothers for Amber, and they'd all live happily ever after on Parry Street.

The doorbell rang downstairs. *Shit!* Who was that? Sam eased himself the rest of the way out of bed and grabbed his sweatpants off a chair where he'd flung them the day before. He tiptoed out of the room, closing the door behind him and cursing when the doorbell rang again. Lydia needed her sleep. She hadn't got much last night. Neither had he, but he felt like a million bucks.

"Hold your horses," he muttered as he dashed down the stairs, then skidded to a stop. There were clothes all over the hallway—Lydia's sweater and gloves, his shirt and pants, her skirt.... He quickly gathered up everything he could see and stuffed it in the hall closet.

He wrenched open the door just as the bell pealed for the third time. "Candace!" His ex stood on the porch, looking perky and wide-awake. "What the hell are you doing here?"

"Well, good morning to you, too, grumpy," she said, stepping inside. "I came to pick up Amber. Didn't you get my message last night?"

Message? He ran one hand through his hair. He hadn't checked his machine since before he'd gone to the airport. "What was the message?"

"I left a message saying I couldn't come for her last night but I'd be here this morning—"

"You were supposed to have her this weekend?" Sam frowned. "But we had the party planned for my parents. You knew we were going to that."

"Yes, I did. But I thought I'd collect her early today and give you a chance to spend some time alone with—well, you know who I mean." Her eyes were mischievous. "A certain somebody."

"I don't have a clue what you're talking about, Candace," he said flatly. "And I'm kind of busy right now. I—"

"Busy? You look like you just got up, Sam. Where's Amber? Having breakfast?" Candace glanced around. She appeared ready to take her coat off and stay a while, which was *not* going to happen.

"She's at Teresa's house. She slept over. I'll be picking her up this afternoon. Look, could we do this another time—" Sam noticed that Candace's gaze had fastened on something under the hall table.

"Oh, what's that?" Candace squealed. It was Lydia's bra, which Sam hadn't noticed when he threw everything else in the hall closet. "A *bra?* My goodness, Sam, I see you *are* busy—" Sam scooped it up and Candace started to giggle, then stopped, her mouth open, staring over his shoulder.

Sam whirled. Lydia, wearing one of his bathrobes, had halted halfway down the stairs. Her eyes were wide, her face pale.

Dammit, this wasn't going how it was supposed to go at all.

"Oh, hi there, Lydia!" Candace trilled, waving one mittened hand gaily. "I just dropped by to collect Amber. Sam tells me she's not here, so I'll be on my way. Bye, you two! Have fun!" She winked at Sam and went out, closing the door behind her.

Sam turned. "Lydia!" She was heading back up.

He raced toward her and took the stairs in threes.
"Lydia, what's wrong?" He realized he still had her
bra in his hand. She looked at it, then at him.

"Nothing's wrong, Sam. I just want to get dressed.
I—I came down to get my things, that's all." She
wouldn't meet his eyes.

"Look at me!" He put one hand on her shoulder.
She met his gaze. The expression in her eyes was
hurt, vulnerable. *What the hell had he done?* "Lydia,
don't look at me like that. I came down because I
wanted to surprise you, make you some coffee." He
smiled and a tiny smile tugged at the corners of her
mouth. But she didn't seem any happier. "Is it Candace?" He gestured with one hand, the one with the
bra, unfortunately. "Because that was just rotten
luck, her stopping by like this. I should never have
opened the door."

Lydia took her bra from him. "It's not Candace.
Although I have to admit I didn't make a great impression, did I, coming downstairs in your bathrobe—"

"Never mind that. Candace doesn't care. Hell,"
he said, before he stopped to think. "She *wants* us
to get together. Ever since you started the job, she's
been after me to—" He shut up when he saw her
face.

"That's just it, isn't it, Sam?" she said quietly.

"*Everyone* wants us to be together. Candace, your mother, my mother, Zoey, your friend Avie—"

"So, maybe they've got the right idea. What about that? After last night—" he said, pausing to swallow. His throat was suddenly very dry. "After last night, I think they *do* have the right idea, don't you?"

She stared at him for a few seconds. "I don't know, Sam. I really don't know." She started up the stairs.

"Look how you already fit in here, Lydia. Look at the changes around here." He waved one hand toward the foyer but she didn't even glance over her shoulder. "You've turned my life around. Amber's crazy about you...."

She kept walking and he didn't try to stop her. He didn't know how he could. Or what he'd say if he did. What he wanted was to take her back to his bed and make love to her all over again, which had been his plan, anyway, after he'd surprised her with breakfast....

It wasn't going to happen. He needed a new plan.

No, his best bet was to retrench. Let her get dressed and think things over while he made coffee and breakfast, as he'd intended. Then they could revisit this entire conversation.

Damn Candace! Her timing had always left something to be desired. This was the clincher.

When Lydia came downstairs, she was wearing

jeans and a T-shirt. Her face was scrubbed and shiny, no makeup, and her hair was pulled back in a pony-tail, tied with a scarf. All business. No more sultry charmer. No more daring lover, surprising and delighting him with her needs. No more eager woman, giving more than he asked, taking all he could offer...

His coffee was okay. The omelette had started out according to the rules, but was now scrambled eggs. The toast—what could you do to toast? He'd placed a pot of jam on the table, beside a cardboard carton of orange juice.

She smiled when she saw the flowers. Sam went to her and took her in his arms. She looked so fragile, so tender and small. "Lydia," he said, gazing deeply into her eyes. "I don't know what's gone wrong but whatever it is, we can fix it."

"Fix it?"

"If Candace isn't the problem, then what is?" She didn't answer and he went on. "I thought things were going great between us. The last week or so, then last night. I thought we finally understood each other."

Lydia pushed away slightly and he released her. "Last night was sex, Sam. That's what it was. I wanted it, you wanted it, now it's over. Okay?" He was so stunned at her statement he couldn't think of a rebuttal. *Sex?*

"Have some eggs." He brought the pan to the table and shoveled eggs onto her plate and onto his. The toast was already cold, stacked on a plate in the middle of the table.

"Thanks. Do you want juice?"

He nodded and she poured out two glasses and returned the carton to the fridge. Sam walked over to pick up the coffeepot and—

"Sex?" He slammed his hand down on the counter. "That wasn't just sex and you know it! It was a lot more than just sex. Don't you understand? We have a relationship that goes way back. Sure, I realize we haven't really known each other all that long. A few weeks. But, hell—I want to *marry* you, Lydia!"

"Sam!" She stood up from the table, her face white. "Don't say that. Please. You don't know what you're talking about."

"You're damn wrong," he said. "I know *exactly* what I'm talking about. I was hoping you had some feelings for me. I was hoping maybe that crush you had on me when you were a kid might mean something—"

"You know about that?"

"Of course, I know about that." Sam sensed he'd made some kind of fatal error but he wasn't quite sure what. "Steve told me. He showed me the note you wrote—"

"He showed you the note!"

He held up his hands. "Don't take it that way, Lydia. It was just kid stuff." He gave her a helpless frown. "It scared me, I admit. I was twenty and I had my eye on women a lot older than me, not a lot younger. Certainly not my best friend's fifteen-year-old sister. But when I saw you on television after Christmas, I knew I wanted to meet you again. Then, when Candace suggested you do some work for me—" He shrugged. "It was perfect. I thought it was perfect. Believe me, if it hadn't happened like that, I'd have tracked you down myself...."

She pushed back her plate. "Sam, thank you for making me breakfast, but I don't think I can eat. I— I just don't feel like eating. In fact—" She stood. "I think I should leave."

"Leave!"

"Yes." She fiddled with the hem of the tablecloth. "Last night was a mistake. I shouldn't have gone to bed with you. I'm supposed to be a professional. What kind of professional falls into bed with her client?" She sounded bitter. "I'm ashamed of myself. Yes, I went to bed with you because I wanted to and because...I've had feelings, *deep* feelings, for you for a long, long time. I thought it was a secret. I guess I wanted to see what it would be like to—" She clasped her hands in front of her, then shoved them in her pockets. "Never mind. I—I've got to go!"

"Lydia. Don't go."

"I have to, Sam." Her face was tortured. "I have to. Say something to Amber. Make something up. I'll finish the job, I promise I will. And I'll help her with her Valentines later, since I already said I would. But I'm going over to Zoey's now, and when my loft's ready, probably in the middle of the week, I'm going to move back. Thank you for offering me a temporary place here—"

"Don't thank me for anything, dammit!" he shouted. "I'm asking you to stay. I'm asking you to marry me!"

"I'm going, Sam," she said. "You say you want to be married, but I don't think you do. You like the *idea* of marriage, not the real thing. You want a cook. And a nanny. Someone to look after you. You want a *housekeeper,* not a wife!"

CHAPTER TWENTY

"BUT IF YOU *LOVE* HIM, Lydia—I don't get it." Zoey leaned forward, a small porcelain cup in her hand. It was Sunday and they were having Chinese tea in Zoey's apartment, where Lydia had been since she'd left Sam's house the previous afternoon.

"I'm so mixed up, Zoey. How can I be in love with him—I've just known him for three weeks! Three lousy weeks and we've had sex once and he's never even *hinted* that he feels anything for me."

"But he's asked you to marry him." Zoey frowned. "Isn't that—" she waggled her free hand "—a sign, or something?"

"Yes, he's asked me to marry him. But that's because he wants a suitable stepmother for Amber, and so does his ex, by the way." Lydia held out her hands, counting off the reasons on her fingers. "He wants someone to take care of his house and he knows that's exactly what I like to do and I do it well. *And* he wants to be married! Or so he says."

"I didn't know there were guys who *wanted* to be married," Zoey muttered. "I thought they had to be brought around to the idea slowly, or hit over the head before they really saw the point.''

''Well, he does.''

''That's—''

''And—'' Lydia broke in triumphantly, marking off another reason on the fourth finger of her left hand ''—his mother wants him married. His whole family does—cousins, sisters, his uncle Manny-who-gave-him-the-fishing-rod, everybody! Even Darlene his secretary told me she thought he should get married again. She feels sorry for him, having to pick up his daughter from school and then come home and make supper.''

''I see what you—''

''As if half the world of single parents doesn't have to do exactly the same thing!'' Lydia broke in again. ''As if he ever does anything except order in pizza and Chinese food.''

Zoey poured them both more tea. ''And now you have to go back there anyway,'' she murmured.

''Yes.'' Lydia reached for her cup. ''I told him I'd skip this week and that was a mistake. I shouldn't have. I'm a professional. I have a job to do, a contract to fulfill. He still owes me a lot of money. I just got off-track a little there.''

''Yes, I suppose you could call sleeping with a guy you love off-track. Or,'' Zoey went on evenly, glancing over the rim of her cup, ''on-track.''

Lydia's best friend was starting to annoy her.

"Listen, Zoey," she said, "are you supporting me in this? Or not? It's kind of hard to tell."

"Oh, I'm with you one-hundred percent, Lydia. Absolutely! If he's a jerk and he's going to break your heart, nobody hates him more than I do. But if he's in love with you, too, and you guys have just got your wires crossed, I'm going to do my darnedest to get you to make it up with him."

"That's just what I mean." Lydia stood up. It was late and she had a lot to do the next day. "It's kind of hard to tell whose side you're on. I'm going to bed. See you in the morning."

"SO YOU ASKED HER to marry you but you didn't tell her you loved her. Have I got that right?"

Avie was punching the bag next to him—or was supposed to be. Sam had talked him into going to Guido's instead of their regular Tuesday-afternoon squash game. Just for a change.

"Keep punching, Av," Sam muttered, throwing a hard left. The bag swung wildly in Avie's direction. "Yeah, that's right. I asked her to marry me and she told me to take a hike off the closest short pier."

"Which is not necessarily a bad thing at this time of year..."

"What?" Sam glared at him.

"Ice, you know." Avie grinned.

"That's not funny."

"Okay, okay. You definitely didn't say you loved her?"

Sam stared at his best friend. Sometimes he had to wonder. Avie had an important, high-up job at a Bay Street firm but there were times he acted like the class dunce. "No, I didn't, Avie. What's to say? I asked her to marry me. Doesn't that pretty well cover it, for crying out loud?"

"Not for women, it doesn't." Avie started working on his bag again. Every second or third whack he'd lose the rhythm and the bag would come flying into his face. If he didn't watch it, he was going to give himself a K.O. For a guy with so little sports talent, he had a pretty gutsy attitude. Avie'd try anything. Except marriage.

"With all due respect, Av, what the hell do you know about women? I'm the one who's been married—"

"I rest my case." He threw Sam a sideways grin.

"Besides, Lydia's beyond all that 'I love you' stuff. That's for...for girls."

"Sorry, pal. You got that wrong. There isn't a woman alive who doesn't want to hear 'I love you.' They train themselves for it, from about six on. Barbie and Ken, sappy movies, romantic novels, it's all geared to getting the guy down on his knees declaring his undying love."

"Av—" Sam got out through gritted teeth. "The fact that you can still talk means you're not working hard enough.'' He accelerated the tattoo on his own bag and ignored the sweat running into his eyes. After this, he was going to skip rope and then run a mile or two on the treadmill and then he was going to take a shower and head home and face his daughter, who held Lydia's departure against him personally. He hadn't planned to spill his guts to Avie, but he had to talk to someone. Ever since Lydia had packed up on Saturday, piled her bags and her bird into that rustbucket of a minivan and driven away, he'd thought of nothing and no one else. Amber had cried her eyes out when she'd come home from his sister's and he had to tell her Lydia was gone.

He just didn't understand it. They got along great. They talked, they laughed. They were fantastic in bed—what else was there?

"Well, which is it, pal? You love her or don't you?"

Did he love her? Of course, he loved her!

"I love her," he managed between punches and the thunder of leather gloves on canvas. "Dammit," he shouted, pushing up the pace a notch, *"I love her!"*

Several guys on the treadmill looked their way and shook their heads sadly.

"Hey, don't tell me, pal—tell her."

THE PHONE RANG at about ten o'clock and Zoey answered it. Lydia was moving back to her loft on Friday, the next day, and looking forward to it. She'd seen the color the movie people had painted her walls—a luscious melon green—and the curtains, floor-to-ceiling cream-colored shantung silk. It was terrific and much nicer than she could have afforded. All she needed now was new furniture. And, of course, the built-ins she planned, for storage.

"Lydia!" Zoey walked toward her, phone in her hand. "For you. I think it's *the man,*" she whispered. Lydia gave her a dark look, but her heart jumped into second gear.

She took the phone into Zoey's dining area. Zoey and Charlotte and Lydia had had dinner together, just the three of them, and Liam, Charlotte's new husband, had arrived a little while ago to take Charlotte back to her condo. Charlotte had told her they'd be leaving for Prince Edward Island right after Zoey's wedding on the ninth of February. "Hello?"

"Lydia." It *was* Sam. And the way he said her name…

"Yes?" Her heart was hammering. She hadn't spoken to him since she'd left.

"How are you, Lydia?" He sounded so serious.

"Fine," she lied. "Just fine. How's Amber?"

"That's what I'm calling about. You know how you planned to come over a week from Saturday to help Amber with her Valentines?"

"Yes. I'm looking forward to it." She gripped the phone tighter. "Is there a problem?" She'd wondered if Amber would still want her to help, now that Lydia was no longer part of the household. Not that she'd ever been.

"No problem. We were—well, I was wondering if you'd come over this Saturday instead. Come in the afternoon and stay for dinner."

"Oh." Lydia's breath caught in her throat. "Do you think that's a good idea, Sam?" she said softly.

"Dinner? You mean, because of you and me?"

"Well, yes."

"I think it's a good idea. We need to talk. Besides, there's something I want to show you when it gets dark."

"What?"

"I can't tell you. It's a surprise I've got planned. Can you come?"

"I'll be there about five. Is that all right?"

"That would be fine." He sounded relieved. *He wanted her to come.* Lydia had thought he'd still be angry with her for refusing his so-called offer of matrimony and taking off the way she had. Plus, she figured she'd been cowardly missing this week, even though she could make it up next week. She didn't know *what* she thought anymore, but she knew she wanted to see him. And Amber.

"There's something else I wanted to tell you, Lydia."

"Oh?" She was trying to keep her voice cool and nonchalant. It was hard, when her heart was pounding like this and her palms were sweaty on the receiver.

"It's about Larry Massullo. You know his case was coming up early next week?"

"You told me that. Poor old guy!"

"Well, there's some good news. I thought you'd want to know. The woman Larry said was being harassed has come forward—"

"That's wonderful, Sam!"

"Yes. She'd disappeared before the police and ambulance arrived. I've been trying to locate her, hoping she'd say something that would shoot a hole in the story put out by those three thugs."

"Do you think she will? Make a statement, I mean?"

"I'm going to convince her that if she doesn't, she'll be helping to send an innocent man to jail."

"Oh, Sam! I'm so pleased for you. And for Larry, of course." She knew how hard Sam had worked on the case and how he felt about possibly seeing his old friend go to jail.

"Yeah, well. I just thought you'd like to know."

"I did. I mean, I do. Thank you for telling me." She paused, then went on, "I—I'll look forward to Saturday."

"Me, too, Lydia."

Lydia pushed the Off button in a daze. She was going back to Parry Street!

"Guess what? I'm making dinner for you and my dad all by myself!"

"That's lovely, Amber," Lydia said. The girl had met her at the front door, along with her father. Lydia could barely allow herself to look at Sam. She'd missed being with him and his daughter so much.

"Shall I hang up your coat?" he asked, his eyes probing hers.

"Yes, thank you." She slipped off her coat, unable to lose the image of the last time she'd taken off her coat in this hallway—or, to be more accurate, the last time *he'd* taken off her coat. Her coat and all her other clothes…

"As you can see, we have a wonderfully organized hall closet in this house," he said grandly, throwing open the door and smiling at her.

She felt enormous relief. He was going to be casual about her visit today. He was going to be casual and relaxed and—and ordinary.

So would she. They'd forget everything that had happened between them. It was over. He was moving on; so would she.

"We're not having chili," Amber went on, skipping down the hallway ahead of her. "My dad won't let me use a knife and do the hamburger and everything unless you're there to help me, he said, so guess what?"

"What?" Lydia carried the bag of extra materials

she'd brought with her to make the Valentines: paper lace, paints, glue, glitter.

"We're having tuna sandwiches that I made all by myself, the way you showed me, and soup out of a can! You get to pick 'cause you're the guest. We've got chicken noodle and tomato and turkey 'n' rice and cream of mushroom—"

Lydia met Sam's eyes over Amber's head. He shrugged. He mimicked dialing a telephone and mouthed "later" to her.

Ah. Take-out.

She felt as though she was at home but not at home. The house was so familiar to her, yet it wasn't hers. She'd cleaned out and organized these cupboards, she'd sent that carpet and those curtains out for cleaning. She'd polished the mirrors. She'd organized that hall closet he was still so proud of....

And now she was a guest. She couldn't forget that for a minute.

"What's in your bag, Lydia?" Amber's eyes were alight. "Surprises?"

"Oh, just a few things I thought we might be able to use when you make your Valentines," Lydia said, taking out some of her supplies and putting them on the kitchen table where Amber had already started work. "How many are you making?"

"Lots. My teacher says if we give out Valentines to one person, we have to give them to everybody."

"That's a good idea," Lydia said, glancing at

Sam, who was standing by the kitchen counter, watching them. He made her nervous. She hoped he didn't intend to stand there the entire time they were working. "That way no one gets left out."

"That's what Ms. Friesen says. She says that's the worst thing in the world, thinking nobody loves you. And Valentine's Day is about love and all that stuff, isn't it, Lydia?"

"Yes, it is." Lydia didn't dare to look at Sam but she heard him clear his throat. "Your teacher's very wise, Amber."

"She is." The girl nodded, sorting through some paper lace doilies Lydia had produced. "She's my very favorite teacher I've ever had." Amber was in grade three; not counting kindergarten, she'd had three teachers so far.

Amber raised her head. "And that's why my dad says we need to start these *now,* even though Valentine's Day is a long way off. Because we need to make so *many.* We might even have to work on this next Saturday, too."

By next Saturday, Lydia hoped to have finished her work in the Pereira household.

"Amber?" Sam stepped toward them, away from the kitchen counter. "Remember what I told you before? I need to talk to Lydia for a while."

"Yep. That's okay, Dad. You can borrow her. Just make sure you bring her back 'cause I need her, too." Sam's daughter laughed.

Lydia looked at him. What was all *this* about?

"Lydia?" Sam seemed nervous. "Could I talk to you for a few minutes? In my office?"

"Of course." She followed him into the hallway and he led her to his office. Once he'd gestured her inside, he entered the room and flicked on a couple of lights before closing the door behind them.

"Why are we in here, Sam?"

"Privacy." He indicated a small sofa in the client area. "I have something to say to you and I don't want to be disturbed."

"Okay." She hesitated, wondering what he had on his mind that was so mysterious and urgent.

"Why don't you sit down?" He took a deep breath and smiled. She had a sudden warm feeling in her stomach. It was wonderful just being in the same house again, just seeing him again, no matter what he might have to say to her. "It would be easier for me if you sat down," he said solemnly.

"All right." Lydia sat down on the sofa and clasped her hands in her lap. Sam started to pace. That was the only term she could think of for what he was doing—taking three or four steps one way, then turning and taking three or four steps the other say.

He stopped in front of her. "Okay. I want us to rewind everything to last week, before you left." He made a turning, cranking gesture with one hand. "Okay? We're going backward now."

"To last Friday?"

"No, last Saturday morning. Forget everything that happened after you woke up that morning."

She shut her eyes. *How could she ever forget?* "Okay."

"Lydia?" She opened her eyes. "First of all, I want to apologize for every stupid thing I've done since we met and before we met and every stupid thing I'm going to do in the future. I just want you to know I don't mean anything by them—"

"Sam, there's no need for you to apologize to me."

"I'm not finished. I did a major stupid thing last Saturday when I asked you to marry me—" He stopped his pacing abruptly. "Do you understand what I'm saying?"

Lydia felt her cheeks grow hot. She didn't trust herself to nod. *He regretted asking her to marry him.*

"I got everything wrong. Everything! So I'm starting over, right at the beginning. Look at me, Lydia—"

She forced her chin up. She met his gaze.

"I love you, Lydia Lane. I love you! I don't know how it happened exactly, but it did. I want to spend the rest of my life with you and I don't give a damn about housekeeping or a nanny service or whether you can cook or not. We could order out every day of our lives together, and I wouldn't care. Do you understand? I love you. Nothing else matters. I want to marry you.''

Lydia stared at him. He loved *her*.... ''We—we hardly know each other—''

''Don't try and talk me out of it!'' He ran his hands wildly through his hair. ''I've thought about it over and over this week. I haven't been able to think of anything else. I missed you. I can't imagine going on, living my life without you—''

''Sam!'' She covered her face with her hands. ''Stop!'' She was overcome.

He sat down beside her and took her hand. ''Do you think it could work between us? I know this is sudden but if you have any feeling for me at all, please tell me....''

''Oh, Sam! Any *feeling* for you? I love you, I've loved you since I was a teenager. I've never stopped loving you—''

He hauled her into his arms and kissed her. ''You mean it? You'll marry me?'' His voice was rough. Lydia rubbed her face on his shoulder, wiping the tears away.

''Yes, yes, *yes!*''

''You really will?'' He actually looked astonished.

''Yes. I love you, Sam.''

He kissed her and, for long minutes, there was nothing else that needed saying. Then he pulled back and released her. ''Now there's one other thing...'' He disappeared into the doorway of his office and returned a few seconds later with a jeweler's box in his hand. He took out a ring, a large solitaire diamond in a white gold setting.

"The engagement ring." He slipped it onto the ring finger of her left hand. "That's how it's done. Okay. Now we're engaged. You've promised to marry me."

"You were pretty sure of yourself," she murmured, smiling. She couldn't *stop* smiling. "Getting the ring and everything."

He laughed. "Prepared. I had no intention of giving up, even if you weren't ready to marry me yet. I wasn't letting that lion-tamer get you—"

"I believe he trains horses."

"Whatever." He gave her a dark look. "You run into a lot of weird guys in your business."

She smiled at him. "I do, don't I?"

He laughed and hauled her into his arms again. "Yes, dammit, you do."

AMBER NOTICED THE RING when they were nearly finished their cream of mushroom soup and tuna sandwiches. "What's that, Lydia? Are you getting married to somebody?"

"Yes," Lydia said. "Your dad."

"Dad!" Amber threw her arms around her father's neck. "You never told me you were going to marry Lydia!"

"I don't tell you everything, honey."

"Yippee! I'm going to call Tania." She ran to the phone. "Now I'm going to have two moms and she's just got one."

"Apparently you have my daughter's approval," Sam said.

Lydia shook her head. "I can't think what Zoey and Charlotte are going to say."

"I can," Sam said, grinning. "'I told you so.'"

After dessert—a Sara Lee cake—Lydia phoned her mother. When Marcia answered, Lydia said, "Mom?" and hummed a few bars of "The Wedding March."

"Oh, Lydia! I *knew* you'd do it, I just knew you would! Is it Sam? Oh, darling, I'm so happy for you. Wait until I tell Ray!"

When the dishes were cleared away—clean ones from the dishwasher in the cupboards, dirty ones in the dishwasher with the door closed—Lydia turned to Sam. "So, is that the surprise you mentioned? I can't imagine anything more surprising happening today."

"Partly. The rest is outside. Amber! Get your coat. Lydia, I'll go get yours. We have to go into the backyard."

They all traipsed out into the dark snowy backyard, wearing boots and mitts and hats.

"You two sit on the patio there, beside the house," Sam ordered, wading through the snow in the backyard. It was too dark to make out what he was doing.

"What's the surprise?" Amber asked her in a whisper.

"I don't know, honey," she whispered back. "Something your dad cooked up—oh!"

A roman candle lit up the night sky, followed by two sizzling bursts, one purple, one green.

"Fireworks!" Amber shouted. "Yippee!"

"You like that?" Sam was smiling as he came back to the patio. "We didn't get to see the fireworks on New Year's Eve." Another bomb burst in the air, with a loud pop. Then another roman candle went off, this one fizzling to the snow without exploding. A window opened next door and Sam's neighbor poked his head out. "What the hell you doing, Pereira? It's not Victoria Day."

"I know," Sam called back. "We're celebrating." He looked at Amber and Lydia, then yelled over the fence. "It's Groundhog Day, isn't it?"

"That's not until next week!"

"Okay," Sam returned. "It's not Groundhog Day. But I'm getting married. How about that?"

"You're crazy, Pereira!" And the window was slammed shut again.

Amber giggled and covered her mouth with her snowy mitten.

Lydia was beginning to get a very clear picture of life with Sam Pereira. It definitely wasn't going to be boring.

EPILOGUE

SPRINGTIME IN ALBERTA was a magic time. There was even a song written about it, by Canadian musician and singer Ian Tyson, who ranched in the foothills near Calgary.

Lydia, Charlotte and their husbands flew to Edmonton, rented a car and drove out to Jasper, and Zoey and her husband met them there. The Donnellys drove to the meeting place from Stoney Creek in B.C.'s Interior.

By the last weekend in May, the alpine meadows near Jasper Park Lodge were clear of snow, covered with the first blush of spring grass. Lac Beauvert had melted and the rivers—Pembina, Sunwapta, Athabaska—ran high with milky blue-green water, melted from the winter's snow and the glaciers higher up.

There couldn't be a better time to spend a long weekend together, just the three girlfriends and their new husbands. Lissy spent the three days of the Victoria Day holiday with her Uncle Ryan and Aunt Mary Ellen near Vancouver, and Amber spent the weekend with her mother on a shopping trip to New York.

Charlotte and Liam had the farthest to go, all the way from Prince Edward Island, with Charlotte seven months pregnant. But, as she told Zoey and Lydia, she wouldn't miss their reunion for anything.

The first afternoon they were together, they strolled through the magnificent grounds and the women pointed out this sight and that sight to their new husbands—that's where Zoey spotted the black bear, eating raspberries on the bushes; this is where Charlotte dropped her paycheck and three of them spent two hours looking for it; over there's where the wrangler Lydia liked...well, never mind that! They had a lot of memories here. Both from their get-together the year before and from eleven years ago, the summer they'd met.

Charlotte and Liam weren't the only ones with good news. Zoey and Cameron were expecting a baby, too. Zoey was three months along, she proudly told everyone the first evening they were together, sitting around the massive stone fireplace in the Lodge's lobby. As for Lydia—she gave her new husband, leaning against the mantel, a loving glance and put her hand on her midriff—she wasn't sure yet.

"Just think," Zoey said, holding up a glass of cranberry juice, "this is where it all started."

"What do you mean?" Cam asked absently. His mind was elsewhere—on his cows, according to his wife. The Donnelly herd had calved and there was absolutely nothing he had to be back in Stoney Creek for, but there you go, Zoey said. You couldn't take a rancher away from his ranch. Not for long, anyway. The others could tell that her teasing was all in good fun and that Cam was enjoying himself as much as anyone. "What all started?"

"Charlotte and Lydia and me and you and Liam and Sam, that's what!" Zoey turned to Charlotte, massively pregnant in her leather club chair. "You tell them, Char."

"We met here," Charlotte said simply. "Three girls away from home for the first time, scared silly—I know I was—and somehow we found each other. Kindred spirits! Friends for life!" She raised her glass of apple juice.

"And thanks to that crazy challenge someone tossed out at last year's reunion about tracking down our first loves, we've all got husbands and babies on the way and—"

"You, too Lydia?" Zoey and Charlotte asked in unison.

Lydia patted her tummy and colored. Sam smiled proudly and reached for her hand.

"Maybe," she went on. "And we're still all friends for life, right?"

"Absolutely!" Zoey said and held up her glass again.

"Forever!" Charlotte chimed in, then they all held their glasses even higher and spoke together. "To reunions!"

The Shannon Sisters

A Trilogy by C.J. Carmichael
**The stories of three sisters from Alberta whose
lives and loves are as rocky—and grand—as the
mountains they grew up in.**

A Second-Chance Proposal

A murder, a bride-to-be left at the altar, a reunion. Is
Cathleen Shannon willing to take a second chance on
the man involved in these?

A Convenient Proposal

Kelly Shannon feels guilty about what she's done,
and Mick Mizzoni feels that he's his brother's
keeper—a volatile situation, but maybe one
with a convenient way out!

A Lasting Proposal

Maureen Shannon doesn't want risks in her life
anymore. Not after everything she's lived through. But
Jake Hartman might be proposing a sure thing....

On sale starting February 2002

Available wherever Harlequin books are sold.

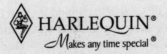

HARLEQUIN®
Makes any time special®

Bestselling Harlequin® author

JUDITH ARNOLD

brings readers a brand-new,
longer-length novel based on her
popular miniseries *The Daddy School*

Somebody's Dad

If any two people should avoid getting
romantically involved with each other, it's
bachelor—and children-phobic!—Brett Stockton
and single mother Sharon Bartell. But neither
can resist the sparks...especially once
The Daddy School is involved.

"Ms. Arnold seasons tender passion with a dusting
of humor to keep us turning those pages."
—*Romantic Times Magazine*

*Look for Somebody's Dad
in February 2002.*

HARLEQUIN®
Makes any time special ®